Maggie's Cottage

Naida Gipson

Printed in the United States of America

First Printing, 2021

FEBRUARY 2000

Virginia struggled with the Yale lock rusted to the front door while I wandered through the weed-choked English Garden, an eclectic mix of Hollyhocks, Violets, and Sweet Williams, English Daisies, Candytuft, Primroses, Sun Flowers, Snapdragons and Bachelor's Buttons. The plants stretched new shoots up toward the pale sun. A breeze moved gray clouds over Deer Harbor. It splattered the surface with staccato raindrops and filled the air with the salty smell of the sea. Gulls flew overhead calling to one another. The prospect of living on Orcas Island in the San Juan Islands of Puget Sound intrigued me more and more. I turned back to the porch and watched as Virginia pushed on the door. It stuck tight. She shoved harder, kicked the bottom panel, and stumbled inside as the door flew open. I heard a crash.

"Damn!"

"Are you all right, Virginia?" I ran up front steps dished in the middle from wear and weather, their blue-gray paint peeling to white.

"Yes . . . sorry. The door's a bit stubborn, isn't it?" Virginia scrambled to her feet, straightened the old coffee table she had fallen against, and turned around. She pushed her blonde hair back from her face, brushed dust from her navy blue pants suit and rearranged the gold and white-patterned silk scarf around her neck.

"Come in, Sarah, come in." She stood up straight and smiled. "This . . . ," Virginia held out both arms and turned in a slow circle, "is the living room."

Late winter sunbeams filtered into the room through unwashed windows and touched an expanse of hardwood floor here, poked into a corner there. The pale sunlight could not disguise the tattered look of the room. Cobwebs hung from the ceiling. Dust covered everything. A row of grayed porcelain figurines lined the mantel. I shivered in the chill air and wished I'd worn a jacket. A musty odor hung over the place, old paint, old furniture, old dust. I rubbed the POW/MIA bracelet I wore on my left arm and wondered why the realty agency hadn't had the place cleaned before showing it.

As if she read my mind, Virginia said, "The house just came on the market and we haven't had time to have it cleaned, yet. But I wanted you to see it before anyone else got to, because I think it's perfect for you."

The once-fine sofa sagged as though tired out at the end of too busy a day, or perhaps, too long a century. Stuffing poked through shredded fabric. A baby grand piano in need of cleaning and polishing, its top down, its keyboard covered, stood facing corner picture windows. A closer look revealed someone had sanded one side down to the bare wood but had abandoned this too difficult job.

I sat on the piano bench, and heard it creak beneath my weight. It moved with a slight tremor. I felt my face turn red, stood up at once and ran my hands through my short, gray hair. "Needs a little glue, I think," I grinned, pushing up my turtleneck sleeves and pulling down my polar fleece vest. "I might be a few pounds overweight, but I don't think enough to break a piano bench," I laughed. "The joints are loose."

"Yes, well . . . yes, I guess it does need gluing." Virginia seemed distracted. "Don't forget, Sarah, the lady who lived here was close to 100 years old. Her things are still in the house, because she had no family left. According to her Will, when the house sells, the money goes to a music scholarship at the University in her name, Margaret McNamara. I guess whoever buys the house will have the job of weeding out her belongings, unless the realty company does it, first."

I nodded, turned toward the piano, remembering the old upright I had learned to play on as a child, longing to play this baby grand. I shoved my hands into my jeans pockets and looked out the corner windows;

an obvious remodel from sometime in the past, for this house was built before picture windows. The rain had stopped. Deer Harbor glistened in the sun, full of white caps. Cumulus clouds scudded across the sky. A small island emerged from the sea in the distance to the right with a steep staircase rising to it's crest. *If only I had a boat, I could go out there, climb the stairs and see all over Deer Harbor and even part of Puget Sound.* To my left and back by the shore, the boat basin was filled with small craft. Rowboats. Sailboats. Fishing boats. *Maybe someone there rents boats.*

How nice it must be to sit here and play the piano with this wonderful view. I stretched one finger out and traced a line in the dust. *Sarah* Dark mahogany wood showed through.

I smiled a smile that would not leave my face and sighed again. After years of apartment living, the cottage seemed like home. It reminded me of the house my parents had when I was a child; a sweet little house just big enough for the three of us. Maggie's cottage was not waterfront property, but almost waterfront. I didn't care. I'm a poor sailor at best. The cottage looked like the perfect place to retire. I wiped out my name in the piano dust with my sleeve and turned around.

"Let's take a look at the rest," I said

"It's not very big, but it's cozy." Virginia led me to the kitchen, where an old wood burning cook-stove stood with an adjoining hot water tank in one corner, the stovepipe hooked in an "L" to the chimney flue going through the center of the building. A small window above the sink peered out over the boat basin. I could barely see above the sill set too high for short people like me. Faded gingham curtains. The countertop consisted of a two-inch solid slab of Douglas fir, two feet wide, bleached, scrubbed and worn from decades of use. Another dusty curtain hid the plumbing under the sink. Cabinets heavy with many coats of paint filled the space on either side of the sink and the window. Even the curved, half-sphere door-pulls were thick with paint, their sharp metal edges rounded with layers of enamel. Although the dated kitchen seemed much older than the kitchen in my parent's house, it had possibilities. It would do.

A small oak table and four spindle-turned chairs, their backs pressed into the intricate patterns of a time gone by, sat by a tiny window in one corner. The door to the back porch stood opposite two doors on the left, one leading to the basement, the other to the attic.

Virginia led the way up the wooden staircase. Steps made a spiral turn half-way up. Tucked under the sloping ceilings at the top was a large irregular room. Some old furniture. A Tiffany lamp with a few broken stained-glass pieces lying in a box. A child's crib. A breath-taking view through two dormer windows facing Deer Harbor. Windows looked out over grass on one side, and the boat basin on the other. A perfect spot for an art studio. My easel by the big window. Good light. Dry and warm.

"This is it?" I asked.

"No, there are two bedrooms and a bath on the main floor, and an unfinished daylight basement under the kitchen and living room."

"I'm glad to hear that!" I laughed. "I was afraid the bathroom would be out back – a privy, you know."

"Well, actually, it's pretty modern, with running water and a flush toilet. The bath was remodeled years ago, so long ago, it's past being dated and is coming back into style, now. There's a furnace and some old concrete laundry trays in the basement." Virginia held onto the rail and headed back downstairs. "Watch your step going down the curved part, there." I followed, taking care to put my feet on the widest part of the pie-shaped stairs.

We went back through the kitchen and living room, past the brick fireplace and into a short hall. Ahead lay the bathroom straight from a House Beautiful Magazine of the 1950's. Green ceramic tile filled with once-white grout, now loose and moldy, surrounded the tub. White pedestal sink with absolutely no place to put anything. White toilet. White tub. Tiny black and white hexagonal tiles covered the floor. Dusty white painted shutters covered the window hung with a green and white valance. A moldy plastic green and white shower curtain hung over the tub.

To the left, the master bedroom looked out on the harbor and the small island. I loved the fact there was a view from this bedroom. Mahogany furniture filled the room. A faded pink satin boudoir chair stood by the window. To the right, a second bedroom had a view of the grassy hillside. More dark furniture and another tattered pink chair in this room.

"It needs some work," said Virginia as we walked back into the living room.

No kidding, I thought, mentally adding up my retirement from work, my savings account, my government allotment and my IRA account.

We walked back into the living room.

The piano.

"It's hard to find anyone on the island during the summer to do remodeling, but in winter when fewer tourists come over from the mainland, you can find good workers."

"I don't know. I kind of like it the way it is, don't you?" I looked around. "It needs cleaning, and I guess a little paint would help." I gazed around the room. "Everything goes with the house? Even the piano?"

"Yes."

"Hm-m-m." I ran a finger over the piano leaving another dark trail in the dust

"I'd like to make an offer."

"Great." Virginia beamed like the Mukilteo lighthouse. "Just let me get the papers." She picked up her briefcase, opened it on the coffee table in front of the sofa and sat down.

"Oomph!" Virginia sank nearly to the floor and sat there, legs sticking out, eyes wide and mouth open. She scooted up, pushed with her hands to scrunch over to the edge of the couch, but fell back down into the broken springs. She sat there, chagrined.

We both burst out laughing.

"Here," I held my hands out to her to pull her upright.

"Oof!" Virginia heaved out of the sagging sofa and sat on one end of the coffee table, the only piece of stable furniture in the room. "Thanks."

While Virginia organized her papers, I wandered over to the piano and raised the keyboard lid. The ivories were yellowed and split, the way my fingernails split sometimes if I have my hands in water too much, or if the weather is cold and damp. A once shiny, now faded gold embossed emblem on the front of the instrument read:

CHICKERING
Boston, USA.

I touched a key. The tone rang out pure and golden. I tried a chord . . . then another. The instrument seemed to be perfectly in tune. How could that be? At its age, close to 100 years, I expected it to be sadly out of tune. Maggie McNamara must have had it tuned regularly. I pushed the bench back, sat down, careful not to make it creak, and played a sonata. The piano responded with notes as clear as diamonds cascading from a necklace.

Did I want the cottage for itself, or for the piano?

I bought the place and didn't go downstairs to look at the concrete laundry tubs. I did not even check out the antiquated furnace. This was it. I had come home.

~~~

1908

Maggie ran up the back porch stairs. "Mama! Mama!"

"What is it, Maggie?" Alice frowned, a worry line between her eyebrows, and wiped her hands on her apron. "Is something wrong?" She tucked a wisp of auburn hair back into its bun with a hairpin.

"No, Mama. Something's right." Maggie panted trying to catch her breath. "It's so-o-o-o right! Did you know Papa had ordered a piano for me for my birthday? All the way from Boston? Maggie danced up and down. She grabbed her mother's arm and steered her to the many-paned living room window. "See the Seattle Ferry leaving the bay – out by the island?"

Alice nodded.

"They unloaded a beautiful baby grand piano from that ferry onto a wagon about an hour ago. Papa paid Mr. Mahoney to bring it to our house." Maggie hugged her mother. "For me!" She whirled around. "Did you know? It was a secret."

Alice hugged Maggie back. "Yes, darlin', I knew. And it was a secret. A nice secret, don't you think?"

Maggie could not stand still. "Oh, I can't wait. Why are horses so slow? Why can't they fly like Pegasus, the winged horse in the story? Did you know they sent the piano by steamship all the way from Boston to Seattle? It must have come all the way down around South America to Cape Horn. Thousands of
~~~

miles. Wouldn't it be *grand* to come all that way with the piano and see the places it's seen?" She laughed as her mother frowned at her. "I know, Mama, a piano can't 'see', but just imagine where it's been."

Maggie ran to the kitchen door and peered out. She turned back letting the door slam shut and shook her head. "Not here, yet!"

~~~

2000

While the property closed, I stayed at the inn high on the hill with a view of Deer Harbor. Every day I drove my Volkswagen Bug over to the cottage and looked in the windows, trying to decide what needed to be done first. Cleaning, of course. Then painting. Better check on the furnace, although the weather had grown warmer. In winter I would need the heat. I worried that I hadn't looked it over when I had the chance. Oh, well . . . it's not as though I'm a heating expert, but I should have checked to make sure it worked.

I walked the property lines and pulled weeds in the flower garden, cleaned out the bird bath and added fresh water. The wet spring days lost their chill and, although the nights remained cold, life renewed itself at Deer Harbor. Wildflowers sprang up along the sides of the roads. Buttercups and violets. A squirrel ran up a fir tree. Water glistened in the harbor, and a few boats ventured out to sea.
~~~

Deer in the apple orchard picked their dainty way through dead leaves and windfall apples. I followed them a little way, careful not to step on a rotten apple, or crunch the dead leaves and frighten the deer, and found myself in the middle of the orchard next to a tree with the scar of a faded heart carved in the trunk. Inside the heart, I could barely make out the letters M.M. + H.A. I wondered who they could be. Maggie McNamara? She had owned the cottage. But who was H.A.? A boyfriend? If so, what happened to him?

Finally, the legal aspects of the sale were completed. Margaret McNamara's cottage and its mortgage payments were now mine. I took my notebook full of "to do" lists and met Virginia in town where we had the telephone and electricity turned on in my name and arranged for garbage service. I followed her car in my Bug to the property and she gave me the keys. We walked up the back porch steps to the kitchen door. I tried the knob.

My mouth dropped open and I felt a frown wrinkle my forehead. I turned around to look at Virginia. "It's not locked!"

"Oh? Well, in Deer Harbor, not many people do lock their doors. It's perfectly safe, don't you know." Virginia looked around the edges of the property. "I was sure I locked it when I showed the house to you." A nervous giggle bubbled in her throat. "Maybe another realtor has shown it to someone and forgot to lock up." She stepped inside and glanced around.

"Everything's fine. Not to worry." Her uncertain smile did not reassure me.

We walked through the house, me holding my breath, but everything did look the same – dusty and unkempt. Virginia went upstairs to the attic and downstairs to the basement, with me hanging over the basement stairs, watching her. Anxious. No one in the house. No itinerant campers.

My breath came out in a big sigh. I grinned. "Thanks, Virginia," I said, walking her back to the door. "I'll just bring in my cleaning supplies. There's a lot to do."

"Call me, if you need help with anything, like who to hire for remodeling, or where to go for paint and things," she said.

"I passed a huge hardware store on the road here from the ferry dock. They'll probably have what I need." I felt selfish. I didn't want to share the place with her or anyone else. Well . . . Johnny, yes . . . but . . . . I twisted the POW / MIA bracelet, wondering if I would ever take it off -- if Johnny would ever come back from the war. Did he still live, or was he being kept in a bamboo cage somewhere in the back country of North Vietnam? Thirty years. I told myself the last letter from the Army must be right. He must be dead, but his body and I.D. tags were not found. Apparently, the whole crew perished in the helicopter crash and burned up. I took a deep breath and tried to get my mind off the war that had been over for years.

A light rain fell as we walked down the back steps to Virginia's car. She drove away. I waved and turned to the house. Mine. All mine – mine and the bank's. I carried in my cleaning supplies, including a new shower curtain for the bathroom. The sun broke through warm spring rain and filled the living room with bright light and dust motes. My vacuum cleaner hummed. The dust motes disappeared, but I couldn't seem to keep my thoughts from when I first met Johnny.

~~~

1968

Ever since that first day at Santa Barbara State, I knew he was the one for me. I think he felt the same way, because he sat across from me in Freshman Lit and stared at me throughout the whole class. I couldn't stop looking at him, either. Some kind of electricity seemed to pass between us. Johnny turned all the girls' heads with his slim, tanned good looks, his black hair and exotic almond-shaped eyes. He waited outside the classroom that first day, smiled showing even white teeth, and said, "Hi. I'm Johnny Hanaeki."

Hanaeki? What kind of name is that? Japanese? I thought Japanese were little people. This Johnny Hanaeki was tall. At least six feet.

I smiled back. "I haven't heard that name before. What country is it from?" I felt my face flush as I realized how rude I was.

"Hawaii."

"I'm Sarah Webster," I said, nodding to him, holding my English books close to my chest with both arms.

"Nice to meet you, Sarah Webster."
~~~

Johnny was a little older than the other freshmen – twenty-three. When he invited me for a coke after class, I could hardly breathe. We walked to the Co-op. I shifted my books to one hand and balanced them on my hip. He reached over to take my free hand. I blushed and sneaked a look at him as our fingers entwined. He bent over to look into my eyes. My breath stopped. I felt my face turn red. I gulped, looked at the ground, and tried to keep a smile from flirting around my face while I watched my feet take one step at a time.

We sat at a window table and held hands. Talk of schedules and our majors revolved around what we really wanted to talk about. Us. His major was engineering; mine, Graphic Arts. We discussed the war in Vietnam, about how unfair it was to our age group to have to go over there and fight. Wars were declared by old men but fought by young ones. I thought if women had been running things, we would not have any wars. Let them play football internationally. We talked in circles, and finally, he told me about himself.

"I'm a surfer," he said. "I've surfed all the best places in Hawaii. Now I want to try the mainland. There're good surfing beaches here in California."

"I'm sure there are, right here in Santa Barbara and maybe south near Santa Cruz?"

"Want to go see if we can find one?"

I held my breath and nodded.

"I brought my long board with me from Hawaii." Johnny let go of my hands, stood up and raised his arms to give me an idea of the length of his ten-foot surfboard. He grinned. White teeth sparkled. "I'll show you how to 'hang ten'."

I smiled and nodded again, shivering at the thought of Johnny teaching me a sport where we would be close together. Touching each other. In swimsuits. My eyes wouldn't focus at the thought. I felt like I had landed on a cloud in heaven.

"My mom raised me with the help of our big Polynesian family. When my father shipped out from Pearl during World War II, Mom was already going to have me, but I don't think he knew about it. They didn't have time to get married."

I must have looked surprised.

"Does that shock you, Sarah?"

My cheeks burned. *An out-of-wedlock child? How would I have handled having a baby if I wasn't married? Abortion? Adoption? No, no, no. I would keep my baby myself.*

"No," I finally answered. "But it probably would shock my parents. They're pretty old-fashioned."

"I guess they don't need to know, then. Not yet, anyway. Right?"

"Um-hm. Right!"

"My father was a Navy fighter pilot. Flew Hellcats. He was shot down over Iwo Jima. Mom always told me how glad she was to have me for a son. I'm the only thing she had left of him – my dad. She always made me feel sort of special, somehow. But I was just another cousin in my grandparent's huge extended family.

"When I graduated from high school, I turned into a total beach bum, teaching tourists to surf, but I decided there was no future in that, so after a couple of years, I made up my mind to go to college. Mom was happy. She didn't want me to be on the beach all my life. My grandparents agreed to help me. They think education is important and they've helped their other grandchildren through school.

He smiled. "Now you." He reached across the table to hold my hand again. "Tell me about you."

"Well, there's not much to tell," I said, feeling my cheeks grow red. *I hate it when I blush like that. Why do I do it?*

"I grew up right here in Santa Barbara and decided to go to Santa Barbara State . . . and . . ." I glanced up into his eyes and felt like I was drowning. "And . . . then . . . I met you." My cheeks burned at my forwardness.

Johnny's eyes locked onto mine, and we sat immobile for a few minutes.

"Guess this is my lucky day," he said. He lifted my hand to his lips and kissed my palm, sending shivers up and down my spine, melting me with his warmth, like a chocolate bar sitting out in the hot sun.

~~~

2000

I made mental notes of things that needed doing as I cleaned. Hardwood floors needed refinishing. I pulled down the tattered lace curtains that disintegrated in my hands. New curtains and shades for the windows. In fact, on closer inspection, new windows seemed to be imperative. Dry rot had taken over their wooden frames. And something had to be done about the kitchen, for sure.

Working warmed me up, but as soon as I stopped to rest a moment, the chill in the house penetrated my bones. A musty odor clung to my nostrils. I kindled a fire in the fireplace to take out the damp. Black smoke poured into the living room I had just cleaned. I probed up the chimney with the fireplace poker, scattering ashes in my hurry, and found the damper closed. By the time I could force it open, I was covered with ashes. The room filled with smoke. Soot had fallen out of the chimney onto the hearth, settling everywhere in minute dots, turning the room into a Nineteenth Century pointillism painting. I sat back on my heels and felt like crying.

The last time I remembered being in black smoke like this was in college. How many years ago? A long time. About thirty years.
~~~

~~~

1969

"I've got a crimp in my hair, Johnny." I frowned. While I lean back in this chair, you iron it out nice and straight. Okay?" I moved a chair close to the end of the ironing board and leaned back on it.

"Yeah, man. I guess." He brushed my long brown hair out straight on the ironing board and laid the damp pressing cloth over it. Johnny licked his finger to test the temperature of the iron. The iron sizzled. I shut my eyes and sat very still. I could smell steam coming from the iron. From my hair. From the pressing cloth. I tried to swallow, but couldn't with my head bent back and my neck stretched out.

"Where's everybody going?"

I swallowed, moving my head forward a little bit on the ironing board. I raised my eyebrows and looked up at Johnny. "You mean you didn't hear about the bonfire at the Quad?"

"No. What's happening?"

"Some of the guys're gonna burn their draft cards."

Johnny set the iron to rest on its heel. He pulled off the cloth and fanned away the steam. He frowned.

I stood up and lifted my hair, letting it fall down straight. "Far out," I murmured, turning around in a circle. I held a hand mirror and looked at my back in the full-length mirror. "Oh, yeah, man, that's cool." My hair hung like a silk waterfall to my waist, cut off blunt
~~~

on the ends, and shimmered in the lamplight. Blouse tucked into a gauzy ankle-length skirt, embroidery around the hem. Long bead necklaces. Dangling roach-clip earrings. Hiking boots. I tied a blue headband around my forehead and painted a thin blue line of eyeliner around each eye with a slender make-up brush. The lid of my lip gloss container snapped off easily. I dipped a pinkie into the shimmering make-up and rubbed it on my lips.

Finally, Johnny spoke. "Well, man, I don't believe in burning draft cards, even if I don't believe in this fuckin' war." He rubbed his beard. "But I'll go to 'Nam if I have to."

I threw my arms around him. "I don't want anything to happen to you, Johnny." My eyes filled with tears causing my nose to run. I sniffed, reached for a Kleenex and held him closer. "What'll I do if you get hurt? Suppose you get shot? Or . . . or killed?" My face pressed against his chest. I smelled the detergent smell of his shirt and the comforting smell of his sweat. His body heat warmed me through the gauzy cotton fabric of my blouse. Tears filled my eyes and spotted his T-shirt with wet drops and blue eyeliner.

"Shit, man. Nothin's gonna happen to me, Sarah. C'mon, let's go."

The sky glowed red like a night battle. Heat from the bonfire rose in waves as we walked through the dark toward the Quad. A slight breeze sent sweet-smelling wood smoke our way. My eyes burned. A loudspeaker screamed in pain. Then an electric guitar filled the air with protest. Protest of the war. Protest of being called to war. Protest of not having a vote about going to war – of being old enough to fight, but not old enough to vote. Jimi Hendrix music, Bob Dylan music. Janis Joplin music.

Two more guitar players joined the first musician who wore a red bandana headband over long, tangled curls. The other two musicians had tied their long hair back in ponytails. Bell-bottomed jeans, patched and ragged, dragged along the pavement. Long fringe on the lead guitarist's leather vest swayed with the rhythm of the music. I clung tight to Johnny's hand as we walked through the maelstrom of frantic bodies all doing their own thing, some dancing to an inner beat only they could hear. A nude body streaked across the Quad in front of the bonfire.

"Hey, man," yelled some girls. "Way to go!" They shrieked and chased the naked boy to the grass where they tackled him and jumped on top of him, laughed and tickled him without mercy.

A group of students hunkered down and passed around a joint while others danced in front of the bonfire. Guys stamped their feet, chanting, "Hell, no, we won't go! Hell, no, we won't go!" Vermillion, a girl from my dorm, reached under her peasant blouse behind her back, unfastened the hooks and pulled off her bra through the blouse's wide sleeves. Her breasts hung loose, soft and visible through the gauze material, swaying in time with the music, rosy nipples at attention.

"Love and peace, love and peace, love and peace," Vermillion chanted as she danced up to the roaring flames, eyes nearly closed, long skirt swaying, beads swinging from her neck, sandals keeping the beat.

She threw her bra into the fire.

I covered my ears with my hands against the roar of the crowd and the crackle of the flames.

Three male students stood in front of the conflagration. Lean bodies in worn-out jeans. Frayed Levi jackets. Long unkempt hair. One wore a cowboy hat with an eagle feather in the hat band. All three stood silhouetted against the red sky. Music played the color red. The color of blood. The color of rebellion. With great care, they took wallets from their jeans pockets, extracted their draft cards, put them on the paved squares of the Quad and squatted down in a half-circle with Bic lighters. Flames licked the edges, turning them brown. The boys tossed their draft cards onto the bonfire.

The music played faster. *"Spinning Wheel",* by Blood, Sweat and Tears. Students yelled. Another girl threw her bra into the fire. Flames reached to the sky. The crowd grew wilder.

Sirens split the air.

"Fuckin' A, man," someone yelled.

"Sooooeeeeepigpigpig."

Scared. I was so scared, I just stood there, frozen, while all around us everyone went crazy.

"C'mon, Sarah, let's get out of here." Johnny pulled me away from the fire.

People scattered as police cars and a fire engine reached the scene. I slipped on the pavement as we hurried away. Johnny helped me up. Someone threw a chunk of pitch-filled pine on the fire, sending showers of sparks high into the sky. The crowd roared, "Hell, no, we won't go!"

The music rose to a frantic, maniacal screech.

Johnny held me close to him, back among the hydrangea bushes at the edge of the Quad, as the police closed in, arresting people in their path. They broke up the marijuana group, scattering weed everywhere.

"Hey! That was good shit, man," protested one of the stoners as the cops put handcuffs on him.

Firemen hosed down the bonfire and any students in their way. I buried my face in Johnny's shoulder, but peeked one eye out to see what was happening. The three draft card burners were handcuffed and put into police cars with the stoners. Black smoke filled the area and covered us in our hydrangea-hide-out with black dots of pointillism soot.

~~~

2000

I shook my head and sighed. Thirty years ago. It seemed like yesterday.

I blinked and looked around Maggie's cottage. Everything, including me, covered with soot.

Well, Sarah, you'd better check out the kitchen stove before you go any further. You'll need that one to cook on, and to heat water, too, if I'm not mistaken. I looked at my grimy hands and felt the soot gritty in my hair as I walked to the kitchen.
~~~

Quaint. Black. Nineteenth century cast-iron stove top. A kitchen cook stove. Two round lids and an hour-glass shaped separator on the fire box could be lifted with a short poker to kindle a fire. A small door under the fire box opened for wood. This door, the oven door with HOME LIFE in raised letters and two doors above the stove top for warming ovens, were covered with blue ceramic. A vintage hot-water tank stood in the corner, next to the stove. Water flowed through the pipes, under the firebox to heat, and back into the hot water tank.

The stove was similar to the one at the beach house where Johnny and I had spent a week, long ago. The summer of '68. I sighed and leaned on the kitchen counter, leaving black fingerprints on the bleached wood, and peered out the high window.

Just before he left for Vietnam.

Tears cut little rivers through the soot and ran down my cheeks. I rubbed my arm across my eyes, smearing the mess on my sleeve.

~~~

1968

The stove in the beach cabin at Rockaway on the Oregon Coast was not blue like Maggie's stove, it was black and cantankerous, hard to build a fire in, but Johnny got it to burn. He opened the draft on the chimney and shaved slivers of wood from a stick of dry kindling with his jackknife. Laid the slivers on top of
~~~

crumpled-up newspaper. Added small sticks of kindling – two or three at a time until the fire took off. Then larger sticks of firewood until the stove glowed and warmed the beach cabin. Even on stormy days, the stove glowed warm, keeping the cabin cozy.

Gray sand dunes. Pale green beach grass. Sunshine and wind. Rain and wind. Fog and wind. Always the wind. We held hands and walked barefoot on the beach, trailing our toes in the sand, making little lines, disturbing sand flea holes that whistled as we scraped our feet over them to take us anywhere. Nowhere. Afraid to think of the future. The War. Vietnam.

John no longer had a college deferment. When we quit school, he lost his deferment. Rather than take his chances on being just another dogface sent out on patrol, he had signed up for helicopter training. If he volunteered, he had a good chance of getting what he wanted. He had to report for duty in thirty days. Most days we were the only ones on the beach. Sometimes we made love in the shelter of a large sand dune, out of the wind, hidden by driftwood, warmed by a small beach fire. Misty salt air clung to our bodies as we clung to each other. The war hung over us like a black cloud. Johnny did not burn his draft card, and I did not burn my bra, although I wouldn't have minded doing that. We felt trapped in a war we didn't want, a war different from previous wars. Why were we in it? Why didn't it just stop?

One day it did. Too late.

~~~

2000

The fire kindled easily in Maggie's kitchen range and brought the hot water tank sitting in the corner attached to the fire box by its umbilical piping, to life. It gurgled and ticked as the water heated. I went into the bathroom and found a dried-up sliver of soap. A wide-eyed raccoon looked back at me from the mirror. I laughed through my tears, stepped into the shower, and scrubbed off the soot. Then I called the Orcas Island Wood Stove Company and made an appointment to have the chimneys swept.

Once in a while I take out the letter sent by Johnny's CO.

4/25/69

Dear Mrs. Haneiki,

I regret to inform you that the helicopter on which your husband, John Hanaeki, was a gunner, has not returned from its last mission. We must presume all aboard have perished. There is a chance, of course, that if the chopper crashed, someone survived, however this is not very likely. For the present, we will list John Hanaeki as Missing in Action, along with the rest of the Huey's crew, but if no trace is found within a reasonable amount of time, we must assume they were all killed.

Please accept my condolences for your loss.
~~~

Major William Walsh
Da Nang Base
Vietnam

If the helicopter had been found, I would have given up hope, but I could not give up hope that Johnny would return to me someday without proof of some kind.

~~~

Music jarred me awake that night. I sat up in bed, disoriented, heart pounding, hands sweating, my room flooded with moonlight. *Piano music in the room right next to my bedroom.* Could someone have come in through the basement door without me hearing him? Maybe a homeless person? Seattle was full of lost souls, why not Orcas Island? I clutched the down comforter and shivered. Pale light streamed across Deer Harbor into my window from the full moon hanging above the water as "The Spinning Wheel" filled the air. This was not the crazy *Blood, Sweat and Tears* song from the 70's, but the beginner's piano piece. Louder. Faster. I slipped out of bed, tip-toed into the hallway and peeked around the corner of the living room. My bare feet turned to ice on the wooden floor, making my teeth chatter.

A young girl about seven years old sat at the piano. She wore her tawny hair pulled back and tied with a blue ribbon that matched the sash on her long-wasted
~~~

dress. Black cotton stockings on her legs. High buttoned shoes. Her toes barely touched the floor. I shivered and clung to the doorframe. Chewed on a ragged fingernail. Breathed in irregular gulps. The old piano looked brand new in the moonlight. Its black finish shone. The ebony keys glistened. The ivories, no longer chipped, cracked and yellowed, glimmered creamy off-white, whole, and new. The child sat up very straight and transposed to another key. "An English Garden" filled the air. I held my breath and stepped closer, but when I stretched one shaky hand to touch this turn-of-the twentieth century child, she disappeared.

I stood in the middle of the living room trembling. Maybe I had dreamed it all and had walked in my sleep. I ventured closer to the piano and touched its worn keys. The lid covering the piano keys stood in an upright position. I knew I had put it down when I went to bed. Hyperventilation made me dizzy as I hurried to check the locks on the doors and even ventured downstairs into the basement to make sure that door was locked. All secure. I ran back to my room and burrowed under the covers, wrapped my icy toes in the down comforter, and pulled one end of the blanket over my head. I shut my eyes tight and lay there, shivering in my moonlit nest. A ghost? No, I did not believe in ghosts. Was I going crazy living all alone with no one to talk to? I certainly hoped not. If she really was a ghost, why was she in my house? I thought ghosts, if they *were* real, appeared if they were unhappy, or had lost their way to another world. This little ghost did not seem unhappy. She appeared to be delighted with the sounds she coaxed from the baby grand piano. Maybe it was all a dream after all. That must be it.

~~~

1908

"The Spinning Wheel" echoed in the tiny cottage.

"Maggie, darlin', that's enough. You'll wear out the piano and yourself if you practice any longer."

"Oh, Mama, I'll never get tired of my piano." Maggie turned around and smiled at her mother. "I never dreamed I would ever have a piano all my own."

Alice wiped the thick wooden kitchen counter with a bleach-soaked rag. "You need to get some fresh air. Go outside. The sun is out. Why don't you find Henry and tell him about your piano?"

"That's a good idea. He'll want to know." Maggie stood up. "I know 'The Spinning Wheel' by heart, now." She put the lid down over the piano keys and walked through the kitchen where she picked up her straw hat and opened the back door. "Did you know Henry's building a sailboat? He says he'll take me sailing when it's finished. Henry's so smart. He can build anything. He wants to build an aeroplane when the boat's finished, and he said I can help." Maggie tied her hat under her chin. "I'll be back soon."

Alice waved and rubbed stove black on the kitchen stove, polishing it. Making it shine.
~~~

Maggie and Henry walked home from Henry's house through the apple orchard. When they reached the tree in the exact center, Henry said, "Stop, Maggie."

"Why?" Maggie looked around, bewildered.

"There's something special on this tree. Close your eyes." Henry held Maggie's hand and led her around the tree. "All right, open your eyes."

Maggie looked, eyes open wide. She saw a fresh carving on the tree bark: Sap trickled down the trunk from the cut. M. M. + H. A. surrounded by a heart.

Maggie blushed. "When did you do this?"

"While you and your mother were in town the other day." Henry looked at her, hoping she liked it.

"It's beautiful, Henry. It must have taken a long time."

"Not so long. Whenever I think of you, time stands still." Henry leaned over and kissed Maggie.

"Oh, dear," Maggie gasped and looked around her. "Mama might see us, Henry," she said.

"We're smack-dab in the middle of the orchard, Maggie. I don't think she can see us."

Maggie smiled and lifted her chin for another kiss. They held hands and walked to Maggie's cottage to see the new piano.

~~~

2000

Walls needed to be washed down again before I could paint. Soot had scattered over everything. I had
~~~

decided not to move my meager furniture from my Seattle apartment, and got rid of it. An upholsterer hauled away all the old over-stuffed furniture to rebuild while I painted and cleaned. Choosing suitable material from so many swatches was mind-boggling, but the upholsterer draped pieces of fabric over the furniture to give me an idea of how things would look. He suggested flower garden chintz for the sofa and the blue of the flowers and the harbor in firm sailcloth weave for the two accent chairs. The worn chairs in the bedrooms looked dowdy and overblown in torn, faded, pink satin, like tawdry ladies of the street. Never mind. Soon they would be respectable again. We chose ivory faille for them. I decided to make ruffled crisscross curtains of off-white muslin for the windows to keep the country look, with old-fashioned roller shades, or perhaps wide-slatted, wooden Venetian blinds to pull down and protect the piano from the late afternoon sun.

I scrubbed the fireplace bricks and sanded the mantel smooth, touched the wood with a little walnut stain and rubbed in teak oil. The collection of twelve porcelain-bisque flower-fairy figurines had baths in warm, soapy water, renewing their bright colors: Hyacinth, dressed in purple; Rose, in rose; Daisy, in green and off-white; Columbine in pink and yellow, and on until all twelve were sparkling clean. I dried them and arranged them once more along the mantelpiece. I wished Johnny could see the house, help fix it up. Ever since I got the telegram, way back in

1969, I'd tried to keep busy and not think about him or the war.

Maybe buying a cottage on an island and living alone wasn't such a good idea after all. Being alone all the time gave me too much time to think. I decided to call Virginia, the only person I knew here, and ask her to meet me for lunch the next day.

That night under a full moon I heard Bach in my living room. How strange to hear music when no one was there but me. I awoke disoriented with my heart pounding, again. I got up and peered around the corner of the living room. Yes, the little girl sat at the piano, playing a minuet. She looked a little older than the first time, but was still a little girl, perhaps 10 years old.

How could there be a ghost in my house when I don't believe in ghosts?

~~~

1910

Maggie practiced a Minuet from the First Lessons in Bach. The precise piece pleased her, and she soon had it memorized. Her mother came in the kitchen door with a basket of groceries. She had walked to the store a mile down the road to buy things that couldn't be grown in the garden. Sugar, salt, baking powder.

"Look what I found, Maggie," Alice said as she set the heavy basket down on the wooden counter. Maggie scooted off the piano bench and skipped to the kitchen, her long hair coming loose from its ribbon. She reached back to re-tie it as her mother lifted the
~~~

small porcelain figure of a flower fairy from her shopping basket.

"This is Hyacinth Fairy. See, her dress is the color of the hyacinths in the garden. Mr. Brown said he plans to have a different fairy every month at the store."

"She's so pretty, Mama." Maggie looked up at her mother. "Are fairies real?'

"No." Alice laughed. "They're . . . like . . . well, like fairy tales – Cinderella, and Snow White. But some people believe in the little folk -- fairies and brownies and elves."

Alice put the salt and baking powder away in one of the high cupboards. "I remember reading one time about two girls who photographed fairies with their father's box camera. They printed the photos and sent them to a newspaper. People really believed their story, but later the girls admitted it was all a hoax. They had set up dolls with fairy wings in the garden and taken pictures of them."

"Well that was sneaky." said Maggie. She looked at the porcelain figure. "I like Hyacinth Fairy. She's so pretty, like a ballerina. And look at her wings, so thin I can see through them," said Maggie. "Shall I put her on the mantel?"

Her mother nodded. "That'd be a good place, wouldn't it?"

Maggie walked slowly, taking care not to drop Hyacinth, and put the statue over the fireplace as Henry walked up on the porch and knocked.

"Come in, Henry," called Maggie. Henry pushed the sticking door open with one shoulder.

"Look what Mama just bought."

Henry looked. "Mm-hmm. That's nice," he said, not really interested. He ran his hand through his thick brown hair, reached over to button one leg of his knickers that kept coming undone, and looked out at the harbor. "Say, Maggie, I thought we could fly kites today. The wind is good out on the point."

"All right." Maggie smiled. "I'll get my kite." Maggie ran to her room for the kite and handed it to Henry while she put on her straw hat. "We're going to the beach, Mama," she called. "All right, Maggie. Be home by suppertime." "Is it all right if I show Maggie the boat I'm building, Mrs. McNamara?" "Why, yes, Henry. I think that'd be fine. Just don't be too late."

~~~

2000

At the hardware store on the ferry road, hundreds of paint color samples overwhelmed me. The paint salesman suggested using off-white to lighten and brighten the dark rusty-colored room and make it seem larger. His advice was good. I painted the room in one weekend. Two coats. I did the bedrooms in off-white, too. All spring I scrubbed and painted while taking care of the flower garden and a small vegetable garden I had planted near the back porch. Strawberry plants grew every which way out there, the runners spreading helter-skelter over the ground. At first, I thought they were wild strawberries, but no, they were domestic.
~~~

Somebody else had had a garden there, once. It was good to find living evidence that someone else had been here before me. The berries were not yet ripe but would be in a few more weeks.

Although my days were full, too much time alone let my thoughts run away, thoughts of Johnny and the War. Vietnam. When he shipped out, I finished my degree and found a job in Hawaii. I needed to be as close to him as possible. Hawaii is in the Pacific. Vietnam is near the Pacific on the China Sea. Yet they were worlds apart. When he was listed Missing in Action, I moved back to the mainland. Mom and Dad were glad to see me and wanted me to live with them while Johnny was gone; but I found a job in San Francisco, so I went to live in a little walk-up apartment on Powell Street. Cable cars rattled and clanged by at all hours, but after a week I got used to their noise. If they had shut down, I would have missed them. Then an offer came from a firm in Seattle, so I moved again.

I discovered a beginning book of Bach in the piano bench. Every evening I took time to play the lovely old piano. Someday I planned to have it refinished and replace the worn ivories with new ones.

~~~

Another month passed. A full moon rose over Deer Harbor flooding its white light over the water and into my house. I went to bed, exhausted from my work, only to be awakened by piano music. I sat up in
~~~

bed, my heart pounding. Fear trickled down my spine in rivulets of sweat. Then I remembered the little ghost girl and slipped down the hall to the living room. She was at it again, only this time, she looked different. At first, I couldn't tell why, but then I realized her feet touched the pedals. She sat taller and looked older, about twelve. Her hair, braided into a loose French braid, held different shades of blonde and brown, woven like spun taffy. Dreamily, she played Debussy's *Clair de Lune – Moonlight.* Moonbeams engulfed her as I stood listening, enchanted by her talent and her promised beauty. I leaned against the door jamb, remembering this piece had been a favorite of Johnny's.

~~~

1912

"I like that one," said Henry, scraping the toe of his boot awkwardly on the hardwood floor. He had graduated from knickers to long pants, and the hems were a little muddy. "Say, do you know anything we can sing?"

Maggie transitioned to *"It's a Long Way to Tipperary"*. Henry sang the words directly to Maggie. She smiled. "Like that better?"

"I like it a lot, but I don't like it *better.* I like everything you play, Maggie." Henry's ears turned pink. "But we should change the words from Tipperary to
~~~

Orcas Island. That's where the sweetest girl I know lives."

Maggie blushed and turned back to the piano.

"How about this?" She played *By the Light of the Silvery Moon.*

"That's good, too." Henry sang along while he looked out the window at Deer Harbor.

"Hey, Maggie, the fog's burned off. Let's go for a boat ride. My boat's finished and I've been practicing sailing."

"Oh, yes, let's." Maggie ran outside where her mother tended the flower garden. "Mama, Henry wants to take me for a ride in his new boat. Is that all right?"

Alice worked bent over. She put one hand on the small of her back, straightened up and looked out at the harbor sparkling with "cat's paws" – little patches of miniature white caps, clues as to where to capture a breeze.

"Are you a good sailor?" Alice impaled Henry with her worried look.

"Yes, Ma'am. I can take my boat anyplace in the harbor. I haven't tried sailing out on Puget Sound yet, just Deer Harbor, but I promise not to take Maggie out in The Sound."

"Very well. Just be careful, you two." Alice sighed and went back to her weeding.

Maggie tied her straw hat under her chin as they walked in the warm sundown the road to Henry's house. Clouds scudded across the sky in the breeze. Gulls circled overhead. Fields of purple and yellow lupine filled the air with their scent.

They stopped at Henry's house. "Goin' sailin', Ma," he said, poking his head inside the kitchen door. His mother waved. Maggie and Henry walked down to the dock. The fourteen-foot boat bobbed gently on the water. White with a blue waterline. Maggie's name on the stern in blue letters.

"Henry! You named the boat for me?"

Henry turned red. "Um-hmm. Like it?"

"I love it. Thank you. I can't wait to tell Mama."

Henry helped Maggie into the boat. She sat on one of two seats that ran down the sides of the boat. Henry untied the mooring line, keeping it snubbed around a dock cleat. He stepped in.

"This is the dagger board," he explained as he let it drop into the water through its housing in the center of the sailboat. "And this is the rudder." Henry unlashed the steering equipment and held on with one hand while he released the sheets for the main sail. "We'll try the jib sail after you get used to sailing."

Henry slipped the mooring line from the dock cleat and pushed the boat away. The wind caught the sail. The wind also caught Maggie's hat, but since it was tied under her chin, it didn't blow away.

"When I say, 'coming about', duck under the mainsail spar and move to the other side of the boat," instructed Henry. "A sailboat has to tack in the wind, or you don't get anywhere."

Maggie nodded.

Wind filled the canvas sail making the fabric snap. They scudded across the harbor like the clouds scudding across the sky. Maggie smiled as she reveled in the freedom of moving so swiftly. The sun warmed her face and arms. Salty sea smells. The cries of gulls wheeling and soaring in the sky.

"I love it," said Maggie. "It's such fun to go so fast. Let's sail every day."

"Every day that's fine," said Henry. "Not when it's rainy or stormy, though."

~~~

2000

Virginia met me for lunch at the gingerbread-trimmed Victorian hotel. We sat by a window overlooking the ferry dock in our go-to-luncheon clothing: nice slacks, sweaters and blazers. Tea in bone china cups. Cucumber and crab sandwiches with the crusts cut off. Tiny macaroon cookies for dessert.

"I'm getting the cottage cleaned up." I held out my work-worn hands, and wondered if I should hide them, they looked so scruffy. I put them on my lap and sighed. "There's so much to do, I haven't had time to go through all Maggie's things, yet. I just stuffed them into the hall linen closet. I'll look through them later." I crossed my legs and leaned back in my chair. "The work is slow, but things look better already. I gave those little statues on the mantel a bath and their colors turned clear and bright. Do you remember them?"

"Yes" Virginia said. "Flower Fairies." The merchants in town promote fairies and elves and
~~~

gnomes to help the tourist trade. Maggie's fairies are delicate porcelain -- real treasures. They don't make many like that anymore. Most are just plastic."

Virginia took a sip of hot tea. "You might like to join the Little Peoples' Group in town – merchants who promote the whole idea. At least come to a meeting at the library. It's a nice way to get acquainted. I'm afraid you're alone too much at Deer Harbor."

I laughed. "I don't believe in things like fairies, but I'm beginning to believe in ghosts!" I shivered. "I'll give it a try. When do they meet?"

"Every other Thursday at seven o'clock." Virginia looked at me, a puzzled frown creasing her forehead. She picked a paper-thin cucumber slice from her sandwich and munched it. "What do you mean you're beginning to believe in ghosts?"

"Don't laugh. I think Maggie's ghost is in my cottage."

Virginia gasped and scooted her chair up closer. "Have you seen her?"

"You're going to think I'm deranged. Cuckoo like a clock from living alone." I squirmed, embarrassed. "Looney Tunes!" My nervous laughter echoed through the room. Other diners turned to look at me. I felt my face flush.

"No, tell me, please. Other people have said the cottage was haunted, but I didn't pay any attention to the stories. Frankly, I didn't want to scare away a potential buyer. Like you." She smiled. "Besides, how would it look on a Real Estate disclosure? *'This house is haunted!'*? Virginia wiped her lips on the linen napkin.

"Seriously, Sarah, I'm sorry I didn't tell you the ghost stories, but you see, I didn't believe them, so I didn't think anyone else would, either." She smiled. "Forgive me?"

I nodded, swallowing a bite of crab. "When the moon is full – and only when the moon is full -- a little ghost girl comes and plays the piano. Plays very well, I might add. Each time she visits, she looks a bit older than the time before, and plays a more difficult piece." I couldn't meet Virginia's eye, so I picked up my teacup, my shaky hands rattling it on its saucer, and gulped Earl Gray tea.

Virginia breathed hard. "Tell me more."

"There's nothing more to tell. She's a very nice little girl dressed in early twentieth-century clothes. Long, blonde hair. Plays the piano. What more could you want in a ghost?" I laughed, trying to make a joke of it, although I found my hands shook even more as I talked. *Stop it Sarah. It's probably just a dream!*

"I've heard stories of people walking past the cottage on moonlit nights and hearing piano music," said Virginia, "but I didn't give it any credit." Virginia laughed.

I made a wry face at her. "She only visits once a month, and if I try to talk to her or touch her, she disappears, just like that!" I snapped my fingers

"That is so interesting, Sarah. I wish I could be there to hear her play."

"I'd invite you to spend the night sometime, but it might spook her – spook the spook!" I said, a little bit hysterical. "Oh, dear, that's really bad."

Virginia laughed and squeezed my arm. "I'm so excited." She wiggled in her chair, making its legs squeak on the dining room's hardwood floor. It's not everyday we have a ghost in our midst." She sighed. "You're probably right. I might frighten her away, but please call me the next time she shows up, will you?"

I nodded, finished my tea, and beckoned the waitress for the check. We added a tip and split the bill. "Got to get back to my restoration," I said. I giggled. "And my little ghost."

We walked to the dining room door. "I wonder if the moon was full when Maggie died. If that's who my ghost really is, could that explain why she only appears on the night of the full moon?"

"I really can't tell you, Sarah, but why don't you meet me at the library tomorrow and we'll look in the archives of old newspapers and see if we can find anything. I can check on the date of her death at the Court House. I have an appointment to show a house at one. Why don't we say three in the afternoon?"

"Good idea, Virginia." I unlocked my car.

"When you find time to paint watercolors again, you should put some of your work in a gallery in town. Paint some flower fairies for the tourists. Paint your ghost for me!" Virginia waved and drove away, her tires scattering gravel along the side of the parking lot.

The next day, I arrived early and applied for a library card. I wandered through the stacks enjoying the smells of the library – of new paper and old, of mildew and mold. The scent of a good read. Books, magazines, pamphlets. I picked out a few novels. Larry McMurtry's Lonesome Dove. Ken Kesey's Sometimes a Great Notion. A new novel called Drowning Ruth.

Virginia came rushing toward me, out of breath. "Sarah!" she said. "I think I've sold another house! Isn't that wonderful?" She threw her arms around me in a bear hug.

"Absolutely!" I hugged her back, wondering if perhaps I should try to get a Realtor's license. Then I wouldn't have to use all my retirement money fixing up the cottage. "I hope you didn't leave too soon just to meet me."

"No, the people want to figure out how to finance it. They need a little time, you know." She looked around the library.

"I think the newspapers from last year are all on microfilm, so let's go into the basement and see what we can find for that date."

Virginia seemed to know her way around, and we soon scrolled through the pages of the Orcas Times for January 2, 2000.

"She won't be in the obituaries on the day she died -- that will be a few days later," said Virginia. "What we need are the phases of the moon and the tide tables."

"Look," I pointed to a page of the paper showing high and low tides; sunrise and sunset; moonrise and moonset. "There's the moon, and it was full on the day she died. Maybe that explains why her ghost comes back only when the moon is full."

"Let's find her obituary."

We scrolled through the copies of the Times for the next few days after Maggie's death. Finally, her obituary showed up.

"Look, Sarah, here it is. See, Maggie was nearly 100 years old. If she had lived another month, she'd have made it."

A photograph on the obituary page showed Maggie McNamara, a young woman seated at a Baldwin grand piano in a concert hall, her tawny hair piled high on her head. She wore a formal evening gown, its train trailing back from the piano bench. A diamond necklace sparkled around her throat.

"She was very attractive, don't you think?"

I nodded. "Talented, too." I sighed, wishing I could have known Maggie in real life, and not just as a ghost.

I gathered the books I had checked out and we walked to the parking lot. An old beat-up pick-up had pulled in beside my Volkswagen. I stopped short and stared. *Déjà vu.* Just the sight of the vehicle dragged memories from my head.

I broke out in a cold sweat and leaned against the truck.

Virginia touched my arm. "Sarah? ...Are you all right?"

"Yeah . . . I think so." I rubbed a hand over my eyes to keep from crying. "It's just this old rusty truck reminded me . . . of . . . something."

~~~

1968

Patches of rust festered through the metal of our dented 1950 Chevy pick-up like scabs on an old scrape. Two bolts holding the right front fender had rusted completely through, and it rattled and clanked along with other loose and worn parts as we navigated hairpin turns on the mountain road. Worn tires skidded in the loose gravel, raising clouds of yellow-white dust, making me want to sneeze. Our worldly belongings banged around in the bed of the pick-up – clothes, bedding, Johnny's guitar carefully wrapped in an old blanket. Thank goodness we'd thought to cover our things with a tarp, or they would be as dusty as the rest of the truck.

I looked back toward the main highway, wishing we were going somewhere else. Anywhere else. But we were headed for our new home deep in the Coast Range of California. Lyle had told us it was a good place to escape the war in Vietnam. A place to hide out. To be safe, even for a short time. He called it a hippie commune, but when I saw Lyle with his friends in their fringed leathers, revving up their hogs, I wondered if it might be more like a bikers' rendezvous.

We could see a cloud rising on the road far ahead of us where the Harleys traveled. Johnny held the pick-up back to keep from breathing their dust. We looked at each other. Was this really what we wanted?
~~~

"Shit, Sarah," said Johnny. "If we don't like it, we'll leave. Don't worry."

I snuggled over next to him, the long stick shift pressed against my stomach. His right arm lay across my shoulder. He steered with his left hand. The truck slid toward the cliff on its threadbare tires. Johnny muttered under his breath, "Fuckin' A, man!", and gunned the engine for more traction. We slewed around the turn, kicking up gravel and dirt, the bald rear tires dangerously close to the edge. He snuggled his nose into my hair and kissed the top of my head. His right hand slipped down inside my blouse and stroked my breast. I pushed my chest up into his palm and looked for a place to pull over away from the road. . . . But then, we'd have lost our guides.

After the bonfire and the arrest of the draft card burners, Johnny and I decided to leave the University and *live* while we had the chance. Mom and Dad were pissed off at us. They practically disowned me.

"Living in sin!" Mom said when we went home to tell them we had quit school. "My only child! How could you?" Her hands shook. Eyes all red and weepy.

"Now, Sarah," said my father. He cleared his throat. "You know nice girls don't do what you and Johnny are doing."

"Why, Dad?" I couldn't help smiling. "What're we doing?"

"Well. . . um . . . you're . . . well, because . . it's " He squirmed in his chair. "It's just not done. Your mother doesn't approve."

I grinned at him. *He's jealous. He'd like to do it, himself! I'll bet he wishes he were nineteen again, too.*

"But, why, Dad? This is 1968. It's a good idea to move in together to see if you can make it. Not so many divorces that way." I couldn't keep from teasing him. "Now tell me, why?"

Dad glared at me. "Because it upsets your mother, that's why!"

I laughed and kissed the top of his shiny head. "Don't worry, Dad, Johnny and I'll get married."

I took Johnny's hand and we skipped down the porch steps. Waved at my parents. "Love ya," I called, blowing them a kiss.

And we did. We got married. On the beach near Oceana. Our friends joined us as witnesses. One of Johnny's friends, Kevin, who designed and made jewelry, crafted wedding rings from sterling silver for us with intertwined peace signs engraved on them. A matched set. I wore a long white *Gunne Sax* dress by Jessica McClintock, trimmed with white hand crocheted lace and white embroidery – almost a Victorian dress. A wreath woven of lupine and California poppies picked from the sand dunes for my hair -- my long, straight, hair shimmering clean, hanging down my back to my waist. More flowers and bunches of beach grass for my wedding bouquet. Johnny wore his same old patched jeans.

We stood near the surf, our bare feet wet and sandy, and held hands in front of our friends as we vowed our eternal love for each other. First Johnny spoke, quoting a poem from Bob Dylan. Then me. I used a poem by Joan Baez and twisted it around to suit myself. Wind blew. Waves crashed onto the beach. The sun dipped down into the ocean, turning the water and the sky brilliant red. Kevin played "Never My Love" on his guitar, while Chastity played the flute and Vermilion sang. I looked deep into Johnny's eyes as the words of the song echoed in my mind and I thought *no, 'I will never stop loving you'.* Johnny kissed the bride – me -- a long, sexy kiss, practically making love right there in front of God and everybody. Our friends cheered and clapped. Gulls cried and hung on the thermals overhead. I finally extricated myself from the kiss, and taking his hand, ran away to the water where I kicked up the surf, splashing him.

"This'll cool you off," I laughed.

Then we all danced on hard-packed wet sand to the music of Eric Clapton while Gordon Lightfoot played on somebody's eight-track. The guys had gathered mussels from the rocks and cooked them in a huge kettle over a beach fire. Grass. Everyone brought food. Mushrooms. Vermillion and Chastity made the wedding cake of granola bars, stacked up and held together with ready-made Betty Crocker cake icing. Beer. People slept where they had fallen, behind driftwood piles, in the dune grass. I hoped above the tide's high-water mark. Johnny and I had our bridal suite staked out a mile down the beach in a nest of driftwood. Later we wandered down there hand in hand by the light of the moon.

We stopped to see my folks the next day to tell them we were married.

"Where is the marriage license?" Mom frowned, twisting her hands together.

"Oh, Mom," I said. "That's so bourgeois. Who needs a piece of paper, anyway?"

"You might, some day. If something happens to Johnny, you'll have no rights without a legal certificate. And the way the world looks now, you might wish you did." Once more, Mom's eyes filled with tears. She sniffed and wiped her nose with a Kleenex.

"For real?" Johnny shook his head. "Awesome!" His long hair bounced. "Well, Babe, we better high-tail it to the courthouse and make it legal." He grabbed my hand. My worry about him must have shown, because he put one arm around me and said, "Shit, man! Nothin's gonna happen to me, but, like, we'll make it legal, just in case, y'know?" He glanced at my mom. "Make your mother feel better, okay?"

Mom heaved a sigh of relief. I'm sure she thought that now she would be able to hold her head up in the neighborhood. I would not be living in sin. What a terrible thought. How can love be a sin?

~~~

2000

There's dry rot in the wooden window frames. All of them, except the attic windows. Rotten. A contractor came out today and showed me samples of
~~~

different double-paned windows. Most people buy vinyl-clad windows, because they're cheaper and more efficient, but they just didn't seem to fit the cottage. I decided I had to have the more expensive wood-framed windows. I also made up my mind to replace the picture windows someone had installed on the front of the house in a long-ago remodel, with windows original to the cottage – "Oriels" -- many-paned windows cantilevered out from the side of the house. They might have to be a little larger than the original windows, because I have to fit the existing openings, but I think they should be wooden framed, suitable to the era in which the house was built. But for the time being, I'll leave the picture windows in the attic for good lighting when I find time to paint. The glass man said he could install a second sheet of glass on them to make them double-paned for better insulation.

A big chunk of money. What have I gotten myself into? This little place sucks money up like water in a sponge. But the windows will be worth it if only to save heat in the winter, which reminds me, I need to check out the old furnace. Maybe next week.

I ordered the windows and shuddered when I thought of the cost. Maybe I won't be able to do everything I want to do to Maggie's cottage. Or I might have to come out of retirement and get a job. But I decided to put corner windows, smaller oriels, by the kitchen table, anyway. The contractor said he could do that by putting in a header where the wall is now. A big, low, garden window will go over the sink looking right out at the English flower garden and the boat basin. Low enough for me to see out without standing on tip toe. This window will need a new header, too, as it will be three times as wide as the original window.

I might as well stop washing windows if I'm going to replace them.

The hardwood floors in the living room, hallway and bedrooms had to be refinished. I decided to have them done professionally, with the new Swedish finish that is practically indestructible. *There goes more of my retirement money. Refinishing takes three to four days, and I'll have to be out of the house because of the fumes from the process. Most of the furniture is at the upholsterers. The workers will put the rest in the attic while the floors are being done. I'll take the ferry to Seattle and do some shopping. It'll be a good opportunity to visit friends. My bag is packed, ready for the 7:30 a.m. boat tomorrow.*

Tchaikovsky's Romeo and Juliet overture awakened me in the night. Once more, the moon was full. Was that significant? I know now that Maggie died when the moon was full and I hear the piano only during the full moon. I slipped out to watch the musician, as she immersed herself in her music, unaware of my presence. I wished she would talk to me, look at me, and let me touch her. Is she just a figment of my imagination? Am I losing my sanity?

~~~

1912

"Did you like that one, Papa?"

"Yes, Maggie. You're doing quite well. I think the piano was a good thing, don't you?"

"The most wonderful thing, Papa. Thank you," agreed Maggie. "I'm going to be a concert pianist some day."

"Well," her father chuckled, "we'll see about that. I'm just glad you enjoy it for your own self."

"Alexander," called Maggie's mother. "Hiram's at the back door to see you. I tried to get him to come in, but he won't."

Maggie's father put down his newspaper and went to the door.

"Well, Hiram, what can I do for you?"

"It's Gretchen, Doc." Hiram rubbed his nose with his sleeve. "She's having pains already, and it's not nearly time, yet. The baby's coming way too soon, I'm thinking. She's afraid she'll lose it. Can you come right now?" He sniffed and used his sleeve for a handkerchief again.

"Yes, of course I'll come. Let me get my medical bag."

"I might not be home tonight, Alice." He breezed a kiss on her cheek and ran out the door. "I think I detected two heartbeats. We might be delivering twins tonight. Don't wait supper for me."
~~~

Maggie watched her father as he took the steps two at a time down to the back yard, sprinted to the shed and threw open the shed door. Tossed his black bag into the Model "T". He reached inside the car and turned the dash lever to 'on' and set the spark on the ignition. Then he hurried around front and made sure the crank handle was in the bottom position. He reached under the radiator for the choke ring, gave it a couple of pulls. He held the crank handle with his palm open, gave it a sharp turn to the top position, and jerked his hand back just in time to keep from breaking his arm as the engine caught, putt-putting softly, kicking out puffs of exhaust. The automobile shook and rattled.

"Get in, Hiram," Alexander called.

But Hiram had already mounted his horse. "Follow me," he shouted, and galloped down the road.

Maggie stood on the porch watching, twisting a piece of her hair. "Mama? Will Gretchen be all right? Will her baby be all right?"

Alice put her arms around Maggie and held her close. "I don't know, Maggie. Your father will do everything he can. We just have to hope and wait and see."

"I'd like to make a present for the baby. Will you show me how to knit?"

"Of course, Maggie, but you need to start with something simple, to learn how to handle the needles and yarn. How about knitting a scarf?"

"All right. I'll make one for Henry. Then I'll make something for the baby. A sweater or booties."

Maggie struggled for the next hour with knitting needles and yarn. Finally, she grew tired and put Henry's scarf away for awhile.

~~~

2000

The window contractor came yesterday to put in the new windows. I never dreamed it would be such a mess. Sawdust and plaster all over everything. I should have had the windows done first. I followed the workers around inside the house with my vacuum cleaner, afraid the dust would get all over everything again.

Such a big hole in the wall above the sink for the garden window. But it's in, now. I love it. Hooray! I can see out.

New headers. New windows. The whole kitchen has opened up. It seems bigger, somehow. Lighter. Airier. Now I need to decide about new cabinets and wall paint and the floor covering for the kitchen. Something light. No more dark rooms.

~~~

1916

"Papa says Gretchen is fine, Henry. Did you know twins nearly always come early? I didn't know she was having twins, did you? Want to walk over there on

Sunday and see them? Two little boys. They are so-o-o tiny. Not very pretty yet, but when they've grown a few weeks, they'll be cute and cuddly." Maggie took a skip between steps, and then stopped, perhaps because skipping seemed too little-girlish to her now she had put her hems down and her hair up.

"All right, I'll go see them with you. But let's go sailing, now. The sun is out and the wind is perfect. Your mother agreed it would be a good day to sail."

"Let's try the jib sail this time," said Maggie lifting her ankle-length, wool tweed skirt to step from the dock to the boat.

"I guess you're ready to help do this. See, when there's just enough wind in the sail you cleat it, like this." He demonstrated how to handle the sheet for the jib.

Maggie nodded. "I can do that."

"Swell. Just remember when we come about, to bring the sheet with you." He put the end of the rope in her hand. "But we'll sail without the jib first for a while, to get you used to the feel of sailing again.

The boat sailed fast with just the main sail. Henry and Maggie sat on the gunwale with their feet tucked under a strap across the dagger board housing and balanced the little boat as it heeled over the opposite way in the wind. Maggie's hat blew off, but stayed tied under her chin, hanging down her back. Hairpins fell out of her hair and it blew loose in the wind. She leaned back laughing. Her hat came untied and blew away. Maggie's long hair trailed in the water.

They tacked back and forth across the harbor. Every time they came about, Maggie tucked up her long heavy skirt and ducked under the mainsail boom to sit on the opposite side of the boat. They sailed around Deer Island, a small green emerald set in a sea of blue.

"Next time let's bring a picnic and have it on top of the little island," said Maggie.

Henry grinned at her. "Will you make the picnic?"

Maggie nodded, pushing her loose hair away from her face as she peered at the island.

"All right," said Henry. "This time let's see how fast this boat will go. Are you ready to try the jib?"

"Yes, I am," Maggie shouted. She picked up the end of the sheet to show him. Henry cleated the main sail and said, "Sit here and steer on this tack, while I raise the jib."

Maggie looked a little unsure of herself.

'It's okay. Sit right here and hold the rudder steady. I'll only be a minute."

Maggie wiped the palms of her hands on her woolen skirt and took hold of the rudder handle. Henry stepped to the prow of the boat, pulled the jib to the top of the mast and tied it off. Then he moved back to the stern, took the rudder from Maggie and handed her the jib line.

"When the sail fills and doesn't luff in the wind, cleat the sheet on the gunwale, there." He pointed to a cleat next to Maggie. "Don't let go of the end of the sheet, though, because this time when I say 'coming about', you need to un-cleat it, cross over to the other side, and cleat it over here." He pointed to the other cleat.

Maggie gulped and nodded.

"O-o-o-kay, here we go. Coming about!"

Maggie uncleated the jib sheet, lifted her long skirt and moved to the other side of the boat, cleating the line on that side. She smiled. "I did it!"

"You did fine," agreed Henry.

They practiced this maneuver several times. The boat went much faster with the jib sail. Maggie reveled in the swiftness of the little craft as it sped across the harbor. The boat heeled over with both sails set, and they had to sit on the gunwale, tucking their feet under the strap on the dagger board housing to balance it.

"Hooray-y-y-!" yelled Maggie, smiling from one ear to the other.

A sudden gust of wind grabbed the boat and flipped it. Henry and Maggie went under, but only Henry surfaced. Maggie's long, heavy skirt pulled her down, down into the cold depths of Deer Harbor.

"Maggie!" shouted Henry. He glanced around in desperation, took a deep breath and dove after her. Maggie's long hair floated up toward him in a swirl of sea-green water, bubbles rising in streams from her hair and clothing. He grabbed hold of her long hair, working his way down to her body, lifting her toward the surface, but her long skirt was too heavy and pulled them like an anchor toward the bottom. Maggie struggled to get out of the skirt. Henry ripped the waistband open, tearing the buttons off, and peeled the skirt away. He kicked hard, and they rose to the top with the bubbles, gasping and choking.

Henry lifted Maggie across the sailboat's upturned bottom, climbed up next to her and pressed her sides to get the water out of her lungs. Her rib cage, encased in a tight corset could not move.

"Damn!" *Why do women wear these things, anyway?*

He ripped the back of Maggie's blouse apart to get at the corset laces. The wet strings would not budge. Henry reached in his pants pocket for his jackknife. *Don't drop this knife now, Henry old man,* he told himself. He opened the knife and cut the corset laces. Maggie's chest expanded. Henry held the knife in his teeth and pressed her sides. In . . . out. In . . . out.

Maggie choked, coughed and vomited. Henry looked around for help. There were no other boats in sight. He couldn't turn the boat over and hold onto Maggie, too. Deer Island loomed in the distance ahead. He closed the jackknife and slipped it back into his pocket.

"Listen, Maggie," he said. "I'm going to swim you over to the island and then I'll come back and get the boat."

Maggie did not answer.

"Did you hear me?" Henry called, struggling to remove his shoes. One shoe came loose and sank to the bottom. Then he got the other one undone and let it go.

"Maggie? Maggie? Hold on to me. We're going to the island."

Maggie choked and vomited sea water. She nodded and put her arms around his neck, the remains of her corset trailed in the water and floated away. Shreds of her blouse floated like kelp on top of the waves. Maggie rested against Henry's back. Henry let go of the boat and moved toward the island, swimming steadily, pacing himself. The tide had turned and would help him if it didn't carry him too far to the left. Deer Island drew nearer. Maggie's arms slipped away from Henry's neck. He turned around, treading water, holding her up.

"Maggie," he whispered. "Wake up. I know you're tired, but try to hang on. Look," he pointed with one hand, holding her up with the other. Waves splashed into his mouth. He spat out salt water and gasped for breath. "Look, Maggie, we're almost to the island. Not much further. Please! Please hold on."

Maggie choked on the waves. Eyes closed, she nodded.

After what seemed an eternity, Henry touched bottom. He stood up and carried Maggie in his arms to the beach where they collapsed on the sand. Henry checked on Maggie. *Yes, she was breathing.* The sun beat down. Gulls cried. Sticky salt water and sand dried on their bodies.

When he got his wind back, Henry unbuttoned his shirt, stripping it off, keeping one eye on the boat drifting toward the harbor entrance. He shook the sand and seaweed from the shirt and put it over Maggie's bare back as she lay on her stomach. The buttons on his soaked trousers were harder to do, but he stripped them off, too, all wet and sandy, and stood, a little embarrassed in his BVDs.

"Maggie," he knelt down to touch her. She opened her eyes and sat up, holding Henry's shirt around her. He smoothed a tendril of hair from her face and kissed her, a long, lingering kiss on the lips.

"Maggie, I'm going back to get the boat. I'll come for you as soon as I can. Understand? The tide's going out, and it's taking the boat with it. I've got to get it before it passes the island. There aren't any other boats out there. We'll be stranded here if I can't bring it back."

Maggie coughed and nodded, clinging to his hand. "Be careful, Henry." She fell back onto the sand.

Henry waded out in the water and dove under the whitecaps, swimming diagonally against the current, taking his time, not panicking, but straining his muscles to make any headway. The boat drifted east of the island. Henry swam harder, exerting all his strength to reach the craft as it was carried out into The Sound. Maggie stood up and followed along the island's edge, stumbling over rocks, seaweed and driftwood.

Finally, the tips of Henry's fingers touched the keel. He lurched forward, grabbed for a hold, and pulled himself up on the dagger board. He lay still for awhile, panting. He could see Maggie standing on the shore. She had scrambled over rocks and driftwood to the east side of the island, the better to see him. The boat drifted with the tide, past the island toward the larger waves of Puget Sound.

Henry stood on the dagger board, holding onto the gunwale of the craft. Gradually, his weight pushed the dagger board underwater. He looked toward the island and Maggie, making sure she was still all right. She stood on some driftwood, watching him. He knew if he tried to hurry the process by jumping on the dagger board, it would break. Slow and steady worked best. Finally, the boat turned back upright, wallowing in the water. Sails dripped. Sheets tangled. Henry climbed in and bailed with an old coffee can he kept in the boat for just such an occasion. By this time the tide had carried him past the breakwater out into The Sound. Although Henry was unable to bail all of the water out, he sorted out the sails and sheets, and using just the main sail, headed back to Deer Island, tacking across the tide's pull. He waved to Maggie as he rounded the end of the island.

Maggie followed his progress, stumbling back around the island to where the boat could land. She picked up his clothing and stood watching him. He drew close, raised the dagger board and ran the boat up on the sand. Maggie walked into the water, carrying his clothing, her wet slip plastered to her long legs. Henry's shirt hung from her shoulders and blew in the wind revealing her young bosom covered with a tangled mass of her hair and seaweed. Henry thought she had never looked more beautiful. He climbed out to help her aboard, then pushed off the beach, jumped back in the boat, lowered the dagger board and set sail for home.

~~~

2000

It took a little time to move Maggie's things from the closets and drawers and make room for my own things. I bundled up her clothes and took them to the Salvation Army. Boxes of photos and letters looked interesting, so I stuffed them into the already nearly full hall linen closet to look at later. My own letters from Johnny went in the top dresser drawer. I couldn't resist taking time to read one of them:

September 1, 1968

Dear Sarah,

We landed here at Da Nang Base last week. The place is crazy, with helicopters and hooches all around. Hooch is what they call the building we live in – a kind of a house. I'm crew chief of a Huey helicopter. It's my job to keep it in perfect running condition. I'm also a door gunner on this bird. I love to fly. When we pull pitch on a mission, my heart jumps up into my throat, and I'm alive as never before. The whump – whump of the rotors make a nice comforting sound.

Sorry I haven't written sooner, but we've been real busy. Keep the letters coming. They mean a lot to me.

Love, Johnny
~~~

~~~

1914

Alice started a fire in the kitchen stove early that morning. Even though it might be a warm day, and they wouldn't need the heat, she needed hot water for the laundry. While the water in the tank heated, she carried the dirty clothes downstairs to the unfinished basement.

"Come and help me, Maggie," she called.

"Oh, Mama, you know I hate doing laundry. Can't I just stay upstairs and practice?"

"No, darlin'. Some day you'll need to know how to do this yourself. Come along, now."

Maggie grumbled as she stumbled down the stairs to the basement.

Dim early morning light penetrated the window above the concrete wash tubs.

"You need to cut the soap like this," said Alice. She shaved thin pieces from a bar of yellow laundry soap with a paring knife. The scalding water melted the bits of soap. Bubbles foamed high in the tub.

"Now we need to sort the clothes as to color. You can help do that."

Maggie made a pile of white clothes, a pile of light-colored clothes, and a pile of dark clothes. Alice rolled up the sleeves of her cotton dress and put the white sheets into the tub filled with hot soapy water. She handed Maggie the clothes pole to push them under the steaming water and swish them around. Alice filled
~~~

the other tub with cool water and fastened the wringer to the divider between the two tubs.

"All right, Maggie. The sheets are ready. You turn the handle of the wringer while I put the sheets through it." Alice lifted one end of a sheet with her pole, set the hem between the rollers of the wringer, and Maggie turned the crank. The sheet went through the wringer, squeezing hot water and suds from the fabric, and fell into the cool rinse water in the other tub. She swished the fabric around, turned the wringer on its pivot to the side of the tub, and fed the sheet back through while Maggie turned the handle again. The sheet fell into a laundry basket positioned underneath the wringer on the floor.

Maggie, darlin', you can put the white dish towels into the hot suds, now. I'll take the sheets out and hang them on the line." Alice picked up her basket and headed out the basement door to the side yard and the clothesline.

Maggie heaved a big sigh and dumped the white dishtowels into the soapy water, poking them around with the pole. She ran to the side yard and handed her mother clothespins and together they hung the wet sheets on the line.

"May I go in and practice, now?"

"No, Maggie. You may not. We're not finished."

Maggie picked up a smooth stone and threw it toward the water but missed. She tried another. The sun sparkled on white caps in the harbor. The white sheets danced on the clothesline.

Alice scrubbed dirty socks on a scrub board. She became hot and sweaty, her hair falling in tendrils about her face. The strong smell of the laundry soap irritated her nostrils. She rubbed her nose with her arm.

"Come turn the wringer again, Maggie," called Alice.

Maggie came back inside and helped her mother. Together they carried another full basket of wet clothes to the clothesline.

"This is the way we hang out our underwear so no one can see them," said Alice as she pinned her under-drawers inside a pillowcase.

Maggie laughed. "Why do you care if anyone sees them?"

"Well, because they're mine. They're private."

"That's kind of silly," said Maggie.

"Silly or not, that's the way it's done."

By the time Alice got to the dark clothes, the soapy water had turned a light gray color, and had become cool enough to put her hands in. She finished the last load and Maggie helped her hang it to dry. The sun broke out of high clouds. Alice stood in a stiff breeze that blew her fly-away hair back and cooled her sweaty body. She took deep breaths of the clean air and looked out over the harbor. Maggie ran around the clothesline in the wind, turning around and around and fell to the ground. A sailboat tacked across the water. Alice's clean white sheets snapped in the wind on the clothesline, as the sailboat's white sails snapped out on the bay.

"Now you may go practice, Maggie," said her mother.

"Come with me, Mama. I want to play my new piece for you. It's a Gnossienne by Erik Satie." She tugged her mother's arm. "I want you to see how the music is written, too. It's really weird with no bars to mark the measures. It was written before they had invented measures for music."

~~~

2000

My shopping trip to Seattle yielded a new, soft green area rug with a leafy border for the living room. I had taken the broken Tiffany lamp I found in the attic with me and had its colored glass pieces replaced, just like new. I felt a little ridiculous driving onto the ferry boat with a hunk of carpet sticking out the back window of my VW. But, never mind. At least it didn't rain. I set the lamp carefully on the baby grand piano and rolled the rug out on the newly finished hardwood floor, remembering how Johnny had liked green. Beautiful.

The furniture arrived the next day, and the upholsterer helped me arrange it around the rug. He even brought pipe clamps and wood glue and re-glued the joints of the creaky piano bench. Everything went well with the off-white paint on the walls and woodwork. The piano received an extra-careful dusting. I decided to wait until winter to make the curtains.
~~~

Sewing is a good indoor activity. Right now, I'm too busy with outdoor things.

That evening, I built a little fire in the fireplace, and holding my plate, ate my supper standing in the threshold of my beautiful room, admiring it and the view of Deer Harbor and tiny Deer Island. The setting sun flooded the water and the room in a rosy glow. The Tiffany lamp competed with the sun, splashing bits of color over the piano and walls. Red, green, blue, and gold. After I had eaten, I played the piano, not as well as Maggie's ghost, but good enough to suit me. Good enough to celebrate my new room.

That night I went to sleep in the light of the full moon. Once again, I was awakened by piano music. This time the piece was Brahms' Hungarian Dance No. 5. The lively Slovakian music made my feet itch to dance. I could picture the Magyars in their colorful costumes dancing, dancing, dancing, the girls' skirts full with yards of petticoats, their clothing rich with hand embroidery. I slipped out into the hall to watch my ghost play. Maggie looked to be about seventeen. I felt as proud of her as if she were my own daughter. The child I never had. A beautiful, young lady.

~~~

1917

Henry clowned around, dancing a gypsy dance to Maggie's Hungarian music. When the piece ended, he
~~~

stumbled against the piano and knocked over the Tiffany lamp. Bits of colored glass tinkled to the floor. He staggered across the room and collapsed on the sofa, smashing through the frame. Maggie and Henry dissolved in fits of laughter.

"Oh, no, Mrs. McNamara!" Henry spluttered. "I'm afraid I've broken your furniture. I'm so sorry."

"Oh, Henry, how could you?" Alice stood with her hands under her apron and looked at her ruined sofa. She tried to pick up the broken end, but it fell apart to the floor. She looked at Henry, big and masculine in the small crowded room. "Well, we can't cry over spilt milk. I'll just ask Dr. McNamara to repair it."

"No, I'll fix it. I'll bring my tools and some nails and lumber over tomorrow and fix it."

Alice rescued the broken lamp and pieces of glass, put them in a box and took the box to the attic. "I'll take it to Seattle next time we go and have it repaired," she said.

Maggie giggled. "Mama thinks you can do no wrong, don't you Mama," Maggie called after her mother's retreating back. "Every day she talks about how you saved both our lives that day, Henry. About how won-der-ful you are." Maggie spread her arms wide to emphasize the word. "How if it had been anyone else out there in the water, we'd both be drowned." She leaned over and whispered. "I didn't tell her how fast we were going or how far the boat had heeled over."

Maggie grabbed Henry's arms and pulled him off the broken sofa. "I've great news, Henry. I've been accepted at the school of music in Seattle. Some day I'm going to be a concert pianist. Isn't that won-derful?" She danced around the room with him.

"You're what?" Henry's face fell. "You're leaving the island?" He stood, arms dangling loose at his sides. He sank to the floor. "You're going away?" His eyes slid from Maggie to Alice standing in the doorway. "Leaving me? And . . . and your mother and father, too?" Henry sat, stunned. "Oh, no. Don't go to Seattle, Maggie."

"Silly. I'm not going to stay there. I'll just take the ferry over twice a week for lessons and come home to practice."

"Well, if that's all, I guess I'm happy for you. I just couldn't bear the thought of you leaving, Maggie." His face turned red as he noticed Maggie's mother watching him.

"Mrs. McNamara, excuse me, but I . . . well, I . . . I love Maggie, and some day, I'm going to marry her, if she'll have me. You see . . . " Henry wiped his hands on his pants legs. "That is, with your permission . . . and the Doctor's, too, of course."

"I see, Henry. It would make us all happy if that's what the two of you want. I know you'd never stand in the way of Maggie's career as a pianist"

~~~

2000

I've been painting the outside wood trim – white to set off the pale blue gray of the house. What a job! At least there's no dry rot in the new windows. I'll hire a painter to help with the second story windows. Tall ladders scare me. The inside of the cottage is coming along. New plank-faced, country-style white cabinets and white paint in the kitchen lightened it along with the garden window. Johnny would have liked the place. The garden produced more than enough for one person, so I froze things for the winter. Along the edge of the property, blackberry vines are trying to take over. I'll have to cut them back, but not until I pick the berries to make jelly and freeze some for winter pies.

~~~

1967

Blackberry vines grew rampant in Blackthorn Valley. The other girls and I would put on our bib overall shorts, lay the babies on blankets on the grass and let the little children play in the fields while we picked blackberries to make pies. The hot sun ripened the berries, filling them with sweetness. Our bodies tanned and our fingers and mouths grew stained with berry juice.

I thought we were among friends in Blackthorn Valley but found out that was not the case. More guys wearing fringed black leather hung around there than guys like Johnny in tattered Levi's. Biker's girl friends wore leather, too. The hippie girls wore sandals and long skirts. Many girls either packed a small child around on their hip, or were pregnant, or both. But not me – not Sarah.

The spring and summer weather stayed warm. We all worked hard. Shared the work. Shared the food. Lyle and his biker friends with the Harleys had already built a large building with a kitchen of sorts. It had a wood-burning cook stove and a sink with a hand pump to use if we needed water. A huge fireplace of river rock. People slept where-ever. Some shared their boyfriends and girlfriends. Johnny and I didn't do that. What we had was too special. I had to watch out for Vermillion, though. She had her eye on Johnny. Since she was a single and others shared with her, she seemed to expect me to share, too.

But I didn't.

We planted a communal garden. I ruined my fingernails. At first everyone helped. Then it got so just the girls did the gardening. Little kids underfoot. Babies. Mothers breast feeding. Single guys gawked, wanted to try it, too. There always seemed to be a baby or small child crying. Most of the guys worked in the marijuana patch, hidden from the Feds way back in the forest, or they lay around getting high on weed and anything else they could find. They spent a lot of time tramping through the redwoods looking for hallucinogenic mushrooms without any luck. Oh, they found a few mushrooms, but no one knew poisonous mushrooms from non-poisonous, so only the hard-core stoners had the nerve to try them. A tiny taste. Just to see if it'd kill them. Thank goodness, Johnny wasn't like that.

Lyle found a market for the marijuana.

The women did the laundry in the creek, downstream. The toilet was out back. I soon realized I had traded civilization for the life of a pioneer. I only put up with this for Johnny's sake. As far as I'm concerned, the flush toilet is the greatest invention ever.

Mountains covered with dark-green Redwood trees hung over us like the hunched shoulders of fairy tale ogres. Blackberry vines grew at the edges of the fields. Salal proliferated on the floor of the forest. Trilliums, their delicate three-petalled faces echoed three-petalled leaves. Bunchberry with small white flowers. All kinds of ferns. Speckled orange tiger lilies. Indian paint brush.

The morning sun took longer to penetrate our commune than it did "on the outside" and by four o'clock in the afternoon it disappeared behind the mountains to the west. We sat in a dark old growth Redwood valley in Mendocino County, isolated from the world, living the way people did a hundred years ago. Our only money crop was illegal. I hated it, but stayed to protect Johnny from having to go to war. I regretted our dropping out of college. At least he'd had a deferment as long as he was in school.

~~~

2000

I kept the wood cook stove with its quaint blue door fronts but installed a small apartment-size electric stove next to it. Certain things baked in the oven of the wood stove tasted better, like homemade bread and apple pie with apples from my own trees. I had the basement floored, and a new electric hot water tank installed down there to produce hot water more quickly than the wood burning stove with the heating coils. It was a nuisance to have to build a fire whenever I needed hot water, especially in hot weather. An automatic washer and dryer near the old concrete wash tubs made laundry a breeze.

New kitchen cabinets updated the kitchen in a hurry. I decided to keep the wooden drain board made of a single slab of old growth Douglas fir, and had it refinished, installed a new kitchen sink and modern single-handled faucet. The garden window enlarged and lightened the kitchen. New vinyl on the kitchen floor.

~~~

1917

"I'm helping Henry build an aeroplane, Mama." Maggie struggled through the door, her arms loaded with yards of linen. "Will you let me use the sewing machine?"

The linty smell of linen filled the cottage. Alice lifted one corner of the fabric and sneezed. "I don't know if my machine will sew through this, but let's give it a try."

Maggie spread the material out on the floor. "See, these pieces have to be sewn together like so." She held them up for her mother to see. "Henry numbered them so I'll have no trouble remembering. And this isn't all of it. Henry's bringing the rest this afternoon. After we sew the pieces together, we'll tack them onto the wooden framework of the plane." She smoothed the fabric. "Then we paint it with "dope" to tighten it up." Maggie sorted through the pieces of linen. "Don't you think Henry's clever to do this?"

Alice pulled the sewing machine to the middle of the living room. She smiled. "Yes, Maggie. He's very clever for a young man only twenty years old. But this time, I have to put my foot down. I didn't mind you going sailing until you nearly drowned, but you really must not try to fly in this aeroplane. Please. Give me your word of honor. Flying is very dangerous, no matter what those Wright brothers say about it."

"Oh, Mama, there's nothing to it. Henry says if he has trouble with the engine, he'll just glide down and land on the beach. We've practiced flying kites for years, so we know all about it. Don't worry. I can't wait to go for a ride."

Alice stood and twisted her hands together. "You'd better ask Papa what he thinks." She went into the kitchen to start lunch.

Maggie moved a handle to switch the sewing machine belt over to connect the wheel with the treadle of her mother's *Singer.* She positioned two pieces of fabric under the pressure foot, let the pressure foot down with its lever, and started the machine with a downward push on the wheel, while rocking the treadle.

The treadle had to be pumped with her feet to keep the machine running. It took a lot of concentration to do two things at once – pump the treadle and guide the fabric. If she forgot to pump, the thread would break and she'd have to stop and re-start it. Sometimes, the bobbin thread would become tangled, or the needle would have to be re-threaded. Maggie grew hot and tired and cross as she struggled with the linen fabric.

Alice poked her head into the room where Maggie worked. "Do you need some help, darlin'?"

"No. I don't need help. I just need . . . Drat!"

Close to tears, Maggie looked up at her mother. "The darned thread just broke for about the hundredth time!"

"Tsk,tsk." Alice shook her head. "You mustn't use bad language, dear."

Maggie took a deep breath, re-threaded the needle and tried again. The needle broke. Maggie put her head down on her arms and cried.

"There, there, Maggie." Alice rummaged in one of the sewing machine's drawers. "Here's a new needle. I'll put it in the machine for you."

Footsteps pounded on the porch as Maggie stood up to let her mother sit at the *Singer.* Her face brightened. "It's Henry! He'll be able to make this horrid machine work right." Maggie smiled and brushed away her tears. "Come in, Henry," she yelled.

"Really, Margaret. It is not lady-like to yell like that," said her mother.

"Sorry, Mama." Maggie gave her mother her sweetest smile and climbed over the heaps of linen to answer the door.

"Come in, Henry," she said, as she tugged the door open. "I'm so glad you're here to help. If anyone can make this sewing machine work, it's you."

~~~

2000

Thursday night, I drove over to the library and met Virginia and the Little People's Group in the library conference room. The owner of the Orcas Island Art Gallery, Michael Hinton sat beside us.

"This is Sarah Hanaeki," Virginia introduced me. "Sarah bought Maggie McNamara's cottage over on Deer Harbor. Do you know the place?"

"I've been by there," said Mike. "Heard rumors of a ghost that plays the piano in that house on moonlit nights." Mike laughed. "Any truth in that?"

My mouth dropped open. My shoulders sagged. I glared at Virginia.

She shrugged. "*I* didn't tell him that, Sarah."
~~~

I took a deep breath and plunged right in. "Well, Mike, I have heard the ghost of Maggie play in my little house," I said. "But I'm not sure I want to tell everyone about it. People might think I'm crazy." I laughed, hoping he would not think that.

"Other people have heard piano music when they go by the cottage on moonlit nights," said Virginia. "I didn't tell Sarah before she bought the place, because I didn't want to freak her out."

"I'm getting used to the ghost," I said. "I'd miss her now, if she didn't show up when the moon is full."

"Sarah has Maggie's porcelain flower fairies on her mantelpiece," said Virginia. "They're exquisite. Much nicer than the plastic ones we get now-a-days."

Other people at the table turned, interested.

"Maybe you'd like to come and see them," I suggested. "You could have your next meeting at my house."

They agreed to meet at Maggie's Cottage in two weeks.

"Sarah's been redoing the cottage," said Virginia. "She has an art studio set up in the attic, where she'll be painting watercolors. I suggested she paint Maggie's flower fairies and put them in your gallery, Mike."

"Let me know when you get some done, Sarah. I'd be glad to take a look at them. Right now, the tourist season is nearly over, but we could use two or three flower fairy paintings, anyway."

Two weeks later, I had things ready for the meeting. I looked around Maggie's remodeled kitchen and ran one hand over the new cabinets. The cottage sparkled. A small fire burned in the fireplace, and coffee, tea and cookies were ready for the Little People's Group meeting. Roses from the garden floated in a low bowl on the coffee table and Maggie's flower fairies stood in a row on the mantel. I had painted watercolors of Hyacinth Fairy, Daisy Fairy, and Rose Fairy for Mike's approval. Guess I needed some incentive to get that done. The three matted watercolors stood on the piano. A gibbous moon hung in the sky over Deer Harbor and would be full in a day or two. I shivered and wondered if Maggie would play for me soon.

The merchants of East Sound arrived in a caravan led by Virginia.

"I can't wait to see what you've been doing, Sarah," she said as I let them in the front door, one of the first things I had had fixed. I was relieved that it no longer stuck when I tried to open it.

"Well, come along. I'll give you a tour," I said. "This is the living room," I waved one hand around and led them to the hall. "Just put your coats on the bed in the small bedroom there. The bath." Another wave of my hand. "And my bedroom with a view of the harbor." Moonlight flooded the room. Then we walked through the kitchen and up the steep staircase to my studio. They loved my little house. Moonlight illuminated the harbor and shone into the cottage.

"I can't believe it's the same house," said Virginia. "When I showed this place to Sarah, it was a wreck," she said. "Cobwebs and dust everywhere. Broken furniture. You wouldn't believe how it looked before!"

Virginia gazed in awe at my sweet little house. "Now see how lovely it is." She stood in the middle of the living room and turned around. "Something's different . . . different windows," she said. "Sarah, you've changed the windows. These are perfect for the cottage."

The fire glowed. The cozy room welcomed them to sit on my newly upholstered furniture. I served the coffee, tea and cookies, and then took the flower fairies down from the mantel and passed them around the circle. A big lump formed in my throat as I heard the praise of Maggie's cottage and figurines. It made all my hard work worthwhile.

"I like the watercolors, Sarah." Mike walked over to the piano. "These are just right – not too big. Something a little girl might like to have in her room. I'll take all you can paint. We may be able to sell some before winter."

~~~

Maggie woke me with Beethoven's Moonlight Sonata. Rich chord changes filled the cottage with intricate harmony. I'm getting sort of used to her visits when the moon is full. She no longer frightens me, although if I'm sleeping, I still wake up disoriented, wondering what in the world . . . ?

I wish I could have known Maggie. She must have lived in the cottage all her life. Why didn't she get married? When she died, she had no family left. I
~~~

wondered if she felt lonely. What happened to H. A. – Henry Anderson? Maybe she liked living alone. The sky clouded over, blanketing the full moon, and rain ran down my new windows like tears.

~~~

1968

By the end of October, the rain had started in Blackthorn Valley. Never-ending rain. What can you do all day with only a kerosene lamp to read by when it rains? No electricity. No radio. No TV. A few books. An old wind-up record player. A stereo that ran on a car battery with an AC/DC adapter. At least we could play 33 1/3 LP's and listen to the *Beatles* on that.

Although we could look up and see daylight around the hand-split redwood shakes on the roof, the rain didn't come in. The grain of the wood funneled the rain down onto the ground outside, and we stayed dry. Bored, but dry. Some spent their time making more babies. Even that got to be routine, after awhile. Although we tried, Johnny and I didn't have any babies. I felt jealous of the young mothers and their babies, but on the other hand, a baby would complicate things if Johnny had to leave for Vietnam.

Vermillion entertained herself and others by belly dancing. She told us her mother was a gypsy, but no one believed her. Vermillion gave Tarot Card readings that always seemed to turn true. She wore long flowing skirts made of chiffon that hung from her hips and
~~~

wound a sheer scarf around her breasts. No bra. No panties.

Numerous strings of beads around her neck. Rings on her fingers. Rings on her toes. Her ears pierced from the lobe to the top, with the largest silver hoops at the lobe, decreasing in size to tiny studs at the tops of her ears. Ankle bracelets and arm bracelets. A small red dot of lipstick in the center of her forehead. A large fake amethyst stuck in her navel with first-aid adhesive tape. Her curls piled up on her head in an artsy manner, helter-skelter, tendrils corkscrewing down over her cheeks, wisps flying away. She carried castanets, a tambourine, and wore absolutely nothing under this outfit. Some days the costume contained all the different shades of red in the spectrum; tonight, there were shades of purple. Vermillion wound the handle on the record player. Then she put one of her East-Indian sitar 78 bakelite recordings on the turntable.

"Vermillion," I called. I tucked my patchwork shirt into my hip-hugger jeans, the ones with a two-inch zipper, as I hurried across the bare floor to her.

"Tonight . . . " Vermillion held out one hand for the joint Lyle had just lit. She inhaled, held her breath for fifteen seconds, and breathed out the word *tonight* on a small cloud of marijuana smoke. She gazed at me with unseeing eyes and smiled.

"Tonight," she repeated, "I am Heliotrope." She held out her filmy skirt. "See? Purple. Violet. Lavender. Heliotrope's colors.

"Tomorrow . . ." She turned around in a slow circle, nearly falling down. "Tomorrow . . . I might be . . . 'Vermillion'. . . or . . . or maybe 'Blue' . . . no, I think . . . 'Turquoise'."

"Cool," I said, irritated. "Heliotrope." I tried to get her attention. "I want to know if you will read the cards for Johnny."

Heliotrope pirouetted, making her gauze skirt bell out like a flower. "I'd love to read Johnny's cards." She smirked at me and reached for the joint again. "I'd love to do anything with Johnny. You're so lucky to have a man like him." She inhaled, and smiled at Lyle, who frowned. Wisps of smoke trickled out around her teeth as her eyes glazed over with euphoria.

I glared at her. I had known all along she had her eye on my man, but she wasn't going to get him. Not if I could help it. All I wanted her to do was tell his fortune. Not that I truly believed in fortune telling, but Heliotrope seemed to be able to foretell what would happen. I had to know. I worried all the time.

Heliotrope let the marijuana smoke, sweet and pungent like burnt grass, drift out through her nose. "Okay," she breathed.

I went outside for Johnny while Heliotrope floated away to get her cards.

"Jeez, Sarah, I don't want that bitch telling my fortune." He pulled away from me. Took a drag on his Marlboro. "She's balling all the guys, and keeps trying to get me, too. Did you know that?"

I nodded, near tears. "But Johnny, I'm so worried about what's going to happen to you with this crazy war on. Maybe she'll give you a good reading, and then I'll feel better. Please? For me?"

"Shit, Sarah!" Johnny squirmed. "Since you put it that way!" He dropped the cigarette butt on the ground and stepped on it, grinding it with his boot.

He grabbed my hand and stomped into the building.

Heliotrope sat down on the floor cross-legged – Indian fashion. Open to the world. The gauzy skirt barely hid a thing. I gulped. Did I want Johnny near someone so blatant? No. But I did want to know *what was going to happen.* I had to know. I'd go crazy if I didn't know. Lyle and the other stoners joined the circle, all eyes, practically panting with their tongues hanging out, like dogs. Heliotrope smiled a secret smile, brushed her arm across her breasts to make her nipples stand out from under the veiling, and laughed to herself as the guys gawked.

She handed the Tarot deck to Johnny. "Shuffle the cards, lover," she said, kissing the air between them. "Shuffle them until they feel right to you."

Johnny rolled his eyes at me. "How can they 'feel right'? That's pretty weird," he muttered.

"Sh-h-h! Just do what she says." I sat still, trying not to look at the place between Heliotrope's legs. I waited. I couldn't look at Johnny's face. I was afraid to find out if he looked at the place between Heliotrope's legs.

Johnny shuffled. And shuffled. Acted goofy and shuffled again.

Heliotrope sighed and drummed her fingernails on the floor, impatient to begin. "Don't they feel right, *yet?*"

"Yeah, I guess." Johnny made a face at me and handed the cards to her. I hid my face in his shoulder to stifle my giggles.

"Far out," she said.

Heliotrope held the cards close to her breasts, shut her eyes and seemed to be praying, or something. She opened her eyes wide and stared up at Johnny. "What question do you want answered?"

"Shit, man, I don't know. What the fuck do you want answered, Sarah?"

Tears overflowed my eyes. "Will Johnny have to go to Vietnam? And, more important, will he come back?"

"That's two questions." Heliotrope looked down her nose at me and frowned.

"Well, can you tell me if he'll come back to me, if he has to go?"

Heliotrope smiled her secret smile. She wrinkled up her nose. "Let's see what the cards tell us."

Heliotrope laid the Tarot Cards out face down in a Celtic cross. One, two, three, down in a vertical row. Number four on the left, number five above number one, and number six on the right. Then, to the right of these, she laid out four more cards, from bottom to top. Numbers seven, eight, nine, and ten.

"This is your present situation," she said. She turned over the number one card. The picture on the card showed an Excalibur sword crowned with a wreath. "The Ace of Swords shows you are courageous against odds. You have intense feelings. You can handle necessary conflicts." She looked into Johnny's eyes and added, "You have a magical use of force and the courage to achieve your goals. Your determination will win against all odds."

I squeezed Johnny's hand and breathed a little easier.

Heliotrope shifted her position, lifting her skirt a little, giving the stoners a tiny look, and turned a card over. "Number two. The Two of Cups. This is a further description of where you are now."

This card had a picture of a young man and young lady on it. Lovers.

"A friend or lover will influence the situation. If the Ten of Cups shows up later, it shows a very intense experience of true love."

Heliotrope looked around the circle, making sure she was the center of attention.

"The third card." She turned it over. "The Eight of Rods." The picture showed eight rods of various lengths.

"Aha," she gloated. "Travel is in the future for you. And maybe you've had too much good stuff, too soon." Heliotrope glanced at me, her look sly and devious.

Jealousy overwhelmed me with its ugly talons, and I wanted to slap her. I leaned closer to Johnny.

The fourth card had a picture of the sun. "This card shows the influence of the past. Where you are coming from, Johnny. What kind of life you've lived. It means joy. Lots of joy and self assurance.

Heliotrope reached for the fifth card. She gasped and put it back face down on the floor.

"What is it?" I grabbed her arm. "Let me see!"

Heliotrope's face had turned pale. She shook her head and pulled her scarves and skirts close around her and shivered. Her eyes wouldn't meet mine. Or Johnny's. At last she turned the card over. A picture of a knight in armor, upside down. "The Death Card," she muttered. "Reversed."

She looked up at Johnny, "But that doesn't mean you're going to die. It's upside down. It could mean something you are trying to do isn't going to work out. Or, a situation needs to be reversed. You will resist needed transformation." She looked into my worried eyes. "Shit, Sarah, don't look so scared. It could mean anything."

Heliotrope hesitated before picking up the sixth card. Her fingertips touched it, and then drew back. Finally, she turned it over. She groaned. A picture of a body appeared lying face down with ten swords stuck in it. Heliotrope's face fell. I couldn't keep from crying.

This is the Disaster Card," she said. "You must try to recover from a hopeless loss." She reached over to pat my shoulder. I flinched away from her and her awful cards. "It doesn't mean Johnny will die, Sarah. It means something bad will happen, though. Maybe not to him, but to someone else."

She looked directly at me. "Maybe you."

Me? What could happen to me? I didn't have to go to war. I just had to sit home and wait and hope Johnny would be all right.

The seventh card showed a man with a bandage around his head. "The Nine of Rods," said Heliotrope. This seventh space is Psychological. You have the strength to wait out a situation, Johnny. You are in a state of readiness, like a soldier ready to defend his country."

The Queen of Rods came next, a picture of a young lady. The eighth card. "This is a relationship card. The Queen of Rods is exuberant," said Heliotrope. "Probably Sarah, or perhaps even -- *moi* -- " Heliotrope preened. "Me!"

Heliotrope's smug smile made me sick. I wanted to throw up.

"This next card, the ninth card, is the Four of Pentacles. Any card with Pentacles is about security. Money. A stable relationship, or financially stable." Heliotrope put the card down, and shifted her legs around, causing the stoners to sit up and take notice.

The last card – the tenth card -- showed a man falling off a tower. "The Tower Card indicates something totally unexpected is going to happen. You are living on the edge of potential disaster." Heliotrope sighed. She sat limp and exhausted from the reading. She reached for the joint Lyle smoked, inhaled and held the smoke in as she gazed around the circle of admirers. She exhaled.

"I'm sorry this wasn't better, Johnny, but it's not all bad. Although the Death card turned up, it doesn't mean you'll die. Not right away, anyhow." Her weak smile riled me. "We're all going to die someday, you know."

Duh, Heliotrope! Vermillion! Turquoise! Whoever the fuck you are!

"What was your question, Sarah? Will Johnny come back if he has to go to 'Nam? She picked up the cards and put them back in their box. "It's hard to answer that from this reading. Looks like he'll be all right, but there're lots of conflicts."

Heliotrope stood up and stretched, to the admiration of her audience. Then she wound up the record player with its little handle, turned it on and set the needle on the record. She danced around the circle of ogling guys, banging her tambourine against one hip. Bracelets jingled on her wrists and ankles, her bare feet kept the rhythm of the eerie sitar music. Toes curled and uncurled. Fingers contorted in weird positions. The amethyst in her navel glinted in the lamplight. She set the tambourine on the floor, clicked her castanets, cast her eyes down, and held one edge of a veil over her face. The guys reached out to touch her feet, the hem of her skirt. She flipped her skirts around, showing her bare bottom and dragged the veil across their faces, stopping in front of Johnny where she wrapped the fabric around his head. He yanked on the veil, trying to get free. Heliotrope tugged him to his feet. She pulled his arm and propelled him toward her sleeping area.

"Johnny," I screamed. "Don't you dare go with her! Man, I'll never speak to you again, if you do." Tears streamed down my face.

Johnny ripped the scarf from his face and turned away from Heliotrope and laughed. "Don't worry, Sarah, I'm not going to go anywhere with that bitch."

~~~

2000

The telephone rang, a rare occurrence. I jumped. Who could be calling me? I picked up the phone. Caller I.D. showed the call was from the Art Gallery in town.

"Hello?"

"Sarah? This is Mike Hinton. My customers love your watercolor paintings of Maggie's flower fairies. I need more."

I sighed. Mike. Someone I knew. "That's wonderful. I'll try to do some this week-end, okay?"

"Good. The sooner the better. Summer's about over and the tourist season will be, too, before we know it."

"In that case, I'll get to it right away." My smile showed through my voice. "I can't believe someone actually bought them."

"You'd better believe it. Someone did. For their three little daughters."

I grinned. "This is really exciting, Mike."

"It is for me, too. I always like to have satisfied customers." He paused for a minute and then said,
~~~

"I've been wondering how many flower fairy figurines you have?"

"Twelve. One for each month of the year."

"Great. When you have time, will you paint one or two of each with the month worked into the painting somehow – maybe something seasonal like holly for December?"

"That sounds good. I'll try that."

"Say . . . I'd really like to see you again. Would you be able to go to dinner with me tonight at the Harbor Restaurant? I have a check for your first three paintings."

"Dinner?" This was totally unexpected. How many dates had I been on since I received the telegram, *MISSING IN ACTION* thirty years ago? There had been that guy with the big glasses whose hands smelled like Dial soap. And the one with the mustache who'd thought I had a lot of money. But, no, no one to speak of.

"Well," I stammered, "Yes. All right, I guess I could do that. What time?"

"I'll make reservations for 7 and pick you up at 6:30."

I panicked. "Oh, no, no that won't be necessary. Deer Harbor is out of your way. I'll just meet you there." *Why did I sound so inane? Didn't I want to meet someone nice? Yes? No? I didn't know.*

"Great. I'll meet you there at 7 then. Bye."

"Good-bye. . . "

I disconnected the call and leaned against the kitchen counter, stunned. *What did I know about him? He seemed nice. Good-looking. Still had hair, but gray at the temples. Took care of himself, not gone to fat like some older men did, well, maybe a little tummy, but then that happens to most of us. Married? Good heavens, I didn't know. I decided to call Virginia.*

"Oh, Mike's so nice," Virginia said. "I'm excited he's invited you out. He must be interested. You know, he could have just mailed you a check."

"You're right, Virginia."

"Well Sarah, he's been married, but his wife died a few years ago. His kids are all grown and gone to live on the mainland somewhere, but he loves the island, so he putters around with the art gallery and his garden. You'll like him."

"Well, I did like him when I met him, but I didn't think about him in that way, you know?"

"Just go and have fun. What are you going to wear?"

"I don't know. I hadn't thought about that. I don't have much. Maybe my black slacks with a silk blouse and a blazer. Sound okay?"

"Perfect. Call me tomorrow and tell me all about it. Gotta run now."

I walked into the living room and looked at Maggie's flower fairies, each one exquisite in its own way. I decided to paint Heliotrope that afternoon.

The large attic window overlooking the boat basin was a perfect place for my paint table. Heat from the main floor of the house found its way up the staircase, and the morning sun shining through the plate glass window took the chill off the attic but didn't get too hot in the afternoon. I used a table when I painted watercolor, because I liked to work wet on wet, dropping pure color into a puddle and watching it melt into the whole. I stood over my work so I could get a good swing at things with my big brushes when doing backgrounds. I'd been dying to paint the boats in the harbor but found their shapes harder to capture on paper than they looked. I did manage a watercolor with a forest of masts and boats reflected in the harbor, and a Douglas fir forest in the background. A few dry-brush strokes with a square brush let some white paper show through and added sparkle to the foreground water.

With that out of my system, I tried some more flower fairies and elves for the Art Gallery in East Sound. I thought about investing in oil paints. I needed something to bring in some money. The things I wanted to do for Maggie's Cottage cost too much for my graphic-arts retirement budget, and I didn't want to dip into my Roth IRA. Not yet. I had a small allotment from the government because Johnny was presumed dead. I would try to make do.

I rinsed my sable watercolor brushes and laid them out to dry. Then I stood my painting up against the wall and compared it with the scene from the window. The dark fir forest in the background needed something – maybe a few more shadows. Dark colors. I'd have to think about that. The sun and wind outside called to me, but still I sat in the warm window staring at the fir trees across the boat basin and soon my mind wandered into the other forest – the Redwood forest.

~~~

1968

Once in awhile, Johnny and I left the valley deep in the redwoods of Northern California and took Lyle and his "product" into town. Then we'd bring back supplies for the commune: fresh meat packed with ice into ice chests, flour, sugar, and salt – things we could not grow. We kept a cow and some chickens, so we had milk for the children and butter and cream and fresh eggs. We even had fried chicken now and then. If the cupboard was bare, one of the guys would go out in the woods and shoot a deer, putting meat on the table.

I sat in the middle of the pick-up's bench seat, the long gear shift between my legs, the knob pressed against my stomach. One day as we wound out of our mountain valley, Lyle tried to put his hand on my thigh underneath the folds of my full skirt, not letting Johnny see what he was doing. I pushed him away and snuggled closer to Johnny who looked down at me and freed his right hand for a split second to pat my knee. Then he grabbed the steering wheel again, concentrating on driving the rough, chuck-hole-filled twisty road.

Lyle put his arm across the back of the bench seat and fiddled with my hair, working his grimy fingers closer and closer onto the back of my neck. I jerked away and glared at him. Johnny would have kicked him out of the truck right there, miles from the commune and miles from the main highway if he knew what Lyle
~~~

was up to. I didn't want to see anyone stranded on a remote mountain road, not even this sleazebag, so I didn't say anything. I just scooted closer to Johnny and rested my left hand on his right thigh.

We wound out of the hills skidding on hairpin turns in the gravel, sending plumes of dust lifting in S's behind us, visible above the switchbacks. I looked forward to seeing the sun rise and set. Looked forward to not being closed in – down in the dark valley, but out where I could see around. See the ocean. The fields. The orchards. The vineyards. See a town and other people. Real people. People who were not stoned.

Johnny and I wandered through the little town of Willits while we waited for Lyle to sell his weed. The sun beat down on us and met hot air rising from the pavement, turning the street into a natural kiln. Smells of dust and sweat overlaid everything. We held hands and looked into shop windows, trying to keep in the shade of the building overhangs. An ice cream cone would have tasted good, but we had no money to buy anything. Not until Lyle got back.

I noticed the townspeople looking at us, at Johnny and me. Did we look so strange, then? I stopped in front of a plate glass window and studied my reflection. Yes, I guess I did look a little strange. Sort of hill-billy hippy. Not too clean, that's for sure. Even though Johnny had rigged a solar shower at the commune with a tub of water and a garden hose coiled on the roof like a long green snake, it was hard to keep clean. I noticed my hair looked disheveled. Not as silky as it had once been. Sun-bleached. No make-up. To tell the truth, I thought I looked a little bit Earthy. Granola even, and I didn't like it at all. Johnny didn't look any better.

The guy coming down the hot sidewalk toward us resembled an early western explorer -- a mountain-man like Jedediah Smith or Zebulon Pike. Frayed jeans, worn-out boots, fringed leather jacket, scroungy beard. I knew he carried a stiletto knife hidden inside one boot. I had seen him sharpen it daily and slide it back into its sheath. An aura of unclean clothes, cigarettes and marijuana surrounded him. Lyle. People moved out of his way on the sidewalk. He grinned showing green-tinged teeth and waved. I shuddered and turned away.

Lyle pulled us around the corner of the building and rubbed his leg against mine. I stepped back, cringing. His pockets were stuffed with money. Green weed. Green teeth. Green money.

Lyle gave Johnny some cash. "Go gas up the truck," he said. "Meet me in the Safeway parking lot. I'll get the things we need there." He leered at me. "Want to come, Sarah? I'll buy something special just for you." He grabbed my hand and started walking away. "Just tell me what you want. Got lots'a *moola*." He pulled a wad of bills from his jeans pocket and waved them around in the air, dropping a few on the pavement. As he stooped over to pick them up, I pulled free of his grasp and ran back to Johnny who stood like a mountain lion, a dark frown on his face, his body coiled and tensed to pounce. He glared at Lyle as we climbed into the oven-like cab of the pick-up and rolled down the windows.

"What's with him?" asked Johnny. "You *like* that guy?"

"Yuk. He's always trying to get close to me. Haven't you noticed?"

"Yeah." Johnny pumped the gas pedal, pushed in the clutch and pressed the starter. The engine coughed and kicked in, rumbling uneasily. We pulled away from the curb leaving Lyle standing there, fuming in the hot sun.

I yelled out the window, "Buy yourself a toothbrush!"

That night we had a party with barbecued ribs, fresh vegetables from our garden, beer, and of course lots of marijuana. Lyle followed me around like a sick puppy, trying to get close to me, grinning his green smile and holding onto the edge of my long skirt.

"Beat it, Lyle," Johnny told him, stepping between Lyle and me. "Get lost."

Lyle shrugged and leered at me. He wandered away to hit on some other girl.

People passed out everywhere, just like they had at our wedding. Back then I had thought it was funny. Cool. Now, I was disgusted. Johnny and I were glad to be rid of Lyle and went to sleep in our private corner curtained off from the rest.

Just before dawn, I awoke to realize someone else was in our corner with us. A filthy hand covered my mouth. I struggled to yell and get away, but only muffled noises came out of my throat through my jaw clamped shut by fingers that stank of marijuana and filth.

"Sh-h-h!" He breathed alcohol fumes in my face, sickening me. His unwashed clothes reeked of dirt and pot. His free hand pulled up my gown and he hoisted himself over on top of me.

I bit his hand and kneed him between the legs.

He screamed and fell over holding his groin with both hands. Johnny woke up. The place came alive as much as it could. Most were wasted beyond help.

"What the fuck's going on, man?" Johnny stood up, pulling on his jeans. He grabbed a flashlight and beamed it on the intruder.

Lyle. A trickle of blood seeped from one hand.

"Why you fucking bastard!" Johnny yanked Lyle to his feet by his t-shirt. "Sarah's my woman." He shook Lyle until his teeth chattered. "You hear scumbag? Mine! Leave her alone, mother-fucker!"

Lyle groaned and doubled over. He couldn't answer.

I stood up. "Let him go, Johnny. He can't do anything, now. I took care of him."

We packed up and left. Right then. We threw our meager belongings into the beat-up truck and headed back up the winding road away from the little valley where the sun disappeared behind the western hills and the mountains closed in around me every afternoon at four. A cloud of dust followed our pick-up and I felt like a big load had been taken from me. I sighed. Free. Finally, free.

All the way to Santa Barbara, we talked. "Communal life stinks," said Johnny. "I wonder if I can get my college deferment back. What do you think, Sarah?"

"I don't know, Johnny. Guess it wouldn't hurt to ask."

"Do you want to go back and get your degree?"

I nodded. I had really wanted to do that all along, but thought the commune was what he wanted.

"Maybe if I sign up for the military, I can get into helicopter training – something specialized – not just cannon fodder. Not just walkin on fuckin' point!" He reached over and held my hand. I squeezed his hand back. "You could go stay with your folks while I go to boot camp. What d'ya think?"

"Whatever you want, Johnny. You know that."

"Okay, then, you finish school while I go into the army. I'm glad that's settled. I should have a chance in helicopters. Shit, man! First Cav!" He grinned. "When I get out I can finish my engineering degree on the GI Bill. Fuckin' awesome!"

I looked up at him, wondering. This is what he has wanted all along. Maybe because his father was in the Air Force. Maybe he wants to be like his dad.

We bought some used tires in Santa Barbara and the pick-up took us where we wanted to go. Some days, when the coastal fog lifted and San Francisco Bay turned into a sparkling jewel, we'd take a picnic lunch and drive to the Presidio or over the Golden Gate Bridge to Sausalito and watch coveys of white sails from the yacht clubs tack back and forth across the bay like flocks of Canadian snow geese.

Johnny decided not to wait to be called up but enlisted in the army. He requested helicopter training. We spent the week before his departure at that beach house in Rockaway Oregon with the cantankerous wood stove. One day I gave him a haircut as he sat out on the beach. I tied one little hunk of hair with a piece of my hair ribbon and saved it in an envelope. Then, when I felt lonesome for him, I could take it out and touch this small part of Johnny.

He left for Fort Benning, Georgia.

Now that I wasn't "living in sin", Mom and Dad were glad to have me stay with them and go back to school. Mom was right, although I hated to admit it. Until I lived in the commune, I hadn't trusted anyone over the age of thirty. Now I knew better. Maybe it's called growing up. I truly did feel thankful I had that little piece of paper. The marriage license. My connection to Johnny.

After boot camp, I left school for a while and we lived on the base in married housing at Fort Rucker, Alabama while Johnny took extensive helicopter training and was commissioned as a warrant officer. Then we came back home on leave before he shipped out for Vietnam.

~~~

1917

"Are you sure you want to sail again?" Henry coiled the mainsail sheet neatly beside the rudder.
~~~

Maggie leaned over and tousled Henry's hair. "Of course, I want to sail, Henry. I love to sail. How else can we go so fast and be as free – free as those gulls up there." She pointed to the seagulls soaring overhead. "It wasn't the boat's fault we tipped over. We just have to be more careful about watching for wind gusts when we're "hiking-out" so far. When we sit on the gunwale and tuck our feet under the hiking out strap to balance the weight in the boat, we fly over the waves like the wind. From now on, we just need to be pay more attention and let wind out of the sail the next time a big wind gust hits so the boat doesn't heel over quite so far. But that's the most fun of sailing, you know

"We'll be more careful, though." Henry's blue eyes clouded with his thoughts.

The sailboat skimmed across Deer Harbor, both sails full of a south-easterly wind as they tacked back and forth to the island for a picnic.

They eased the boat into the little cove and pulled up the dagger board, scraping the bottom of the boat on the sandy shingle. Henry took off his shoes and socks, rolled up his pants and tied the mooring lines to a tree. He helped Maggie out of the boat, carrying her through the surf. The hem of her long skirt made of light-weight cotton instead of the heavy woolen tweed, trailed in the foam. The picnic basket. A blanket.

The wind.

"Let's not go to the top of the hill today." Maggie shivered. "We can find a sheltered place on the beach in the driftwood and build a fire."

They spread the blanket down behind a pile of drifted logs. Henry kindled a fire while Maggie unpacked the lunch. Cold fried chicken, apples, cheese, and Snicker Doodle Cookies. The wind hummed and spread inquisitive fingers around the driftwood, but couldn't find its way through the pile of logs. The sun shone down, warming them. They huddled close together on the blanket, feeding each other bites of chicken, chunks of cheese, and pieces of cut-up apple. Now and then Henry leaned over to kiss Maggie's lips, her eyes and her neck.

"Thank God you didn't drown that day," said Henry. "I'd have never forgiven myself." He stroked her forehead and nuzzled his nose into the warm curls that fell from the hairpins holding her hair in its bun. "I love you, Maggie."

"I love you, too, Henry." Maggie put her arms around him and pulled him toward her. They kissed. Touched. Hands made gentle explorations of each other's bodies. The waves crashed on the beach, but they did not hear them. Wind whistled around the driftwood barrier unnoticed. They were too engrossed in each other's scents to even smell the salt air. Somehow, Maggie's blouse came unfastened, slipping from her shoulders, causing Henry to catch his breath at the sight of her. Her skirt came off, unbuttoned this time.

Maggie unfastened Henry's shirt. Soon they were naked under the warm sun in their driftwood den. They lost track of time and the world around them as they became lost in each other.

Later they pulled Maggie's full skirt over their nakedness and slept in the warmth of the sun and the fire's flame. Wind crooned softly around the driftwood. Waves ran up on the beach in a regular rhythm.

Gulls hung on the thermals overhead, swooping to the shore to grab an unsuspecting clam – then winging high in the air to drop the crustacean on the rocks, breaking its shell, screeching and diving for the tender morsel before a rival bird could reach it.

A gull cried, scolding another bird for taking its clam. Maggie awoke with a start. She looked around at the sky turning pink in the west. Deer Harbor showed white caps here and there. *Henry.* She snuggled down and kissed him, smoothing his brown hair back. *How can people frown on this – this wonderful way of two people showing their love for each other? I know Mama would be angry with me, but since Henry and I love each other, I think what we did is right. It hurt for a brief moment and then the heavens opened up.*

But . . . suppose we have a child? No I don't think that can happen the first time – but then again, the feelings we had were so overwhelming they might create a child. I won't think about it now. Tomorrow will be soon enough. Now I'm just going to love Henry.

Henry sat up and blinked at the red sky, the whitecaps on the water and the lights turning on around the half-circle shoreline of Deer Harbor.

"Maggie, it's late. We'd better get home."

They hurried into their clothes, Henry's eyes drawn to Maggie's body like a moth to a flame. Maggie smiled and cast her eyes away from his, shy, but all of a sudden aware of her power. She dressed in a hurry and packed the remains of the lunch. Henry shook sand from the blanket and noticed a spot of blood near the center. When he carried the blanket to the surf to try to rinse it off, he looked over at Maggie to see if she had noticed the blood. Her cheeks blazed red as her eyes met Henry's. He folded the blanket over the wet spot and put it in the boat. They climbed aboard and skimmed over the whitecaps, the jib sail held out with the whisker pole, the main sail perpendicular to the boat, going with the wind.

A light glowed in the cottage living room window.

"Oh, dear," Maggie said. "Mama's worried."

Henry raised the dagger board and ran the boat up in the shallow water of the beach across the road from the cottage. Maggie slipped her shoes off and jumped out, splashing up to her knees, soaking her stockings and skirt.

"We're here, Mama," she called. "We lost track of time. Sorry we're so late."

Alice ran to them, tears streaming down her face as she dried her hands on her apron. She hugged Maggie. "I was just about to ask the Browns down the road to take their boat out and look for you. You were very thoughtless to worry me like that, Maggie."

"I'm sorry, Mama," Maggie patted her mother's back. "I'm truly sorry we worried you."

"It won't happen again, Mrs. McNamara," said Henry.

"You be sure, Henry Anderson. It's difficult to always be the person waiting at home with no way of finding out what's going on, wondering where you are, if you are dead or alive. I don't think Maggie should sail with you anymore."

Henry nodded, looking sheepish.

"But, Mama," Maggie said, tears filling her eyes.

"No, Maggie." Alice stood with her hands dangling at her sides, tears running down her cheeks. "It's too dangerous. We'll have to speak to your father about this."

Henry helped Maggie bring the wet blanket and remains of their lunch to the cottage and hung the blanket over the porch railing to dry.

"I'll come by tomorrow, Maggie," he said. "Don't worry. Your father will understand. He likes to sail, too."

Maggie walked to the boat with him. The dusky-rose twilight enveloped them, hid them from Alice's view. Henry lifted Maggie's hand and held the palm to his lips. Their eyes locked together in the wonder of love they had discovered that afternoon.

~~~

2000

Money is becoming a real worry. Winter will be here soon, and people won't vacation in the San Juan Islands again until late spring next year. That will give
~~~

me time to paint many flower fairies for next season, if only I can manage to get through the winter.

I wouldn't think of taking the piano away to be refinished now, even if I could afford to have it done. Maggie's ghost wouldn't know where to find it.

~~~

1968

"Where the hell's my door gunner? My number one gunner?" The helicopter pilot pushed back his black Stetson trimmed with a black leather braided hat band, reminiscent of the original First Horse Cavalry, and picked up his helmet, as the co-pilot and second gunner climbed aboard the Huey, still housed in its revetment.

John looked up from pumping fuel into the Huey. "Here! Sir!" He shut off the pump. Overly aware of the honor of wearing the First Cavalry Horse Patch on his sleeve, he stumbled, all left feet, scrambled to attention, and saluted.

"At ease soldier. Let's go – on the double. M'name's Hammond. Major Greg Hammond." He returned the salute with a wave of his right hand and glanced over at John. "Yours?"

"My what? . . . Sir!"

"Name, buddy. Name."

"Yessir! I'm SP4 John Hanaeki. . . Sir!"

"Okay, John. Let's go."
~~~

"Yessir!" John's shirt showed dark sweat stains under his arms and in the middle of his back from the humid 80 degree weather. "Just as soon as I finish fueling, we'll be ready, Sir."

"Well, SP4 Hanaeki, if you're in charge of my bird, you need to know it's a designated 'DUSTOFF' back-up, and needs to be ready on 'hot' standby at all times." The major pushed his black Stetson hat up on his forehead and glared at Johnny.

"Yes, sir!" Johnny breathed in JP4 fumes. His face turned pale. "I just got here, sir." Johnny gulped, "But that's no excuse. Sir!" Beads of sweat formed on Johnny's brow.

"We don't have any red crosses painted on this bird, but we do fly wounded, if necessary."

"Yessir! From now on, it'll be on 'hot' standby, at all times. You can count on me, Sir!"

John finished fueling quickly while Greg set his prized black Stetson in a corner of the revetment and put on his helmet, adjusting it comfortably to his head. John shut off the fuel pump and signaled to the ground crew who slipped a dolly under the helicopter, jacked it up and pulled it away from the revetment. Greg and Johnny climbed inside the bird where the co-pilot and the number two gunner waited. Greg started the engine and lit a cigar. Johnny, sitting by the open door, put his helmet on, straps dangling. The crew slid the dolly out from under the bird. Johnny gave Greg a thumb's up, and they pulled pitch on a skewed slant, leaning toward the northwest. Greg hummed a bit of "Mr. Tambourine Man" in an off-key baritone, his voice a low rumble in the headphones installed in the crews' helmets

"Goin' up near the Cambodian Border to evacuate a family of Montagnards," said Greg.

"Sir?" Johnny squirmed around to look at the aviator. "What are they . . . those Montagnards, sir?"

"They're our allies, buddy." Greg blew cigar smoke. They're good people, native to the mountains and loyal to the U. S. of A."

"Oh," said Johnny. "But why are we evacuating them? Sir!"

"Must a been able to do some damage to the Viet Cong. We gotta get 'em outta there."

Johnny scanned the area below as he sat in the Huey's doorway listening to Greg's singing and the "whump, whump" of the rotor blades. Sun beat down on the helicopter making him sweat. John thought again how lucky he was to be assigned to aviation and not infantry. Back at Fort Rucker, the sergeant had scared the piss out of the guys when he told them, "Now, you cain't go runnin' to yore momma or yore antie in this here army." Sarge had stood arms akimbo, glaring at them. "*No,* sir! If ya'll fail this class, Ah *guarantee* ya'll'll be walkin' point in a week."

Johnny didn't need any more incentive than that to study his ass off. He felt lucky to be a good mechanic, a good engineer and a good marksman. Maybe he'd have a chance to get through the Vietnam War alive in a gunship -- a chance to come home to Sarah and start their family.

After an hour, they overtook a small LOACH that looked like a bumblebee flying ahead of them near the mountains. One of its airmen hung from the skids and looked up eyeball to eyeball at Johnny sitting in the open door of the Huey as they passed. The airman quickly turned back to the business at hand, which involved dropping bombs down a hole in the mountain, a hide-out for Viet Cong.

Two Cobras – helicopter gun ships -- waved the LOACH away. From his vantage point in the door of the Huey, Johnny could see the Cobra pilot's helmet with stickers that read: *Bomb Saigon Now*

Bomb Hanoi Now

Bomb Disneyland Now

Bomb Everything

When the LOACH had flown clear, the Cobras roared down, unleashing their rockets into the hole.

"Awesome!" breathed Johnny, glad he was not the enemy in that tunnel.

Major Hammond nodded. "I kinda like to have a couple a' them Cobras near me in case this Huey gets into trouble."

They drew near the Cambodian border.

"Wait'll you guys see these Montagnards," said the co-pilot. "They live up here in the mountains with goats and pigs, and not much else. But they're our friends. Once in a while the VC come in and harass 'em. Take their food, rape their women, you know, the usual drill. This family must be pretty important to be air-lifted out. Maybe they'll send 'em to the states. They're real gutsy people but can't keep very clean.

They probably all have lice. Don't get too close to 'em."

"You and Booger help us find 'em, John," Greg tossed back a map. "These're our coordinates.

Johnny and the number 2 gunner studied the map and the area ahead of them.

"Looks like an LZ at 10 o'clock, Sir," said Johnny.

"Ole eagle-eyes with us today. You are so-o-o right."

"Doin' good for an FNG," said the co-pilot.

John looked puzzled and punched the number 2 gunner's arm. "What the fuck's an FNG?"

"You know, *a Fuckin' New Guy!*" Number 2 gunner grinned and picked his nose with his pinky finger. "That's you!"

Johnny turned away, disgusted when Booger lived up to his name and wiped his finger on his pant leg. Johnny scanned the jungle for enemy.

Booger laughed making the brass peace symbol he wore on a chain around his neck clank against his dog tags, his khaki undershirt dark with sweat stains. "You're okay as long as you don't fall outta this bird." He reached up to fasten his helmet on which he had written *Booger.*

Johnny motioned to the helmet. "That your real name?"

"Yeah, sure. That's it, all right-ty."

Johnny shrugged and looked back out the Huey's door, concentrating on his job of watching for the enemy.

Major Hammond slanted the 'copter toward the pad. Green Berets waved them in. The Special Forces scurried under the rotor wash with an extended family: grandpa, grandma, mom, dad, kids, grand kids, uncles, aunts, and cousins, all exceedingly frightened.

One of the Green Berets in the 5th Special Forces Group handed Johnny a primitive bush axe made from a piece of sharpened metal wedged into a handle formed out of the root of a bamboo plant. Intricately braided grass trim formed a pattern around the handle and held the metal axe blade in place.

"They want you to have this – it's a gift so you won't hurt them."

Johnny looked from the axe to the Montagnard family huddled under the helicopter's rotors.

"They're afraid you'll kill 'em," said the Green Beret. "None of us can speak their lingo. Just a combination of pidgin garbage: French, Cambodian and American. We tried to explain that they'll be taken care of. You're saving them from the Viet Cong. These folks've been helping us. They hate the VC. Hate 'em like poison."

The Green Beret smiled at the Montagnards and motioned them to get in the helicopter. They hesitated in front of Johnny, sitting in the doorway. Johnny jumped out, jammed the bush axe handle into his belt, and helped the small people in. Then he stepped back inside and hung out the door as Greg pulled pitch out of there. Johnny watched the Special Forces evaporate into the foliage. Inside the Huey, the family clung together, hushing the youngest children.

Johnny smiled at the Montagnards, trying to encourage them. Booger fished a Hershey bar from his shirt pocket, opened it and broke off pieces that he handed around.

"Fuckin' Numbah Ten," said Booger.

"Yeah, man, Numbah Ten. Bad," agreed John.

"We'll take 'em to the base at Ben Hao. They'll be okay." Greg headed south toward Saigon singing snatches of *Mr. Bojangles.*

Johnny showered and ate and went to his bunk. Sarah, he thought. God, but I miss you. He tossed around and couldn't sleep, his mind whirling like the blades on the chopper. Finally, he got up and walked to the mess hall with a note pad and pen where he found an empty table and sat down to write.

Dear Sarah,

I got a letter from you today. You don't know how much that means just to get mail in this God-forsaken place. I'm beginning to think we're nuts to even be here. These gooks don't want us. We're just in the way of their civil war. Maybe we should butt out. I can't wait to get home to you. We'll build a little house somewhere on the Russian River or the beach and raise us a passel of ninos.

Love, Johnny

~~~

1917

Maggie helped her mother pick green beans from the vines supported by bean-pole tepees. Hot sun beat down on top of her new straw hat, making her sweaty and uncomfortable. The buzzing sound of bees annoyed her. She sniffed and wiped an arm across her forehead.

"This would be a good day to sail. I'm surprised Henry didn't come over to invite me to go with him." Maggie pouted. "I told him Papa agreed to let me sail again." She looked out over Deer Harbor sparkling in the sun. "I promise to be back on time, Mama."

"Perhaps Henry's busy, darlin'. Didn't you tell me he's nearly finished with that flying contraption you've been working on?"

Maggie nodded. She looked around her as the buzzing noise grew louder. *I hope there aren't any bees around here.*

A small bi-plane sputtered out of the clouds and swooped low over the cottage and the vegetable garden.

"What in the world . . . " Alice pushed back her hat to get a better look.

Maggie laughed. "It's Henry! Just look at him flying!" She ran out the garden gate into the open yard and waved at him.
~~~

Henry flew low and waggled the wings as he flew over them. The scarf Maggie had knitted dangled from his neck. His eyes sparkled behind his goggles. He grinned and waved to them. The plane banked, turned around and headed back, disappearing over the headland jutting out into Deer Harbor.

"Oh, my!" Alice sat down on the garden bench, holding one hand to her chest. "Henry gave me a start. He really knows how to fly that thing, doesn't he?"

"Yes, Mama. Don't you think I could go up for just a little ride? I'd make him promise not to do any tricks. Please say yes."

"Absolutely not, Margaret Mary McNamara. I'll not hear another word about you flying in that contraption with Henry."

"But, Mama, it's perfectly safe. Henry's a good pilot. You saw him fly."

"I can understand how you would want to go for a ride, Maggie, I think I'd like to try it, too, but I must insist you don't go up in that aeroplane. For the life of me, I can't figure out what keeps it up in the air."

"But, Mama . . ."

"No. Maggie. Don't argue with me. That's very disrespectful."

Henry landed on the beach as Maggie and her mother hurried to him.

"Flying looks wonderful, Henry," said Alice. "But isn't it terribly dangerous?" She looked up at the blue sky full of scudding cumulus clouds. "What keeps that contraption up in the air?"

"Well, you see, Mrs. McNamara, this is the way it works." Henry picked up a piece of driftwood to demonstrate. "The air moving across the wings causes an upward force called *lift.* The pressure of the air decreases as the speed of the air increases. The top of the wings are curved, causing the air to move faster across the top than beneath it, so the airplane rises. It's really simple. You just need a good shape to the wings and some pretty good speed." Henry waved to his plane moored out on the beach. "My airplane will go about 80 miles per hour."

"80 miles an hour?" Alice was incredulous. "That's faster than a mile a minute! Are you sure it's safe to go so fast?"

"Yes, ma'am. I'm positive. You and Maggie just saw me do it."

Alice fidgeted. She longed to fly. Soaring like a bird through the air seemed miraculous to her. As a young woman, she had always done what was expected of her. Always done what was right. Always obeyed the customs and rules of a rigid society. She wanted more for her daughter, but flying seemed too dangerous for Maggie, as if nearly drowning wasn't bad enough. Nothing else must happen to her. She listened, enthralled by Henry's explanation of flight.

"Well," Alice stalled. "If I go up first and think it safe, then perhaps Maggie can go for just a short ride." *Then, if anything happens, it will be me who is dead, not Maggie.*

Maggie held her hands to her face, eyes shining like stars, afraid to say anything for fear her mother would change her mind. She looked at Henry and nodded her head at him.

"I'd be happy to take you up, Mrs. McNamara. You'll need a warm sweater or a coat. The higher we go, the colder it gets."

Alice looked at Maggie standing there, wanting so much to fly. She looked at Henry. "All right. Let's go."

Maggie ran for Alice's sweater and they hurried to the aeroplane.

Henry helped Alice into the front seat of the two seater and climbed into the seat behind her. "Okay, Maggie. Can you turn the propeller so the engine will start?"

Maggie stood, hands on her hips and made a little face at him. "Of course, I can." Maggie stretched up on her toes to reach the top propeller blade and pulled it down in one swift motion. The motor caught, sending out little puffs of exhaust, making a racket. Alice clung to the sides of the cockpit. The aeroplane taxied along the hard-packed wet sand of the beach.

"Ready?" Henry yelled to her.

Alice nodded. Her knuckles white.

Henry revved the engine and headed down the beach, into the wind. The little plane lifted off and flew out over The Sound.

"Oh, my!" said Alice. "Ohmyohmy!" She looked down at white caps on the water. Toward the shore a boat set sail. Henry turned the craft in a circle and they flew over Maggie's Cottage, a doll house set in a miniature garden, then back over Henry's house and touched down on the beach.

Alice sat mesmerized, her face flushed. Her whole body seeming to smile. "Henry ," she said when she could get her breath. "That was wonderful. I can see why you like flying. I felt like a bird up there." Henry grinned and helped her out of the plane.

Alice hugged Maggie. "You won't believe how exhilarating it is, Maggie. Oh, I can't wait to go again."

"Then it's all right for me to go?"

Abashed, Alice agreed. "Just for a short trip," she said. "No somersaults or dives, mind you, Henry. Just plain flying."

"Yes, ma'am."

Delighted, Maggie reached up to climb into the aeroplane. Henry hurried to help her.

"Wait," called Alice. "Here, put on my sweater so you won't get cold." She looked into Henry's eyes. "Now you be careful with her, you hear me?"

Henry laughed. "Don't worry, Mrs. McNamara, she'll be safe with me. You can sit right here on this drift log and watch."

Alice laughed and sat down hugging her arms around her body.

~~~

1968

Reveille sounded at 4 a.m. John groaned, stood up, shook his head, and stumbled to one of the piss tubes dotting the compound. He splashed cold water on his
~~~

face at a hand-washing station, dressed, had breakfast, picked up his helmet and stumbled out to the revetment to warm up the Huey. He'd been up late the night before making sure the copter was on 'hot' standby. Another 12-hour day loomed before him.

Wonder what the guys in the commune are doing about now. Shit, man, they're probably stoned out of their gourds. Glad I got out of that mess. Right into this mess! Ha, ha! Like my old tutu used to say, "Out of the frying pan and into the fire!" That's me, all right.

Thank God, I get letters from Sarah.

"Everyone here?" Major Hammond ran up to the revetment with a medic. "We're goin' into Indian country and dust off. On the double!" He looked sideways at John as he stashed his black Stetson in a safe corner and grabbed his helmet. "You seen wounded before?"

"No, Sir." John slammed his helmet on his head and ran to the helicopter's door.

"Well, if you get sick, don't do it in my bird. Puke out the door if you have to." Greg climbed aboard the Huey. "Let's fly!"

The crew and a medic followed, fastened helmets, checked machine guns and ammo as Greg revved the engine and lifted off, flying into Northern Vietnam to bring back wounded.

John and the number 2 gunner studied the map and the area ahead of them.

"Okay, Sir," said John. "I think I see shelling to the left. See? Over there, Sir?" John pointed with one hand.

Booger nodded agreement. "A-yeah, John." Booger peered out the open door. "Yeah, I see it, too, Sir."

"Roger. You've got sharp eyes. Man, we got ole eagle eye with us again today. D'ya see the L Z, yet?"

"Yes, Sir," said John. "Left a bit more. See the green smoke? That soldier down there is waving us over. The Landing Zone's over there. Sir!"

"Hang on, we're goin' in," said Greg.

The helicopter headed for a cleared space in the heavy forest. As soon as they touched down, medics and four litter bearers moved up with wounded and ducked under the rotor blades. John and Booger, aiming above the American soldiers' heads, blasted the terrain around them to discourage enemy fire. A mortar exploded close by, rocking the earth and the helicopter. Soldiers outside the bird hit the dirt. John flinched. He ground his teeth, swallowed hard, and hung on tight to the M -60 machine gun. His ears rang as he fired at the unseen enemy. The medics scrunched over, ran out from under the rotors and waved them away. John held onto the door frame while Greg slewed the Huey out of the battle zone past another helicopter hovering near-by, ready to land.

All the way back to the base, John kept a close watch on their charges. *That could be me, all torn up like that. Fucking bloody bandages. Missing arms and legs.* His stomach lurched and he swallowed hard at the sight of a soldier whose eyes were covered with a blood-soaked bandage. The medic started an IV in the man's arm. Bile came up into John's throat. He gagged and leaned out the door of the Huey, but nothing came up. Just dry heaves. *What chance do these guys have for a normal life when they got back home? If they live to get home, that is.*

This whole fucking war pisses me off. There are soldiers dying in the mud down there. What's the point of all this killing? Haven't we had enough fuckin' wars? John's head felt full of cobwebs and he couldn't shake them loose. He smashed his fist against the side of the Huey.

John breathed a sigh of relief that he was Chief on this Huey and not some poor grunt down in the jungle. Again, he checked the machine gun that he kept oiled and in spotless condition, and scoured the terrain for the enemy, alert to protecting the injured men in his care from further harm.

Major Hammond touched down at the Dong Ha field hospital where they unloaded the wounded. John stood exhausted as he watched medics take the soldiers inside. Greg threw an arm over John's shoulder.

"Well, you done good, kid. Didn't even throw up." He pounded John's back. "Good job."

"Thanks, Sir. I guess having the dry heaves doesn't count? I might do it now though. Want me to use your helmet, Sir?" John's grin was shaky as he grabbed for the Major's helmet.

"Nah," Greg laughed, pushed him away and headed for the hooch.

"Here, you can use mine," Booger offered.

"Thanks, but no thanks, Booger."

By the time they returned to the base at Da Nang, John's head throbbed. Sweat running down the middle of his back itched as it dried. He checked the bird over, looking for shrapnel or bullet holes, and refueled the Huey to be ready for the next mission. He climbed into the pilot's seat and started the motor, listening to the pitch of the rotors and the rumble of the chopper's engine. Satisfied that everything sounded okay, he shut the engine down and motioned to the ground crew to move the Huey back into its revetment.

~~~

2000

I felt like a schoolgirl on her first date as I dressed for dinner with Michael Hinton. I fastened my gold chain around my neck and put in pearl earrings, something I usually forgot to do while working on Maggie's cottage. Two flower fairy watercolor paintings, matted, but not framed, were ready. I looked forward to getting a check for the first three paintings, as well as dinner and companionship. I kept going back to the mirror, trying to see if everything I wore looked okay. Finally, I decided it had to be okay, or I would be late.

A large plastic bag protected the watercolors in case of rain and laid flat on the back seat of the Volkswagen. It seemed strange to be going out in the evening, although it was not yet dark. The sun set in
~~~

the west, turning the sky and the harbor vermillion and gold.

The ride to East Sound at the top of the horseshoe-curve shaped island offered a change of scenery. I found the restaurant decorated with sea anchors and hawser lines and pulled into the parking lot, next to a few other cars. As I turned out the Bug's lights, I wondered which car was Michael's, or if he had even gotten to the restaurant yet. The setting sun filled the sky with reds and yellows, blinding me. I stumbled over a curbing and nearly fell but grabbed the branch of a small tree beside the parking space to save myself, and went inside feeling a bit ruffled.

Michael stood up from the table where he waited and walked over to meet me.

"I'm so glad you were able to make it, Sarah," he said.

"Well, my calendar is not exactly what you'd call full," I laughed, as he pulled a chair out for me. "I seem to spend most of my time working on the cottage."

"You've done a terrific job."

"Thanks, Mike, I've become so fond of the place I want to make it perfect, but I've spent too much of my retirement money on it. I'm getting a little worried about finances. If I can sell some paintings through your gallery, it will certainly help."

Mike reached into his inner jacket pocket and pulled out an envelope. He smiled. "Here," he said and handed it to me.

I opened the envelope and grinned. "Three hundred dollars for three small watercolors? Great!"

"Well, actually, I took the usual commission off the top for selling them."

"Of course, you have to do that. I can't believe I've earned some money doing something that was so much fun." I sipped my water as the waiter hovered closer. "I have two more paintings in the car for you, when we're through here."

We ordered dinner – Mike had the grilled salmon and I had filet of sole with lemon butter on the side. A nice Chardonnay wine complimented both meals.

"A family with three little girls bought the first paintings," said Mike. The children loved the flower fairies and wanted to decorate their rooms using the colors in the paintings."

"I'm flattered." I blushed, thinking about the little girls I might have had. Wondering how it would be to help a daughter decorate her room. I poured lemon butter over my fish and sighed.

"Everything all right?"

"What?" I looked up. "Oh, yes. It's just that I've always wanted a child of my own, but my husband went to Vietnam and didn't come back."

"He was killed?"

"I'm not exactly sure. He was missing in action and presumed to be dead." I held my left arm up to show him my bracelet. It clinked and rattled, its finish worn smooth. "The helicopter he was in crashed and burned. Only three sets of dog tags were found, and only one of those legible." My eyes misted over. "That one belonged to the pilot. Maybe John did die in the crash, but it's strange they could not find a fourth I.D."

I looked up into Mike's eyes. "John's probably not still alive. I think if he were, he'd have tried to contact me some way -- that is unless he's a prisoner who has been overlooked in North Vietnam. But, when the United States pulled out, all the prisoners were supposed to have been sent home."

"I'm so sorry Sarah. I had no idea."

I reached over and patted his hand. "Not to worry, Mike. I've lived with this so long; I don't know if I can let it go. You know?"

"Yes. When my wife died, I felt lost without her. But life goes on, and I have the Art Gallery and my garden." He put his fork down and gazed at the remnants of the sunset sinking below the horizon.

We ate in silence for a while, both of us a little bit uneasy. Finally, Mike said, "Tell me about your ghost, Sarah – the one that plays the piano in Maggie's Cottage."

"There's not much to tell," I said, feeling like I was betraying Maggie's ghost by talking about her. "She only appears on nights when the moon is full, but each time she looks a little bit more grown up." I buttered a bit of French bread and put it in my mouth.

"Does it frighten you to be living in a haunted house?"

I swallowed the bread, took a sip of wine and shook my head. "No. I'm really very fond of my little ghost. I'd miss her if she didn't show up some moonlit night."

"Other folks have heard music coming from the cottage, but no one ever dreamed it was a ghost."

"If she isn't a ghost, then I don't know how to explain it, except that maybe I'm losing my mind living alone on an island!" I laughed at what I hoped was a joke.

"Well, the other merchants and I would like to have you join us at any of our every-other Thursday night meetings." Mike re-filled our wine glasses. "And you're always welcome to drop in at the Gallery, too."

"Thanks Mike." I put my napkin on the table and sat back, my stomach full, my need for companionship satisfied. We sipped our wine. I looked around the room. A fire in the fireplace. A few other customers. Mike called for the check.

"Let me get my share," I offered, opening my handbag, not sure of the protocol for dating in the 21st Century.

"No, this is my treat." Mike said as he gave the waitress a credit card.

We walked out of the restaurant to my car. I watched the curbing, careful not to trip over it again.

"The new paintings are on the back seat," I said, as I unlocked the Volkswagen and lifted them out.

"Great, Sarah. Let's take them under the parking lot light."

Mike held up my paintings of Heliotrope and Pansy.

"Very nice, Sarah. You're really talented. I hope you'll keep painting more things for the gallery – not just flower fairies."

"I'd love to paint other things. Tell me what you want. Something Orcas Island-y, I'm sure. I have one of the boat basin at Deer Harbor I could let you have."

"Great. I'll come by for it next Monday."

I hesitated for just a beat, wondering what to do. Then I said, "Come for lunch, then," and wondered what I would feed him.

~~~

2000

Music awoke me once again, and I tiptoed out to watch my ghost. Maggie sat ramrod straight at the piano playing Chopin's Prelude in A. Moonlight highlighted her face and hair. Her face looked pale and drawn. Maggie looked quite grown-up. Straight posture. Long black skirt. White blouse buttoned high at the throat. Taffy-colored hair piled high on top of her head. The toe and ankle of her right foot protruded from under her skirt, revealing a row of buttons up the side of her shoe. Her eyes filled with tears and spilled over onto the ivory keys.

Why did she look so sad?

~~~

1917

"What's the matter, darlin'," asked Alice.

Maggie wiped her nose with a tatted-lace-edged linen handkerchief and looked into her mother's eyes.

"Henry's joined the Expeditionary Forces. He told me today. I knew he wouldn't be able to stay away from the war once the United States got in."

Maggie then played Chopin's Funeral Dirge, crashing out the minor chords in a thunderous storm. Alice stood by, silent, wondering what she could say to help. When this piece was over, Maggie continued, "He thinks it's his duty to go, because he knows how to fly. Not many people do, you know . . . " Maggie wiped a tear from her cheek and gazed at the moonlight sparkling on Deer Harbor.

"He leaves for training next week. They're desperate for pilots over there. Do you know why?" Maggie let her hands fall onto the piano keys. She turned around on the bench and looked at her mother, her arms limp on her lap, her mouth drooping in an upside down 'U', her eyes brimming tears.

"B-because . . . the s-survival rate is so . . . l-low" Maggie gulped and smoothed her skirt over her lap. "Flyers don't last long over there . . . over in France. Aeroplanes are so fragile. Not safe a bit when they're shooting at each other. It's s-suicide."

Alice sat on the piano bench with Maggie and put her arms around her, rocking to and fro.

"I helped Henry build his aeroplane out of wood and linen. I know how fragile they are." Maggie blew her nose, stood up and paced around the room like a caged animal. "Not only that, but they're highly flammable. Do you think . . . " she stopped, twisted her handkerchief in a knot and whispered, "Do you think he'll come back, Mama? I just don't know what I'll do if Henry is killed."

~~~

2000

The pie baking in the oven of the wood stove filled Maggie's cottage with the warm aroma of apples, sugar and cinnamon. Michael Hinton arrived promptly at noon for lunch. He shook hands with me, holding my hand a little too long. I extricated my fingers from his, brushed my hair back with my left hand, causing my POW bracelet to tick against my watch as it slid down my arm. *Reminding me of Johnny.*

Mike walked to the piano and ran his hands over the smooth mahogany. "So, this is where your ghost appears."

I nodded, not wanting to talk about Maggie's ghost. Afraid Mike would try to see her. "Only when the moon is full," I said, nervously pushing back my hair. *Tick-tick* went the bracelet.

Mike touched the piano keys as he admired the view of Deer Harbor and Deer Island from the new Ariel windows. The piano responded with its clear perfect pitch.

"I think you told me the other night that your ghost doesn't frighten you. Is that right?" He played a C major chord.

I smiled. "Not this ghost. I'm really very fond of her." My bracelet ticked again.
~~~

"Nice old piano," he said. "The tone is amazing and it is still in tune." He motioned to the piano bench and asked, "Do you mind if I try it out?"

"No, not at all."

Mike sat down, flexed his fingers and played some Dixieland Jazz. *Goofus. Ain't Misbehavin'. Honeysuckle Rose.*

My foot tapped with the rhythm. "Very nice, Mike. I love Dixieland. In fact, I like most all kinds of music. I just don't care much for Rap."

"Thanks." He stood up." How about you now?"

"Oh, I'm not that good. I just play for my own amusement."

Mike raised one eyebrow. His eyes twinkled. He grinned. "I'll bet you're better than you think." He turned around and paused to look at Maggie's flower fairy figures, lined up on the mantel. "You certainly have provided these little statues with a beautiful setting."

I fidgeted with the dishtowel. My POW/MIA bracelet ticked on my arm. "I can't take the credit. Remember they were Maggie's before I bought this house." I moved the fireplace screen and put another stick of wood on the small fire. Maybe I didn't really need a fire, but I liked the cheerful, cozy way it looked.

"Lunch is ready," I said. "Come into the kitchen."

Mike followed me. "It smells wonderful in here."

"Apple pie for dessert made with Granny Smith apples from my own trees," I said, pointing out the back window at the orchard. *Tick-tick.*

I had set the table with placemats and flatware and a bowl of Sweet Williams, their tiny clusters of spiky magenta and white blossoms cheering the room. I showed him to one of the bentwood kitchen chairs at the table by the windows overlooking the orchard and garden.

"Sarah, this is so nice. Just like home."

"Thank you. I truly love this little house, Mike." I walked back to the stove. "Grilled cheese sandwiches and tomato soup okay?"

"Wonderful."

I brought the food from the stove and sat opposite him.

"All this and homemade apple pie, too?"

"Mm –hmm. "

"Guess this is my lucky day."

I jumped.

Mike reached over to grasp my arm. "Are you all right, Sarah? You look like you've just seen a ghost." He looked around, perhaps hoping he would see Maggie's ghost. I didn't want him to see my little ghost. *Go home, Mike. Leave me here with my memories of Johnny and my ghost.*

He turned back and looked at me in concern.

"Y-yes. I'm all right, Mike. An old memory just flashed before me, is all. It's funny, but Johnny, my husband, said those exact same words to me the first day I met him." I pulled my arm from his hand and brushed it over my forehead. *Tick-tick.*

"What exact words?"

"You know, 'Guess this is my lucky day.' He said just what you said. Isn't that eerie?"

"Well, he must have been pretty astute. Like me." Mike laughed and tried to touch my arm again, but I put my hands in my lap, not knowing how I felt about this man, only aware of all the minutes, days, months and years I had waited for Johnny, longing for some word – anything, sure he would come back to me if I waited long enough.

We finished our lunch and I cleared the table, leaving the dishes in the sink. "Come up to my studio, Mike. I want to show you the boat harbor painting I told you about."

We climbed the staircase and I pointed out the pie-shaped steps on the curve.

"Right. I'll be careful." Mike stepped on the wide part of each step as he followed me. "More beautiful views from up here," said Mike looking out at the boat basin and Deer Harbor.

I had set the watercolor on an easel next to the window overlooking the docks.

"Say, I like this one." Mike grinned at me. "Can you do more of this type of thing for the gallery?" He stood close behind me and rested one hand on my shoulder as he looked out to compare the boat basin with the painting. I felt his breath stir a few gray strands of my hair and thought how nice it would be just to lean back against this man. But he wasn't Johnny. I ducked away from him and nodded. *Tick-tick.* "I'll take a sketch pad and roam around the island."

I handed him a large plastic bag to protect the fragile watercolor. "I'll try to have some more things ready, soon."

"Good." Mike lifted the painting from the easel, slid it inside the bag, and headed back down the stairs. We walked down the back-porch steps to his car. He looked around at the property. The apple trees were in bloom. Birds trilled their spring songs. The old shed sagged in upon itself and looked in danger of being overgrown by blackberry vines. Mike glanced at it.

"Have you checked out the shed, yet?"

"No, I've been so busy with the house. Want to help me get the door open so we can see what's in there?"

"Okay, but first I'll put the painting in the car." Mike laid the painting on the back seat and shut the car door. Then he took my hand. His touch electrified me. We walked to the decrepit building through tufts of grass and dandelions still damp with morning dew. The door hung crooked on rusted and broken hinges. Mike let go of my hand and leaned his weight against the door, lifted, and swung it open. My hand tingled from his touch.

"Sarah," he said. "Did you know you had a second car?" The open shed door revealed an automobile covered with a rotting canvas tarp. Brass headlights and radiator peered out from under the canvas and, glinted in the sunlight.

Still in a daze, I looked into his eyes. "Ah . . . well . . . Virginia told me Maggie McNamara used to run all over the island in her vintage Model T. I thought it might be here, but I couldn't get the shed door open."

Mike lifted the tarp from the car raising a cloud of dust. He coughed, but his eyes sparkled as he took the tarp outside away from us and shook it. Then he came back and stood, hands on his hips, looking at the dusty automobile.

"I wonder if it still runs."

"I don't know. Maybe Virginia knows when Maggie stopped driving it. It would be hard for Maggie to start as she grew older, as I think you have to crank it, first with that crank, don't you?" I pointed to the handle protruding from the front of the automobile.

"Yes."

I brushed dust from the brass headlights. "It's beautiful, isn't it?"

Mike nodded and grinned. "When I was in high school, I worked for a Model T club. I've always wanted one of these things. Want to sell it?"

I glanced at him and laughed. "I don't think so, Mike. Not right now, anyway. Maybe someday . . . if my paintings don't sell, and I'm really strapped for money."

Mike reached over and held my hand again. He squeezed it. "Your paintings will sell, don't you worry. People love your watercolors." I gulped and dared to look at him. He smiled, and still holding my hand, we walked together back along one side of the automobile, stumbling over old gas cans and boxes, bumping into the unfinished wall made of two by fours and planked siding, getting dirty. Spider webs hung in lacy doilies from the rafters and corners, their builders clinging to trap lines on delicate gray and yellow legs, waiting for unsuspecting prey. The place smelled like old automobile oil and grease, dust and mold. I sneezed.

Mike ran his hands along a fender, his eyes shining. "I'd really like to fix it up and see if it runs, Sarah. That okay with you?" We walked back to the front of the shed and he let go of my hand to brush off his dusty hands and clothes.

"I don't know. I guess that'd be okay, but right now, I don't know if I can afford to buy parts for it. I've spent so much on the house," I murmured.

Mike didn't hear me. He was too engrossed in the Model T. He unfastened two clips on one side of the engine cover to look inside. Mike looked around and found an old rag hanging on a nail.

"Look here, Sarah." He rubbed dirt and grease from the engine block with the rag. "See the serial number here? It looks like . . . " He rubbed some more. "Yeah, it looks to me like 14,399. When Henry Ford built the first cars on the assembly line in 1908, he started at number 1 and went to 309 cars that first year. In the year 1909 the number had reached 14,161. This flivver had to be built in 1910. You know Sarah, between 1908 and 1927 there were over 15,000,000 model Ts built."

"I didn't know he put numbers on the engines." I stepped back to admire the car. "All I've ever heard is that Henry Ford said you could have any color car you wanted, as long as it was black." I laughed and brushed dust from a fender. "But this car is green, dark green –

almost black, but never-the-less, green. Like that forest of Douglas fir over there." I pointed to the hillside above the boat basin.

Mike laughed. "Well, after 1916 he painted 'em all black. Easier to do it that way."

Mike was as excited as a kid at Christmas. "I'd love to take it home and work on it in my garage. We could have fun riding around in it when the weather is nice. Maybe even join a Model T club. The people in those clubs put on old clothes from the turn of the twentieth century and go on tours."

He looked toward the house. "Did Maggie leave any clothes in there from the early part of the twentieth century?"

"I don't know, Mike. When I cleaned out her closet, I gave everything to the Salvation Army, but they were pretty up to date, maybe only twenty or thirty years old. There are some boxes up in the attic. Maybe they have old clothing in them."

"Well, could I come back tomorrow night after work with a trailer and take this Tin Lizzie home to work on in a nice heated garage?"

What did I know about this man who wanted to take Maggie's antique car away with him? I pushed back my hair with my left arm. The chain links of my bracelet clicked. I walked around the vehicle stalling for time to think. Virginia said Mike was a good person.

"Okay," I said. "It would be fun to see if it still runs." I kicked a dandelion gone to seed, scattering fluff over the grass. "I'm afraid I can't help with the expense right now, though, Mike. You understand that?"

"Don't worry, Sarah. I'll take care of it."

I sneezed again, as I helped Mike cover the car with the dusty tarp. He picked up the corner of the broken door and closed it.

"Thanks for lunch, Sarah." Mike held my hand a little longer than necessary. My bracelet clicked at me. I shivered.

"The homemade apple pie was delicious."

"Thanks Mike. Good-bye. Come back again. I'll call you when I have more paintings."

"Don't wait too long. Drop by the gallery if you're in town, and we'll have coffee."

"Sounds good."

"And come by anytime to see how your car is progressing."

I grinned and walked with him back to his car.

"Good by, Sara." Mike kissed me, a long tender kiss that sent shivers clear to my toes and awakened dormant feelings I had thought might never return. "I'll be back tomorrow night with a trailer to haul the Model T into town. Okay?"

In a daze I nodded. "Okay."

Mike backed up his car and turned down the road to Eastside. We waved, and he drove away. A minute or two passed as I stood there with the fingers of one hand touching my lips. Soft breezes blew in from the harbor as I wondered about my mixed-up feelings. Maybe I wasn't ready for a new relationship. Maybe too much time had passed. Why was my bracelet so noisy when Mike was around? Every little click reminded me of Johnny. Usually, I didn't even notice it.

And what about Johnny? He really might have been killed in that helicopter crash, and no one found his body. Maybe the second letter I received from the Army was right. Maybe he really wasn't Missing in Action but Killed in Action. Too many maybes.

My bracelet clicked. *Funny, but all the time we looked at the Model T, I hadn't been aware of my bracelet at all. If it had clicked to remind me of Johnny, I had not heard it.*

That second letter . . .

10/3/70

Dear Mrs. Hanaeki,

The wreck of the helicopter in which your husband, John Hanaeki was crew chief, has been found near the Cambodian border nearly a year after it failed to return to base. The helicopter had crashed and burned. It is now overgrown by the jungle. There is no evidence of any survivors. Three sets of I.D. tags were found, but only one set, belonging to the pilot, Major Greg Hammond, was legible. We must assume that everyone, Major Hammond and his crew, perished. They are all officially listed as dead, not missing in action as previously reported.

Please accept my condolences on the death of your husband.

Sincerely,

Captain Jed Winslow
U.S. Army First Cavalry
Da Nang, Vietnam

~~~

I rummaged around in the basement under the light of a bare bulb, looking through a box of old paint brushes. Bright red and yellow paper in a dark corner caught my eye. A box kite appeared when I pulled this apparition over under the pale light from the basement window. The paper still seemed to be strong, and the kite string, neatly wound in a figure eight pattern around a piece of doweling, did not look rotten. Spiders had built nests in the kite's corners, leaving small silken egg sacs ready to hatch. I brushed away the cobwebs and threw the spider's nests out the basement door.

Could this have been Maggie's kite? Maybe she liked to go out on the beach in the sun and the wind to fly it. Although the colored paper covering the wooden frame felt dry and brittle, the kite was in good condition. The kite's tail, made of scraps of cotton fabric tied together, had turned gray with dust that lifted into a cloud making me sneeze. I carried the kite outside and shook the kite tail in the wind, sneezing again.

Sun-drenched cumulus clouds scudded across the sky over Deer Harbor, beckoning me. I ran back into the cottage for a jacket, took the kite to the end of the road and walked out on the beach.

How does one fly a kite alone? I had always thought it took two people – one to hold the kite and one to run with the kite string. I set the kite up on a
~~~

driftwood log and eased the string out a bit, running into the wind. The kite lifted off.

I ran faster, letting out more string. The kite soared high with the seagulls. What fun! I had been working too hard. All work and no play makes Sarah a dull girl. I stood in the wind, watching the kite reach for the clouds.

The wind freshened, carrying with it the smell of rain. As the kite danced among fluffy clouds, giant raindrops splatted down on me and dimpled the sand. The kite tugged harder. The string snapped. Wind carried it out over Deer Harbor, past the harbor entrance and far away over The Sound where it went into a spin and disappeared into the water. I stood dejected, holding the dowel with its bit of string still attached. I sighed, put the dowel in my pocket, zipped my jacket closed and walked back down the beach toward Maggie's Cottage, getting soaked through, feeling guilty about losing the kite, and wondering how to build a new one.

The wind and rain blew my hair about and I lifted one hand to smooth it out of my eyes. *What is that? My mother's hand poking out of my sleeve? No, no, it couldn't be her's, it's mine.* My hand, the knuckles of the first joints knotted with osteo-arthritis. Fingernails cut short, but still split and torn. Gnarled blood vessels woven in and out over and under tendons visible beneath papery skin. I don't remember seeing two strange brown spots like freckles out of control the last time I looked. I turned my hand over. Rain pelted down. The lifeline was unbroken. A row of calluses along the base of my fingers. My palm still smooth. The carved, silver wedding band had worn thin in thirty years.

Thirty years since Johnny had put the ring on my finger and we had vowed to be true until death.

Thirty years since he had shipped out for Vietnam.

Thirty years since the telegram arrived: "Missing in Action". The POW/MIA bracelet clattered on my wrist, weighing down my arm like chains on a prisoner. Tears flooded my eyes as I stood in the rain. I chewed on a hangnail and looked out over Deer Harbor to Puget Sound, strained to see through the mist and rain, tried to penetrate the dark clouds, watching for him to come home.

Knowing he wouldn't.

~~~

1968

The colonel stopped Greg and talked to him, pointing to a map. Greg nodded, folded the map and put it into his shirt pocket. He squinted at the sun low in the afternoon sky. His shadow grew long on the tarmac.

"Hey, John!"

John crawled out of from under the Huey. "Yessir?"

"We got another mission. Right now. ASAP."
~~~

John groaned. They had just spent another 12 hour day bringing in wounded. Fatigue pulled him down. He felt his face sag.

"I know you're beat, buddy, but we gotta do it. Come on, get a cuppa coffee. Let's go."

"Yessir!" John turned to the ground crew. "Make sure you top off her fuel tanks." John dragged himself to the mess shack.

"Our mission tonight's hush-hush." Greg pierced the co-pilot, John and Booger with a dagger-look as they walked back out on the tarmac holding their muddy coffee. "Ya got that?" His voice was quiet. "Be like those monkeys -- y'know -- See no evil, hear no evil, speak no evil. 'Kay?"

"Yessir," they muttered. John trailed his helmet by one strap.

"Good. It'll be just us. No other bird. I chose you guys 'cause I like what I see -- soldiers who take care of their equipment." The Major punched John 's upper arm and grinned at the others. "S'secret. 'Kay?"

The ground crew crawled all over the helicopter, checking everything. Greg walked up to a Vietnamese standing to one side. "Ready?"

The man nodded.

"Let's fly!"

Greg motioned the passenger and crew aboard, waved the maintenance crew off, and took the pilot's seat. Started the engine. JP4 fumes. Exhaust fumes. The rotors *whumped* around, shaking the bird. John's head ached. He felt a little bit sick and sipped the murky coffee. Coffee helped, even if it did taste like shit. Greg checked to make sure all personnel were out of the way, lifted off, and staying under the enemy's radar, flew above a strip of jungle and headed out over the South China Sea.

John's sweaty hands slipped on his door gun. He gulped and wiped his hands on his pants legs. Fatigue covered him like a foggy blanket. He took several deep breaths and looked around at their passenger. The man sat, impassive. Calm. Not seeming to worry as they skimmed at 115 knots four feet above the tops of the waves. John was afraid they might dip too low and be pulled down into the Gulf of Tonkin, never to be seen again. He pulled his eyes back to the job of scanning the terrain and the horizon for enemy planes or gun emplacements.

Who is this guy, anyway? Can't tell a South Vietnamese from a North Vietnamese. Shit! Maybe he's Charlie! What the hell's he doing in our bird? John's imagination ran wild. But Greg didn't seem worried about their passenger, so John decided he shouldn't worry, either.

They stayed under the radar for forty-five minutes. Then the pilot leaned the helicopter over to touch down on a beach. He unloaded his passenger and gear and pulled pitch out of there as fast as possible. The man vanished in the tropical forest before John even had time to look for him.

"Sir? . . . Are we just gonna leave him there, Sir?"

Greg nodded, lit a cigar and winked at John through the smoke. "S'secret, remember?"

"Oh . . . yeah . . . Yessir." John automatically checked the horizon for the enemy.

Oh-my-God! The man must be a spy! That's it. Numbah ten, f'sure! He has a radio with him. Bet he's gonna send back info to our troops. John shivered in the warm tropic air.

Greg whistled, off-key "The House of Blue Lights". The Huey flitted back over the whitecaps and headed toward land and the tropical forest. "Piece of cake," said Greg, speaking around the cigar clamped between his teeth as they lifted higher to clear the forest.

John grinned and nodded, his head clearing a little. "Piece of . . . " A tracer bullet whizzed by John's peripheral vision. More tracers streamed toward them from the dense foliage below.

"Six o'clock, Sir! Six o'clock!" John yelled. He and the second gunner rattled their teeth with bursts of machine gun fire.

Greg leaned his craft to one side and dove. Bullets followed, hitting empty air above the helicopter. Greg slewed the bird sideways. A row of bullets stitched a pattern in the side of the Huey above John's head. Another burst of gunfire followed them as Greg zigzagged fast and low, following the contour of the ground, getting out of range. John leaned out the door of the Huey and threw up, one sweaty hand slipping on the metal opening.

"It's all right, man," Greg reassured him. "No prob-lem-mo. We got it made, now." Greg's gruff voice sent the strains of *Puff the Magic Dragon* rumbling through their headphones.

~~~

1917

In September 1917, the Americans joined the allies. Henry was sent to ground school at the University of Texas. From there he went to Kelly Field, Texas, a makeshift camp consisting of six canvas hangars, some barracks and tents where the would-be pilots practiced flying in dual-controlled Jennies. The landing field was a flat piece of desert cleared of sagebrush and cactus. The allied blockade kept supplies and raw materials from Germany while Henry trained in Texas. Then he was sent home on leave before going to France to join the La Fayette Escadrille.

Henry bounded up the porch steps and rapped on the door of Maggie's Cottage.

"I'm coming," called Maggie, a little bit annoyed. She had been practicing scales and didn't like to be interrupted. She looked out the window, her fingers still moving along the keys. "Just wait a minute . . . Henry?"

"Henry!" she screamed as she realized who it was. Maggie stood up, tipped over the piano bench that crashed to the floor, and ran to the cantankerous front door that always stuck when she least wanted it to stick. Maggie tugged. Henry pushed. Finally, the door opened. Henry stumbled in to grab Maggie around the waist and kiss her. Hairpins slipped from Maggie's hair and her hair escaped from its bun. Henry buried his face in the tendrils of curls around her neck.
~~~

"Ah, Maggie, Maggie, I've missed you so."

"You couldn't have missed me more than I missed you!" she said, kissing his face all over – his eyes, his cheeks, his forehead – as she ran her hands through his hair.

Alice came up from the basement. "What's all the ruckus? Maggie, I don't think . . . Henry? Henry, you're home! How wonderful. I'm sure your parents are as happy to see you as we are. Come in. Come in. I just baked some cookies. Maybe you and Maggie would like some with a glass of cold milk."

"Thank you, Mrs. McNamara. That'd be keen." Henry grinned, stepped closer to Alice and shook her hand. Maggie stood back to admire him, tanned and fit from training camp. She couldn't get enough of looking at him, storing up memories for when he would leave again, for when he went overseas to France and the War.

Alice went to the ice box in the kitchen and took out a bottle of milk. The sweet smell of sugar cookies filled the kitchen as they sat down at the kitchen table.

"These cookies are swell, Mrs. McNamara," said Henry, stuffing his mouth full. He drank half a glass of milk and reached for another cookie. "It's so good to be home again." He reached across the table and held Maggie's hand. Maggie blushed, looked at her mother, and gently pulled her hand away.

"I'm home for two weeks." He shoved another cookie into his mouth. "If the weather is nice tomorrow like it is today, I'd like to take Maggie sailing

-- that is, with your permission?" Henry looked at Alice.

"If you will promise to be very careful, Henry. Don't try to win any races out there."

Henry laughed. "I know, I know. I'll try my best not to drown us."

Maggie nudged his leg with her foot under the table and made a little face at him. *Let's not remind Mama about my near drowning, please.*

"Tomorrow then, Maggie?" He smiled at her. "I'll come for you at 10 o'clock in the morning."

"Shall I pack a lunch?"

"I'd like that." Another cookie disappeared. "Come with me to my house now. My parents want to see me, and if you come, I can see you all at the same time."

Maggie went for her sun hat.

"'Bye, Mrs. McNamara. Thanks for the cookies and milk."

The next morning, Henry sailed along the harbor to where he could moor his boat across the road from Maggie's cottage. He crossed the road and knocked on the door.

"Come in, Henry," called Maggie. "I'm just finishing the lunch. See? Cold ham and pumpernickel bread, and cheese and fruit. And cookies." She smiled as she handed him the basket and picked up her straw hat.

Henry helped Maggie aboard and set sail for the island where they spent another afternoon in their driftwood nest. Every sunny day of Henry's leave was spent on the island, but they were always careful to be home before the sun set.

His leave over, Henry was sent to Europe with hundreds of other aviators on troopships for final training. Here, aviators learned to fly the "Rouleur", a single seated normal in every way plane, except for the fact that its wings were too small to lift the plane off the ground. After gunning his Rouleur along the ground, Henry was given an unclipped plane and told to fly it.

"Gladly," said Henry, anxious to have at it. An American aviator, Billy Mitchell had already led a force of 1,500 fighters and bombers to support an American ground attack near Verdun. Henry felt like he wasted his time running around the field in clipped-wing trainers. A row of aeroplanes including a single-seat British Sopwith Camel F-1 Scout, a few Spad 7's, and some Neuport 28 flying craft stood at the end of the field tied to stakes to keep from being blown over by the wind. These were planes that had crashed and been quickly repaired, planes with engine trouble, planes with weakened struts, planes the French and British could spare. Henry wondered why there were different kinds of planes as he stood with the other American pilots, admiring them. The British commander strode up with his aides.

The squadron leader yelled, "Attention!"

All the American aviators stood in a line, heels together, toes pointing smartly at 10 o'clock and at 2 o'clock, heads up, shoulders back.

A row of ribbons ran across the top of the upper left-hand pocket of the British Officer's tan coat, the left sleeve empty and pinned up to the shoulder seam. A "Sam Browne" belt encircled his waist with a leather strap that went from front to back over one shoulder. Fawn-colored jodhpurs flared out at the hip and fit close around the lower leg underneath highly polished knee-high boots. The British officer wore a military hat with a brim trimmed in gold braid. He slapped a riding crop against his thigh and turned to face the American pilots who stood at attention and saluted. The officer raised the riding crop to his cap in return.

"Ah, yes . . . At ease, men."

The pilots stood, hands clasped behind their backs, feet apart. Wool uniforms with high stand-up scratchy collars made it difficult to turn their heads. Khaki jodhpurs ended in knee-high boots.

"Welcome to your airfield, Yanks. There are no words sufficient to express our gratitude for your courage and dedication in coming to our aid. Britain and France will be eternally in your debt."

He waved the riding crop toward the row of planes. "These machines will be your aeroplanes. Sorry this is such a hodge-podge, but we are sorely pressed for equipment. As aviators, you need to be aware that although the one Sopwith Camel in that row is a remarkable fighting instrument, it is a bit temperamental, due to the extreme torque of the engine. Never forget that. Whoever draws the Sopwith Camel should know your plane will serve you well, if you keep the torque under control." He paced back and forth in front of the flyers.

"Try to stay with your squadron – don't let Jerry catch you out alone. The Germans like to come at you with the sun at their backs. Damn difficult to see them, you know."

He stood at ease for a moment and looked them over. "Any questions?"

The American pilots shifted uneasily but were silent.

"No? Very well. Just one last bit of advice. Sight your own guns. The armorer hasn't got to do the fighting." I'll turn you over to your leader, Captain Holcom, of the "Hat in the Ring Squadron". Best of luck and God bless you." He raised the riding crop in a salute. Henry detected a tiny sparkle of tears in his eyes. "Godspeed."

The Americans came to attention and returned the salute. The British officer strode away, his empty sleeve flapping with each step.

Captain Holcom assigned planes to the new American pilots. Henry drew the Camel, fifth in the row of the motley group. Red, white, and blue stripes painted on the tail, and red, white, and blue circles painted on top of the wings identified them as American. A top hat within a circle designated these planes were a part of the "Hat in the Ring" squadron.

The American aviators climbed into their planes, wrapped warm scarves around their necks, and adjusted leather helmets and goggles made of tinted splinter-proof-glass. Ground crewmen spun the propellers to start the planes. They held up the tails of the aeroplanes to keep the rear skids from snagging on the rough terrain, as the planes taxied in a row to the grassy field that served as a runway.

Henry unfastened the tight collar of his tunic and rubbed his neck where the wool fabric irritated his skin. He tucked Maggie's knitted scarf inside his collar, inhaling her lingering scent. A sudden longing for her overwhelmed him. With an effort, he forced his thoughts away from Maggie to focus on the task at hand and pulled his goggles over his eyes. Henry's turn, fifth.

Now.

He revved the engine, bumping across the uneven field, his crewmen running along to hold the tail up as long as they could. The Camel gathered speed and was airborne. Henry struggled with the temperamental Camel's strong engine torque. The plane nearly flipped over as he tried to control it, concentrating so hard, he forgot to watch for the enemy. He looked up in surprise to see scarlet flying machines coming out of the sun toward him. Henry maneuvered to get around the German planes and put his back to the sun. He held the stick between his knees, his heart pounding, and emptied his machine gun at a Fokker D VII.

Fifty rounds! Not nearly enough. Hardly two or three bursts of gunfire. Drat! I'll have to change the drum.

Henry banked the plane away from the German fighter and flew into a cloud. Stick between his knees again, he struggled with the ammunition drum. It would not budge.

Henry swore under his breath. "Tarnation! How do they expect a pilot to change this drum when it won't come apart?"

He yanked harder on the drum. His knees parted, releasing the stick. The weight of his body tipped the aeroplane and the torque of the engine flipped it over. Henry clung to the machinegun drum, feet dangling in the air. A patchwork quilt of farmland and hedgerows spread out far below him as the plane flew upside down out of the cloud. Henry looked around for enemy planes, knowing he made a tempting target for the Red Baron and his squadron.

Oh, Lord, please don't come loose, now!

The red triplane swooped out of the clouds, machine gun rattling. Bullets whizzed past Henry tearing a hole in his jodhpurs and nicking one wing of the Camel. Still upside down, the plane flew into another cloud away from the Fokker D VII. Henry's arms ached from the strain of holding onto the drum. He swallowed hard, took a deep breath, and struggled to swing one foot up into the cockpit above his head. Right foot in; then the left. Both knees gripped the stick. He let go of the drum with one hand and rolled the Sopwith Camel back over. Sweat poured down his face although the atmosphere at 3,000 feet was not warm.

Now, Henry old man, this time keep your knees together on that blasted stick. He grasped the drum, yanked it loose, and tossed it overboard. Then he replaced it with another loaded ammunition drum and headed out of the cloud searching for the German triplane.

The Fokker DVII had disappeared.

Henry flew his Camel back to the base, still trying to get used to the way it handled. He touched the two front wheels down and eased the back skid onto the grassy air strip in a perfect landing. Henry taxied to his place in the line of aeroplanes and cut the engine. He sat with his head on his arms, drained from his upside-down ride and the skirmish with the German pilot.

The ground crew ran to help him climb from the Camel. He stood on the soil of France, his knees shaking, sighed and rubbed one hand across his face. Henry would like to have knelt down and kissed the ground.

The maintenance crew secured the plane. They patched the machine gun hole in the wing with a piece of fabric and some dope paint, so it would be ready to fly the next day. Henry's fingers found the bullet hole in the wide flare of his jodhpurs. A little closer and he would have lost a leg.

Two empty spaces showed in the line of Hat in the Ring planes. The thought of the missing flyers gave him an empty feeling in the pit of his stomach, as he stumbled to the tents. Pale red sky faded to dusk. He tried to remember which of his friends had flown the missing planes. Were they dead? Wounded? Captured?

Sunset filled the horizon with a hazy after-glow. Henry tried to imagine just how high 3,000 feet was. *I wonder how long it would take to fall that far. There wouldn't have been much left of me if that ammunition drum hadn't been stuck tight.*

Henry expected to see two empty places at the dinner table that night, but the spots were filled with new aviators, fresh from the States, eager to do their part, unaware that the life-span of a flyer in World War I was eleven days.

~~~

1968

Dear Sarah,

The weather is hot and humid, sort of like Hawaii in the summer. I stay busy, keeping the chopper running. We go on a mission when ever they need us. Can't tell you where we go, though. Everything's a military secret. I'm so lucky to be on this bird, and not walking point in the jungle. Those poor guys we evacuate from the war zone don't have a chance. Greg, our pilot, is awesome. He can take our chopper anywhere. No place is too tight for Greg. He likes to sing and knows all the really good songs like "House of Blue Lights*". I wonder if he even knows that we can all hear him on our helmet headphones.*

I miss you. My tour of duty will be over some day, and I'll be home. Look around for a place to settle down when I get there.

Love, Johnny
~~~

~~~

2000

One fine day in July, I took a trip to Seattle to visit the Pike Place Market, where I watched the fish mongers toss whole salmon through the air to each other. I acted just like any other tourist to the Northwest, gawking wide-eyed, buying fresh fruit, looking at the craft displays. Then I wandered down to Pioneer Square and poked around the art galleries just for fun. What looked like a band of gypsies had set up some kind of a fair in the square.

After browsing through several art galleries and strolling through the booths, I bought chicken on a skewer and a caramel apple for my lunch. I dawdled over glass cases of hand-made jewelry reminiscent of the ornaments I had worn down in the Blackthorn Valley. Dangling roach-clip earrings. Sterling silver rings and necklaces set with turquoise. We had worn things like these with embroidered gauze peasant blouses and the "balling" jeans the guys liked – jeans with buttons that went up and down both sides of the center seam. How strange it was to see those things again. Thoughts and feelings of life in the commune at Blackthorn Valley overwhelmed me. I felt nineteen again and terribly in love with Johnny. I sighed and looked around me at all the people dressed like hippies. I felt a little out of place in my Nike running shoes,
~~~

khaki walking shorts and navy blue collared t-shirt with a machine-embroidered emblem on the pocket.

A group of people stood around a woman seated on the bricks. She had laid out a Celtic cross pattern of Tarot cards on the small rug in front of her and spoke in an earnest manner to the girl seated across from her. I stopped to listen.

That voice.

I looked closer at the fortune teller. Her weather-beaten face showed years of living in the hot sun. Dry climate skin. Vegas or Arizona. Wrinkled smoker's skin – skin like leather.

Still she looked familiar to me under her aging mask.

"Vermillion?"

She looked up at me and then back at the cards.

"Heliotrope?

"Turquoise?"

"What the fuck!" muttered the gypsy. She glared at me. "Can't you see I'm busy with a very important reading? Why don't you be quiet?" She sighed in exasperation. "I must have it quiet to concentrate. She stopped and stared at me.

"Sarah?" She peered at me, squinting her eyes the way people do who need glasses, but won't wear them. "Is that you?"

I nodded. "Sorry. I didn't mean to interrupt."

Vermillion looked a bit miffed. She scooted into a more comfortable position on the bricks and settled back into her routine. How could I ever have taken her fortune telling seriously? But, when I thought about it, some of it actually came true, bad things definitely happened.

I leaned against a tree and watched her. Vermillion looked tired. Jaded and worn. But then, so did I, and I didn't have to make my living giving Tarot readings. She wore the same sort of gauzy outfit she had worn in Blackthorn Valley, but now I detected a bra strap and a thong panty line underneath the filmy fabric. Her hair had turned salt and pepper like mine. She wore it in a crew cut spiked up with gel on top, and nearly shaved around her ears and the back of her neck. Her bangle bracelets clicked and rattled. Silver rings on all her fingers and toes. Vermillion sat up and stretched, showing her pierced navel. Myriad hoops in her ears. When she looked up at her customer and talked, a stainless steel stud glinted from the center of her tongue. I stood a few minutes and then decided I didn't want to renew this acquaintance and slipped away behind the trees.

"Sarah!" Vermillion finished the fortune and ran after me. "Sarah! Wait! Can't we talk?"

"I don't want to interrupt you, Vermillion. It looks like others are waiting for their turns."

"They'll wait." She lowered her voice. "I just tell the first one exciting things about a new lover or a trip and they all want their fortunes told."

"That's not what you told Johnny," I said.

"Well, Johnny's wasn't commercial the way these fortunes are. I was dead serious about this occult stuff, then. To tell you the truth, I'm bored with it now.

Burnt out, if you must know." She looked around the park. "Where is he, anyway? Johnny? Where's he at?"

I didn't want to talk about Johnny, but I said, "Do you remember the fortune you told him? Travel was in his future. Something bad would happen – a disaster, I think you said."

"Oh, yeah. Well, did he travel?"

"Um-hum. To Vietnam. And he didn't come home." I held up my left arm to show my POW/MIA bracelet. "Missing in action." Tears filled my eyes. "I still don't know what happened to him." I brushed away the tears. "His helicopter didn't come back from a mission. A year later the wreckage was found, but only three sets of dog tags, two of which were illegible. The other one wasn't Johnny's. I keep hoping he might have got out before it exploded."

"Oh, Sarah, I'm so sorry." Vermillion held my wrist and looked at the bracelet, rubbing her fingers over Johnny's name and ID number. "You know, I was always so jealous of you. You seemed so perfect, so, like . . . so . . . absolutely*!* . . . Like you didn't belong in that commune. . . . like . . . *a lady!* Besides, you had Johnny. I could never get him to take a tumble with me, you know. Not like those other guys. Johnny was always true to you."

"I know, Vermillion."

"Oh, I don't go by that name anymore." She grimaced. "Now my name is Mystic."

"I'll let you get back to your customers, Mystic. Gotta go." I tried to pull my arm away, but she hung on tight.

"Don't go, Sarah. Stay until I'm through here. We'll go to your place and have a drink and something to eat." She squeezed my hand. "Lyle's here. Remember him? Come on, you gotta see him. He'll be pissed if he doesn't get to see you. He'll want to talk about the old days at Blackthorn Valley." She sighed and her eyes glazed over. "Those were the days."

How am I going to get out of this? Lyle is the last person I want to see. And she wants to come to my place. To Maggie's Cottage? I don't think so! I don't want Vermillion coming to Orcas Island with me. She'd probably try to exorcize my ghost, and I'd hate that. I don't want anything to happen to Maggie's ghost. What am I thinking? If I don't believe in her fortune telling, how can I believe she could exorcize my little ghost? I brushed one hand over my eyes.

"There he is!" Mystic jumped up and down and waved. "Lyle!" she shouted. "Look who's here!"

I cringed as other people turned to look at me and then at the scummy guy waving and hurrying toward us. My heart pounded at the thought of the last time I had seen this man. I turned away.

Too late. There stood Lyle, grinning at me, showing two missing teeth. Ready to envelope me in a bear hug. I shivered, moved back a step and thrust out my right hand. Better to shake hands than hug this creep.

"Watssa mattah? You too good to give old Lyle a hug?" He grabbed me and picked me up, whirling me around in a circle, trying to plant a wet kiss on me. I turned my cheek just in time to avoid his beard-framed lips on mine and extricated myself from his embrace.

"How are you, Lyle?" I managed, trying to pull myself together.

"Gettin' along. Just gettin' along." He spat a stream of tobacco juice on the ground and brushed one sleeve across his beard that I now could see was spotted with brown tobacco stains mixed in with the gray hair. "You know, Sarah, I always had a thing for you. You knew that, didn't you?" Lyle's eyes pleaded with mine.

"If you call *attempted rape* a thing for me, yes, Lyle, I knew it."

"Attempted rape?" Mystic's eyebrows shot up and she stared at me.

"Awrr," Lyle leaned over to spit again. The round Copenhagen container formed an embossed circle in his back jeans pockets. "I was stoned that night, Babe. Didn't mean nothin' by it." He put an arm around me. "You'll forgive ole Lyle, now, won't you? Come on, give us a kiss!"

I pulled away. The tobacco juice was sickening enough, but he smelled like he hadn't showered in days, or washed his clothes, either.

"Let her alone, Lyle," said Mystic. "Can't you see she doesn't want you?" Mystic put an arm through Lyle's and pulled him close to her. "Why would she want an old thing like you when she can have Johnny?"

I felt my face turn pale. I wished I could have Johnny. Lyle frowned. He turned again and spat.

"Lyle and I run this little art show," said Mystic. "We had to do something when the commune broke up."

"Oh, when did that happen?"

"Not too long after you and Johnny left. Johnny sort of kept things going around there, he was so good with mechanical things," said Mystic, a dreamy look crossing her face.

Lyle laughed. "Anyone who could keep that old pick-up running had to be a good mechanic. So, how's ole John doing?"

Tears welled up in my eyes at the question. "Not very 'how'," I managed to choke out. "He's missing in action in Vietnam." I lifted my arm so my POW / MIA bracelet jangled.

"No way!" said Lyle, peering at the bracelet. "That fuckin' war's been over for years. You mean to tell me you ain't heard from him yet?" Lyle shook his head in disbelief.

I nodded and brushed away tears.

Mystic clutched my arm. "What a bummer, Sarah," she said.

I gulped and took a big breath. "I'll probably never know what happened to him. It still hurts. I still miss him."

We stood in uncomfortable silence for a few minutes thinking of Johnny.

Finally, Mystic ventured, "Did you ever go back to college?"

I nodded. "When Johnny joined the Army, I decided to finish my degree and then I worked for graphic arts firms in San Francisco and Seattle until I retired last year. I've been doing a few watercolor paintings on my own that sell well in local galleries."

I settled my handbag strap on my shoulder and moved back a step.

"I'm in town just for the day on a shopping trip. I know you two are busy so I'll let you get back to work. It was nice seeing you again." I smiled and extricated my arm from Mystic's talons. "Gotta catch a ferry." I waved good-bye and walked away.

They watched me go. Mystic looked like a forlorn child standing there with only Lyle for company. That I felt sorry for her surprised me, but she had made her own choice. She could have finished college, too. I guess she'd rather still be a hippie. An aging hippie. A bummer, for sure.

I walked away, my heart pounding as I remembered Lyle's attempted rape so many years ago. I gagged at the thought of him forcing himself on me. When I had gotten out of sight, I sat down on a bus stop bench and held my reeling head in my hands. Bile retched at my throat. When I had calmed down and caught my breath, I found where I had parked my Volkswagen and went back home to my cottage on Deer Harbor.

~~~

1968

John heard voices from far away. An alien language muddled his brain. Smells of sweat, blood and oiled metal made him want to vomit. Another
~~~

smell, the pungent fumes of JP4 helicopter fuel floated inside the wreckage. John lifted one hand sticky with blood and dropped it, too weak to hold it up. Time seemed to stand still. The voices became louder. He felt hands on his ankles and hands on his shoulders. Through his good eye he could make out Asian faces. *Viet Cong?* A sharp pain stabbed his chest.

They moved John out of the crashed helicopter and ran for cover, jostling him in their hurry. He clamped his jaw tight to keep from screaming as the chest pain dug in white-hot talons. The Huey exploded, licking the sky with red, yellow and orange flames, filling the rain forest with debris. Black smoke soon blotted out the conflagration. John's vision blurred and he lost consciousness again.

~~~

1917

Maggie cried. "I guess I didn't think . . . "

"You didn't think? Didn't that boy think, either?" Maggie's father paced the floor. "You both have grown up near farms with animals around. Surely you know about conception. I distinctly recall our talk before you started your menses. Do you?"

Maggie nodded. She glanced sideways at her mother whose face was red from crying.

"Do you not remember your old text book Gray's Anatomy? I did not want my daughter to be ignorant
~~~

of the facts of life the way so many girls are nowadays." Alexander stopped and looked out toward the island. *And have her pregnant before she's married, for God's sake! She's still a child. I know girls marry at 14 or 15, but in my opinion, even seventeen is too young for motherhood, married or not.*

"Yes, Papa, and I thank you for not keeping me in the dark. I appreciate that." Her eyes pleaded with his. She took hold of his hand and squeezed it. "You should understand the feelings Henry and I have for each other. We love each other. Surely, you and Mama felt that way. Maybe you still do feel that way." Maggie looked at her mother whose face became more flushed.

"Yes, I understand those feelings, Maggie. I certainly do. I just hoped you would wait for marriage."

Maggie stood, arms folded, defiant. "I don't see what difference a piece of paper and a few words spoken by a minister could make. When you love a person, that's all that counts." Maggie stood defiant, arms folded. "I don't think I've done anything wrong."

"You don't think you've done anything wrong ?" Maggie's father ran his hands through his hair and paced around the living room.

He stopped and frowned at her. "We still have to get along in society, Maggie, and not ostracized by the rest of the community. Henry's thousands of miles away from here, fighting in France. There's no way we can have a wedding ceremony."

Tears welled in Maggie's eyes. "I know, Papa, I know. He's gone, and he'll probably never . . . come back." Maggie tried not to cry and pressed her lips with her clenched fist, but sobs wracked her body.

Alice sat on the edge of a kitchen chair wringing her hands, eyes blurred with weeping. "What will the neighbors think? The doctor's daughter with child? Out of wedlock? Oh dear. . . oh, dear."

"Mama, don't worry. Henry and I love each other. This is our baby. Who cares what the neighbors think?"

"Well, I do," snapped her mother. She looked up at her husband in desperation. "Can't you do something?"

The doctor patted his wife's shoulder. His pained thoughts twisted his face into a frown. He sighed. "Yes, I could do something, but would I want to? Abortion is very dangerous, besides being illegal. Sometimes the mother dies." He knelt down next to Alice's chair. "Besides, this is our own flesh and blood – our grandchild, Alice – part of you and me. Part of Maggie and Henry. The Andersons, too. We have all gone into the making of this new human being."

Alice buried her face in her apron and sobbed.

"Please don't worry so, Mama," said Maggie. "I want Henry's baby. Then I'll always have a little bit of Henry." Maggie put her arms around her mother's shoulders. "You see, Mama, Henry won't come back. His chances are not good, flying in France. I hope and pray every day he'll be safe, but I may never see him again." Maggie trembled and held both hands to her face as tears once again flooded her eyes. "I love him so much."

"Remember, Alice," Alexander said. "You were not much older than Maggie when you married me – eighteen. And Maggie was born the next year."

Alice puffed up, her face red. "That was different. We were married and I had not committed a mortal sin. I was not like Maggie, then . . ."

Alice broke down and cried some more.

Alexander patted her on the shoulder. "There, there," he murmured. "There, there."

Alice hiccupped and dried her tears. "Maybe you could live in Seattle with Auntie Kathleen until the baby is born, and then find someone to adopt it," she suggested.

Horrified, Maggie shouted, "Give up my baby? Never! This is my child – my only link with Henry. I can't give up my baby." Maggie paced the room, twisting her handkerchief into a damp rope. "I'll earn my living playing piano, if not in concert halls, then in . . . taverns . . . or . . . or . . . places like that. . . .dance halls . . . maybe. . . bordellos!"

Her parents looked at each other in alarm. Alice nearly fainted. If Maggie didn't know about conception, how on earth did she know about bordellos?

Alexander shrugged. "Very well, Maggie. We'll support you in every way we can, but don't be surprised if no one else on the island has anything to do with you. A lot of folks would think what you have done is a sin. Perhaps my liberal thinking has not been the best influence on you, after all."

~~~

1975

The chef on the TV cooking program I watched in my Seattle apartment closed her show by raising a glass of wine and wishing her viewing audience "Bon Appetit". I took my notes on how to poach salmon in *court bouillon* to the kitchen and filed them in a recipe folder. Poured another cup of coffee. Looked out the kitchen sink window at my tiny view of Puget Sound. Rain clouds hung over the water forecasting April showers and turning everything Payne's gray. While I walked back to the living room, I wondered if I needed to invest in a salmon poacher – a long rectangular lidded pan. Then I decided it was ridiculous to buy such a huge piece of equipment for only one person. When on earth would I need to poach a whole salmon?

I stopped in front of the television set. The Cookie Monster was busy scattering crumbs on *Sesame Street.* The numeral two jumped around the screen in different sizes, forms and colors while background people chanted *"Two! Two! Two!"* Bright colored numbers flashed on the screen with more chanting, "*one, two, three, four, five, six seven eight, NINE, ten.*" Then Bert and Ernie, two Sesame Street Muppets said, "*This program has been brought to you by the NUMBER TWO!*"

I flipped from the PBS channel to see what else was on. *Leave it to Beaver* on one channel. Another rerun: *I Love Lucy* on another. Not much on daytime TV. I flipped the channel button again. Yogi and Boo
~~~

Boo Bear, a kid's cartoon show popped up. I sipped coffee while I watched the antics of these two bears. If Johnny and I had had a child, wouldn't he have loved these characters?

A newscaster interrupted the scene. He looked as though he had forgotten to comb his hair or check his on-camera make-up.

"Good morning, ladies and gentlemen. This is Frank James with an important news bulletin." He stood in front of a map of Vietnam.

Vietnam?

I leaned closer to the set. *What's going on in Vietnam? There hadn't been much in the news since the United States pulled nearly all their men out in 1972. Thousands of U.S. soldiers were shipped back home. But not Johnny. Johnny wasn't shipped home. There had been peace talks. U.S. air strikes. Henry Kissinger. President Nixon.* My bracelet slid down my arm with a little "click".

"The United States Embassy is evacuating Vietnam," the newscaster continued. "All American civilians, the remainder of our servicemen, and those Vietnamese loyal to the U.S. who are in danger of being executed by the Viet Cong are being flown by helicopter to our ships at sea."

Film clips ran in the background behind him showing North Viet Cong tanks lined up outside Saigon, ready to roll into the city. Smoke from bombs and fires filled the air above the buildings. A lowering sky threatened the arrival of the monsoon rainy season that would make rescue by helicopter difficult.

The camera panned back to the announcer. "Now to Saigon and Jim Everly for a first-hand report."

Faint crackling noises accompanied a ghostly image of a reporter streaked with snowy lines. His lips moved, but no sound came out.

"One moment, please," said Frank James. "We're having some difficulties here." He looked off camera and frowned, his eyes pleading with the technicians off screen. Then the line between his eyebrows smoothed out. He turned back to the camera and took a deep breath, "Now, to you, Jim, in Saigon."

"I read you, Frank," Jim said, his words coordinating with lip movements. "All hell's breaking loose here -- Oops. Sorry for that slip, Frank."

The thunder of bombs filled the airwaves.

"We're anxiously awaiting your first-hand report," said Frank James.

I, too, waited anxiously as I stood watching the film clips behind the newscaster. *What's all this mean? If Johnny doesn't come back now, he must be a prisoner or dead.* My bracelet clicked.

"Saigon is falling. For the past week, ARVN soldiers have been deserting at the rate of a thousand a day. The Viet Cong rocket-bombed the airport at 4:00 a.m. this morning, and their tanks are on the way into the city,"

I heard the chatter of machine guns in the background. The whump, whump, of a helicopter's rotors. Screams. Cries. The crackle of small arms fire. A helicopter lifted off from the Embassy roof with people clinging to its skids. I gasped as some of them fell to the ground when the helicopter veered toward the sea. In the background American soldiers sang to the tune of "The Camp Town Races":

We're goin' home in freedom birds,
Doo-dah, doo-dah"
We ain't goin' home in plastic bags,
Oh, doo-dah-day.

Another film clip showed the line of tanks now rolling toward the city center. I shuddered, thinking how defenseless a person on foot would be in the face of all that armored might. How defenseless Johnny would be all alone in the jungle.

The reporter continued, "The first load of people to be evacuated were the children of U.S. soldiers. Indo-Chinese do not want these children and have been know to brutalize them. They are being taken to America.

The TV clip showed black smoke and bits of paper pouring from the Embassy chimney. "Inside the Embassy, they're burning money from the safe so the Viet Cong can't use it. Charred pieces of hundred dollar bills are blowing out the incinerator"

Someone had turned on an American Forces Radio in the background of the newscast. I could barely hear, "The Temperature in Saigon is 112 degrees and rising". Then the strains of Bing Crosby singing "*I'm Dreaming of a White Christmas*" drifted on the air.

Jim Everly continued from Saigon, "People are sitting by the pool drinking champagne while they wait to be evacuated."

I wanted to scream at them as I watched this film clip. How could they be so calm, sitting there drinking champagne? Didn't they know their lives were in danger?

'More people are lined up to the embassy roof's helipad watching for the helicopters – Chinooks and Jolly Green Giants -- to return and take them to our ships anchored off-shore," said Jim Everly. I could see the choppers on the film clip like dragonflies in the distance, flitting toward the Embassy roof. My hands grew sweaty as I worried about how they could possibly rescue all those people.

Jim Everly continued, "Former Special Forces men and CIA officers chopped down a 100 year old giant tamarind tree, to make room for the big birds to land." The camera panned to the roof of the building showing remnants of the demolished tree.

I twisted my hands together. The tree had been shredded in the soldiers' haste to make room for the large helicopters.

"'Operation Frequent Wind' helicopters are supposed to carry fifty personnel, but at first they took seventy. Now they're cramming in at least ninety. With that many people on each flight, there's no room for baggage," Jim Everly told the viewing audience. I hunkered down in front of the TV set. Abandoned boxes and suitcases littered the area inside the Embassy compound. The camera swooped up to show helicopters flying against a background of gray sky. "In addition, the monsoon season's here already, and we're socked in under dark clouds, adding to the difficulty of evacuating these people."

The camera panned to another part of the building. "Oh, my God!" said Jim. "They're locking the doors to the building! The South Vietnamese who've been helping us can't get to the helipad! We promised these people safe transport from Saigon." The reporter shook his head and groaned, "What's going to happen to them?"

I pushed my knuckles against my mouth. *And what's going to happen to Johnny?*

Once again I heard the American Forces Radio in the television background announce: "The temperature in Saigon is 112 degrees and still rising." The strains of "White Christmas" seeped through the static and accompanied desperate people climbing to the Embassy roof to be rescued.

Why did they keep playing the same song and giving the same temperature reading over and over . . . ? Oh . . . I think . . . it must be a code to let the Armed Forces know that America is leaving Vietnam.

I sank to the floor, stunned. Yogi and Boo Boo returned to the screen, playing tricks on the Park Ranger. I stared at them unseeing. Was it over at last? This terrible war that could not be won and made no sense and took the best of our young men? The war that must have taken Johnny? I sat with my legs crossed Indian fashion, my arms limp on my thighs, slumped in front of the television set. Tears streamed down my face as I thought of Johnny. *If we are completely out of Vietnam, why isn't he home? . . . He's not coming home?*

Bing Crosby's voice singing "White Christmas" echoed in my head while Yogi and Boo Boo Bear swiped "pic-a-nic" baskets in Jellystone National Park.

I shut off the TV.

Automatically, I checked the clasp on my POW/MIA bracelet, still fastened securely. I brushed tears from my face and hoped the dog tags that were missing when Johnny's helicopter crashed would turn out to have been his and that he was still alive and wearing his dog tags on a chain around his neck. I hoped he was coming home to me.

~~~

2000

My days continued to be full. When summer ended, I finally found time to go through the hall closet where I had stashed all the things I didn't know what to do with when I moved in. Way in the back on the top shelf, I found a small chest closed with a hasp and a tiny padlock. Locked. Where was the key? I put the chest aside and continued sorting through the things in the closet. Bed linens trimmed with hand-crocheted lace. A quilted satin glove case containing gloves for every occasion. Soft, black kid leather that must have fit like a second skin, fawn colored cotton suede
~~~

trimmed with matching buttons and embroidery work, and several pair of long white satin gloves for evening wear. Linen handkerchiefs edged with delicate handmade lace tatting. A dress box of old photographs. I set that aside to look through later.

As I put the box on the floor, it tipped, and a sepia photograph of a young girl fell out. Long blonde hair. Old fashioned dress. High-buttoned shoes. I smiled as I recognized the same little girl who had played the piano that first night in the moonlight. Her name, Maggie McNamara, and a date were written on the back in beautiful copperplate script. Other pictures fell out of the box: a baby, a toddler, a young girl, and a woman seated at a grand piano and dressed in what looked like black silk. She wore a diamond necklace around her throat. These all bore her name, Maggie McNamara and a date in the same delicate handwriting.

Photographs of the girl, Maggie, and a boy working on a sailboat. Sailing in the boat with "Maggie" painted on the stern. Other photos of the same two young people building an airplane. On the backs of all these was written *Maggie McNamara and Henry Anderson.* Photos of Maggie and Henry in a plane on the wet packed sand of the beach. Another picture of a woman in the airplane with Henry. The back of this one read *Mama with Henry.*

Photographs of another baby with blonde curls fell from the box. One golden curl, as fine and soft as a baby's breath, tied with a faded blue ribbon nestled inside an envelope.

A key.

I gasped as a key fell out.

I held my breath and picked up the chest. The key fit. I unlocked the padlock. Inside were letters postmarked Paris, France, dated 1917 and 1918. I opened one. The paper felt stiff and brittle, the edges flecked away in little bits.

January 2, 1918

My darling Maggie,

Oh, how I miss you. I long to see you with the sunlight shining on your sun-streaked blonde curls or under the white light of the moon. I long to see you in any kind of light. Candle light, lamp light. They're all the same to me. You shine in my memory like a guiding star. That's it. You are starlight. At night, I lie on my cot and try to re-live those sunny afternoons on the island when we built a campfire and made a small fort from drift logs.

Sometimes I hear your music inside my head, and it helps me through these hard times. I can't wait to get home and see you again. I want to go to one of your concerts. I'm so proud of you, a famous pianist. When I get home, will you be satisfied to live back on the island with me? If I ever get home, I never want to leave it again. But you can still give concerts in Seattle. Or even San Francisco. Maybe New York. Trains are fast now, but Orcas Island will be our home.

The French and the Brits are glad we're here to help them but the war seems to be at a stalemate. I don't think anyone can win. We lost six more planes yesterday.

The thought of you keeps me going.

Love, forever, Henry

Maggie stared at the page she had read a hundred times. She smoothed it out on her lap that grew shorter with each passing week and tried to read words into the letter that would tell her Henry was safe. She sighed, wondering if she should tell him about the baby. Would it help Henry to know he would soon have a child? She didn't want to distract him from his job and have him killed. She folded his letter back into its envelope, smelled the faint tobacco aroma still on the paper and tucked it inside her bodice, next to her heart. She buttoned the buttons high around her neck and stood up, her long black skirt trailing on the floor, and went to the piano to play very softly, "When Johnnie Comes Marching Home Again." Tears filled her eyes. Stars blinked over Deer Harbor and reflected on the water.

Next, she played Rachmaninoff's Piano Concerto, reveling in the deep chords, exulting in the depth of sound her piano produced, putting all her fears for Henry into the music.

~~~

Crashing chords awakened me, and I sat up in bed, the room bright with white moonlight. My heart pounded for a few minutes, and then I slipped out of bed and tiptoed into the hall to watch Maggie play the piano. She looked like a young lady, now, dressed in a high-necked white blouse and long black skirt pulled too tight around her waist, the hooks and eyes straining to stay together. A tendril of tawny hair escaped from the bun twisted on top of her head. Tears glistened on her cheek. I wanted to put my arms around her so we could cry together, she for Henry, me for Johnny, but I knew now she would disappear if I tried to touch her.

~~~

1968

The two men padded out a steady rhythm as they trotted inexhaustibly along the trail toward the setting sun. The music of their feet lulled John and he dozed a little even as the jogging motion made his head and side ache.

"Water," whispered John. His throat felt like sandpaper, rasping when he tried to swallow.

One of the bearers hissed at him and frowned, looking back at his companion carrying the other end of John's make-shift stretcher. They picked up the pace, jarring John further. His head wound bled, his teeth clicked together inside his jaw, and he lost consciousness.

Finally, they stopped. John opened his eyes, his head reeling. For a moment, he wondered where he was. Yellow-white sky became tinged with red. In the distance, sporadic machine-gun fire peppered the still evening air. One of the stretcher-bearers held John's head and shoulders up to give him water. Fire coursed through his chest. He fell back, exhausted. His guards each took a rice ball from a pack and ate. One of them put a few rice grains into John's mouth. He swallowed and laid back. His head throbbed. He couldn't see from his left eye. His chest was on fire and a Saharan thirst rasped in his throat. He lifted his right arm and mimed drinking. They gave him more water and then one man settled down to sleep while the other stayed on watch. A night bird called its four-note song. The dense forest whirled like the Huey's rotor blades above John's head, and he became unconscious again. A night owl called its fournote song.

During the night, John heard the guards shift places. He was not sure if they were North or South Vietnamese, Viet Cong or what they were. They didn't look young to John, but it was hard to tell how old the native people were. The sinewy muscles on their arms and legs showed like taut ropes wound round their skeletal frames. Gnarly veins stood out on their hands and biceps and on the calves of their legs.

With his right eye John could see a few stars in the sky above them through gaps in the dense foliage.

He thought he could make out the North Star on the edge of the horizon to the north. John tried to get his bearings, but stars in the equatorial skies were not familiar. He thought he should try to escape before they took him all the way to Hanoi. He had heard of the "Hanoi Hilton", the infamous prison camp in North Vietnam. But pain stabbed through his chest if he tried to move, and his head whirled if he tried to raise it.

He wondered why his chest hurt so much, and gently explored with his blood-caked right hand. He hit a tender spot and groaned. The guard immediately stood over him. He feigned unconsciousness. A rib must be broken. It was hard to tell. It hurt to breathe. His heart pounded. The guard sat back down, and under cover of the dark, John reached up to touch his forehead. Sticky blood greeted his fingertips.

In the morning, the men gave John another drink and helped him stand to urinate. They picked up the makeshift litter and jogged through the forest to a break in the trees bordering terraced rice paddies. Here they stopped to rest a moment, peering through the foliage.

Looking for their buddies, the fucking Viet Cong, I'll bet! John looked with his one good eye, but could see nothing.

Sure-footed, the men trotted along paddy dikes edged with thick, tall elephant grass, traveling faster now. Every bounce caused pain in John's side. He tried not to make a sound, but sometimes a groan slipped out.

When he was able to open his good eye and look around, he saw a farmer riding on a wooden rake pulled by a water buffalo through a flooded rice paddy. The farmer's weight held the rake down under the water. He wore a conical straw hat and carried a switch to urge the animal on. John shut his eyes. It exhausted him to watch this primitive method of farming. The smell of the muddy paddy water gagged him. *Shit, man, they must fertilize it with shit!*

They stopped at a village.

People gathered around them. John was surprised to see young men as well as the old men who carried him. As they talked among themselves, John looked at everything with his one good eye. *Something's different. These people don't look like the Vietnamese I've seen. They are not big people by any means. But why are the young men here? All the young Vietnam men are in one or the other of the armies.* John's brain spun around in his head. *We were flying along the border of Cambodia. Maybe they're Cambodian.* The strain of thinking exhausted him and he passed out again.

When he woke, he found himself inside one of the small houses. Hard-packed dirt floor. Boards along the walls for beds. The two litter bearers had gone. John lay on the stretcher inside the dark hut and worried about his fate. *Would these people put him in a prison? A bamboo cage? Would they torture him?*

At least it's not Hanoi, he thought, but where the hell am I?

A young woman came inside carrying a basin of water.

John raised his head and motioned to the retreating men, his body tense, his heart pounding, and said, "Viet Cong?

The woman shook her head. "Kampuchea."

John's head fell back. His body relaxed. *Oh? Cambodians. I thought they were Viet Cong. That's why they looked too old to be soldiers. They're trying to help me, not take me to Hanoi.*

The woman washed the blood from John's face and hair, making little Ts! Ts! noises with her tongue against the roof of her mouth all the while. A flap of scalp hung loose over his left eye. She went out for a minute and returned with a needle and silk thread. She forced the needle through the flap of skin and then through the skin on his forehead. John winced. His head spun. He fainted.

When he awoke, John's head throbbed, but he could see from his left eye. He worried the wound would become infected. The woman came back and gave him sips of green tea. She helped him sit up and he winced in pain. "Ts! Ts!" said the woman again, helping him lie back down. She unbuttoned his uniform shirt, admiring the horse patch on the left sleeve. A large bruise spread over one side of John's chest. Her fingers touched here and there as gentle as the feet of a butterfly. She nodded and called to someone outside, "Sovann?"

"Eh, Chi?"

A man came into the hut. The two talked a minute in the unintelligible tongue. Chi lifted John's t-shirt and described his injury to this man. Sovann helped

John stand on his feet. He teetered back and forth, holding on to Sovann to keep from falling. Bile rose in his throat and he gulped gushers of saliva, swallowing hard to keep from vomiting. Sovann and Chi removed his uniform shirt and t-shirt and wrapped his rib cage with wide strips of cotton cloth.

"Thank you," said John. "That feels better. I guess I broke a rib, huh?"

Sovann and Chi looked at each other and shrugged, then bowed and smiled.

Chi helped John into his uniform shirt and patted him on the shoulder. Sovann spread clean matting on the boards and helped John lie down again. A thin soup of chicken broth and mushrooms settled his stomach, but over the following days, the sparse diet of rice and vegetables with an occasional bit of fish left him feeling empty. John's stomach rumbled. *Don't they eat any meat here? I'd give a month's pay for a nice juicy steak or a hamburger.* His gut rumbled at the thought, embarrassing him, because he was afraid he was taking food needed by these people.

Chi went about her work while keeping one eye on John. When he caught her looking at him, she would look away and study the ground or the clouds in the sky. At mealtimes, she gave John a portion of her own rice and always the best part of any fish they happened to catch – the head with its succulent eyes.

In a few weeks John's rib felt better but was still tender if he touched it. He could walk around and help with some of the chores in the village. Every time he looked around, there was Chi gazing at him. She quickly looked away when he turned to her. Desperate to learn her language, he followed her around and pointed to things saying the English word for them. He indicated he wanted to know what they were called in her language. *House, woman, man, rice, boy, girl. Soo*n they had both picked up a smattering of each others' tongue.

One day two small village boys raced home from the rice paddies. They waved their arms, and gasping for breath, blurted out words unintelligible to John, but Chi understood them. Alarmed, she looked out toward the rice paddies. John looked, too. Down below, Viet Cong soldiers marched along the terraced dikes.

Chi turned around, panic in her eyes. She hissed at John to duck down, and taking his hand, ran toward the house. He ran in an awkward manner, holding his side with one hand to protect the healing rib. It was difficult to keep up with her. Sovann ran up to them, questioning her in whispers in their native tongue. John could understand a little of it: *Viet Cong. Hanoi. Hurry!* Families sent their daughters to hide in the jungle while Chi took John into the forest, too. Sovann removed any sign of a fugitive from their home.

The Viet Cong soldiers marched through the compound, hungry, fierce, arrogant and entered the small houses, taking whatever they needed. A Viet Cong soldier foraging for food found Sovann's pig near Chi and John's hiding place. Chi held a finger to her lips for silence, and motioned John to run away. John melted into the foliage and circled around the rice paddies. He headed south, straight into a Cong patrol.

~~~

2000

I got into the habit of reading one or two of Henry's letters to Maggie, each night before I went to sleep. It became a kind of ritual, like checking the clasp on my POW/MIA bracelet. John's letters had stopped so abruptly, I had nothing tangible of him to hold onto. Maggie and Henry had a love that transcended war, like my love for John.

May 20, 1918

Maggie dearest,

There is only one thing I love more than flying. You. My Maggie. You are the love of my life, but to be up there alone with my life in my hands, playing the best game ever, facing death every day I fly, I become something else – like I'm part of my aeroplane. My Sopwith Camel and I are one and are invulnerable. Even though our losses are great, I think it can't happen to me. Death will come to someone else.

On moonless nights, I light a candle to dispel the blackness of our tent and the war with its terror and the death that surrounds us, and I think of you and home on Orcas Island. Then your music plays inside my head.

Love,

till the end of eternity, Henry
~~~

Maggie read Henry's latest letter over for the hundredth time while Alice fussed with her Red Cross cap in front of her bedroom mirror. The veil would not settle down in a way to suit her. Exasperated, she frowned and took the hat pins out to try once more.

"Mama, it looks fine." Maggie heaved a sigh, tired of waiting. Wanting to get this over with. Worried about Henry's talk of death in the letter.

"That's easy for you to say, Maggie. You're young and beautiful" Her eye swept from Maggie's face to her rounded stomach. *And so pregnant!* Alice stifled a sob and stabbed another hat pin through the cap into thick hair piled on top of her head.

"There. I guess that will have to do." Alice shook her head, causing the veil to billow out and fall in a soft fold on her shoulders. She looked at Maggie again and hoped her pregnancy was not noticeable, but it was. Alice sighed. "Let's go. Is Papa ready to take us to the Library?"

Alexander poked his head into the hall. "Ready if you are, my darlings," he smiled encouragement at them and raised his right arm high up in the air, pointing to the door. "Onward to the Library!" Alice forgot her troubles for a moment and smiled at her husband.

"I really don't know what all the fuss is about," said Maggie, frowning. "Those old biddies don't have to like me. I'm not going to talk their daughters into a life of sin, you know."

"Oh dear, oh dear," murmured Alice. "Oh deary me. I'm sorry I said we would help roll bandages today.

But someone has to do it. Our boys in France need them. Even Henry might need a bandage, you never know."

Alexander frowned at Alice. "Not now, dear."

"Oh!" Alice put an arm around Maggie. "I'm sorry, darlin', I shouldn't have said that, but Henry's the only 'family' we have over there in the war."

"It's all right, Mama. Let's go shock those witches." Maggie smoothed her dress over her stomach, held her hands under the baby's bulge, and waddled out the door, a mischievous grin replacing the worried frown on her face as she muttered a skewed jump rope rhyme from her childhood:

"Old lady witch fell in a ditch,
Picked up a penny and thought she was rich
Old lady witch fell in a ditch,
Picked up my baby and thought she was rich!"

Alice gasped and turned pale.

"Stop that, Maggie," her father frowned. "Your mother is having a hard enough time with this."

Alexander's Model "T" pulled up at the Library, its engine putt-putting. The automobile shook and rattled. He set the hand brake, stepped out and walked to the passenger side of the car where he helped Alice and Maggie down. Other ladies wearing Red Cross hats and veils minced up the steps to the library in long hobbled skirts. Their stiff corseted figures dressed in scallops, tucks and lace, stood ramrod straight as they looked at Maggie and turned to whisper among themselves.

Maggie felt her face grow warm. Although Alice had discussed the stigma of being an unwed mother every chance she had, she realized for the first time her mother's concerns. But Maggie stood straight, held her head high, and took her mother's arm to help her up the steps.

"Don't even pretend you know who they're talking about," Maggie hissed. Alice's face had turned ashen. She looked at Alexander getting back in the Model "T" and took a step toward him.

"No, Mama. Let Papa go. We're not going to let these gossips get the best of us." They took a few tentative steps up to the door where one of Alice's friends, Bessie Sanford, stood greeting her helpers.

"Good morning, Mrs. Sanford," Maggie called out gaily to her. "Lovely day for rolling bandages, don't you think?"

Mrs. Sanford stared down her nose at Maggie and then at Alice who seemed to shrink down inside herself. "Why yes, Maggie, it is, indeed."

"Please walk in with us," Maggie lowered her voice. "Mama is feeling very uncomfortable about my condition."

Shocked speechless at her candor, Mrs. Sanford took Alice's other arm and escorted them into the library to a table. Ladies sat at other tables, all piled with strips of cotton, rolling bandages. An ornate sterling silver tea service sat on the Librarian's desk midst tea cake and cookies. Somehow the dark mahogany book stacks comforted Maggie. She had always loved the library and felt at home there.

"Thank you, Mrs. Sanford," said Maggie, her voice low. "You know, I am not a bad person. I'm just so in love with Henry, I lost sight of what was proper. I'm afraid Henry will not come back, but I'm proud to be carrying his child. Poor Mama is having a terrible time, though. Maybe I just shouldn't show myself around the island anymore."

"Now, my dear," Mrs. Sanford held a chair out for Alice and patted Maggie's hand. "Don't you worry. Young love is special, but I realize sometimes things happen out of our control. You know, your mama's friends will always stand behind her – and you, too, no matter what." She looked around the room where other ladies whispered behind their hands, staring in Maggie's direction.

One matron stood up and towed her daughter toward the door. "Come along, Charlotte," she said.

"I can't believe you would bring your unwed daughter *in the family way* to a meeting of decent women," she told Alice, as she sailed past them.

Alice's face fell. She looked as though she would faint.

"Mama, are you all right?" asked Maggie. She picked up a piece of paper and fanned her mother with it.

"Ida May Evans! You go sit back down this minute," thundered Mrs. Sanford. "We'll not have that kind of behavior here. Every pair of willing hands is needed to help our men suffering in the Great War. Wed or unwed, we need their help."

Ida May Evans stopped short and stood a moment with her mouth open. "Well, I . . . Well! . . . ," she managed to say, her mouth opening and closing like a fish gasping out of water, but she tugged Charlotte back to their table and sat down in a huff.

Maggie tried to hide her grin as she looked at her mother. Alice had turned from gray to white, and now a little color seeped back into her cheeks.

"Ladies," said Bessie Sanford, rapping a pencil on the table for attention. "I want to thank all of you for coming today. Remember our country is at war, and everyone must do his or her part. We are all in this together and must do everything we can to help our men and boys fighting in France. I know all of you will do your very best to make this day a success.

"We will be serving refreshments at two o'clock. I want to thank the ladies who were kind enough to prepare the food, with special thanks to Mabel Cartwright for her delicious one-egg cake. I'm sure you all will agree a person would never know it's a wartime recipe." Mrs. Sanford smiled at Mabel Cartwright. "Please stand as I call your name. Mabel?"

The gossips stopped whispering as the ladies stood when their names were called. They smiled, pleased to be recognized in front of the group. The others applauded. Then Bessie Sanford said, "When we stop for tea, I should like to ask Alice McNamara to help pour."

Stunned silence greeted this request as shocked looks fluttered around the room. Alice glanced from her friend Bessie to Maggie, her face now a rosy red.

"Well, I . . ." Alice twisted the bandage she held, in anguish. Maggie smiled encouragement to her mother. "I - I'd be happy to help you, Bessie," she said, near tears.

"Thank you, Alice. Now ladies let's get to work."

Still standing, Mrs. Sanford demonstrated the proper way to roll the bandages. "Try to keep the fabric rolled tight with the edges neat, so they are easy to pack and send to France," she said. She walked around the room, her heels tapping on the hardwood floor of the Library, helping the ladies make neat rolls. Then she came back to the table where Alice and Maggie worked, and sat down.

Alice, near tears, reached for a strip of fabric with hands that shook, and rolled it up. "Thank you, Bessie," she murmured. "You are a true friend."

~~~

Rain fell during the night bringing a close to the Indian summer that turned vine maples fiery red and sent the squirrels scurrying to store enough food for winter. The air breezed up with the smell of fresh rain hanging over the island, dampening the dusty roads,
~~~

and blowing reluctant seagulls in from the Pacific Ocean.

"Mama," called Maggie. She stood on tiptoe to peer out the kitchen sink window. "Mama, hurry! Someone's coming!" Maggie turned around, impatient for her mother to see. "It looks like Henry's parents." She stood limp and helpless while her mother peered out the window.

Sven and Mina Anderson made their way carefully around chuck holes and mud puddles. Mina wore a knitted cap to protect her ears as the wind blew leaves from the trees and chopped the harbor water into white caps. Her grey coat came to the tops of her high buttoned shoes. She struggled with the wind to keep the coat from blowing open. In her arms she carried a package wrapped in brown paper and tied with string. Sven wore a wool cap with a small bill. His heavy canvas work coat and pants looked worn, but clean. He held Mina's elbow and helped her navigate the rough road. They stopped as the package slipped from Mina's arm toward a puddle. Sven caught it and tucked it under his coat. Mina looked up at him and smiled. Bits of her hair escaped its knitted prison and blew around her face. Now she had no package to carry, she could hold her coat closed easier.

"Oh, dear," said Alice. "What do you suppose they want?" She looked at Maggie with panic in her eyes.

"Maybe people have been talking."

"Probably that Ida May Evans," Alice muttered under her breath. "Here, Maggie, grind some coffee beans while I stoke up the fire in the cook stove and put the kettle on. They might like coffee instead of tea." She handed Maggie the coffee grinder.

Maggie nodded and poured coffee beans into the grinder. She turned the little handle on top of the grinder to crush the coffee and release its fragrant aroma. Although Maggie loved the smell of coffee, she hadn't yet learned to like its taste.

The Andersons navigated the steps to the front porch and knocked on the door.

"You answer it, Mama," begged Maggie, her face white and drawn.

"All right, dear." Alice worried about her daughter. Although Maggie no longer threw up every single morning, her ashen skin did not look healthy. She handed the coffee pot to Maggie. "Can you finish the coffee?"

Maggie nodded. Alice held one hand over her heart as she walked past the piano to the front door. The cold weather made the door stick. She tugged at it and finally got it open.

"Mr. and Mrs. Anderson! How nice to see you. Come in. Come in out of the wind."

Sven and Mina wiped their feet carefully on the door mat and squeezed through the door, bringing the brisk air with them. Their faces red with cold. Mina unbuttoned her coat. She pulled off her knitted cap and laid the cap and coat on the chair. "Oh, so nice and warm in here," she said, rubbing her hands together in front of the fireplace. A strand of baby-fine hair had come loose from its bun, and she reached up to reset the hairpin.

"Yah," agreed Sven removing his cap and coat. He put Mina's package on top of the coats and combed his fingers through his thick sandy-colored hair.

"Please sit down," said Alice, indicating the sofa. She ran a hand over the piano, noticed with dismay it was a little bit dusty, and brushed her dusty hand off on her apron. "Would you like some tea or coffee?"

"Kaffe, please, if it is not too much trouble, Misses," said Sven.

Alice looked at Mina. "Yes, kaffe, please," she said.

"Maggie," called Alice. "Is the coffee about ready?"

"In a few minutes, Mama." Maggie filled the coffee pot with cold water, put in the coffee and set the pot on the stove. "Do we have any of those butter cookies left?"

"Yes, dear. In the cupboard above the sink."

Maggie's hands trembled as she took the plate of cookies from the cupboard. Cups and saucers rattled in her unsteady grip. She set them down on the counter. *Why are they here? They must have heard about the baby. I don't care about myself, but poor Mama. She looks ready to have a heart attack.* Maggie looked through the kitchen door to the living room. Alice sat with the Andersons, her hand at the throat of her dress, fiddling with the high button on the collar. The fire crackled and popped on the hearth, the only sound in the room.

The kitchen clock ticked away the seconds as the coffee pot boiled over, hissing on the cast iron stove top. Maggie grabbed a dish towel to protect her hand from the hot handle and moved the coffee to a cooler spot. More dishes rattled as she took the sugar bowl and cream pitcher from the cupboard. She went to the ice box for a bottle of cream and filled the cream pitcher, put the dishes on a tray, smoothed her skirt over her tummy and carried the tray into the living room.

"Good morning, Mr. and Mrs. Anderson," she said. "How nice to see you on such a blustery day."

Sven stood up and helped Maggie set the tray on the low table in front of the sofa. "Yah, it is cold and windy."

Maggie went back for the coffee pot and poured. She set the pot on top of the stove away from the direct fire to keep it warm and returned with tea for her mother and herself. Alice poured the tea while Maggie passed sugar and cream to Sven and Mina. They put a tiny bit of sugar in their coffee and lots of cream. "Sugar is hard to come by in war time," said Sven. He sipped the hot coffee and shut his eyes, savoring the rich aroma. "But just a little is good in kaffe."

Maggie passed the cookies. "Yah, and we have cookies, too?" He smiled at Alice. "Now-a-days cookies are a real treat."

"Good cookies," said Mina. "Did you make them, Maggie?"

"I'm afraid not. I must learn to do that. Mama is the cook around here."

"Very good cookies, Mrs. McNamara," said Mina. "If you have time some day, maybe you would be so kind as to write down the recipe for me?"

Alice nodded. "I'd be happy to do that, Mrs. Anderson."

They sipped their coffee and tea. The room was quiet. Only the crackling fire and the ticking of the kitchen clock could be heard. The silence grew.

"It rained last night, but we've been having nice weather until then," noted Alice.

Sven nodded and munched a cookie.

"The fishing boats were able to leave the harbor this morning, even though it rained," said Maggie.

"Yah. Yah," agreed Henry's father. "They go. The weather will clear up."

Alice passed the cookies around again. The clock ticked. A log fell forward in the fireplace, sending up a shower of sparks. A thin tendril of smoke found its way into the room. Alice stood up and grabbed the fireplace poker to shove the log further back, directing the smoke up the chimney. She replaced the poker and sat down again. Alice and Maggie looked at each other, desperate to know what to do or say. Maggie's cup rattled when she put it on its saucer. She wiped her sweaty hands on her skirt, and then realized this brought attention to the small rise in her belly. She held her hands together in front of her. *Why don't they say something? I can't stand this. Poor Mama. She might faint if Henry's father doesn't talk pretty soon. Maybe the Andersons think it's not polite to just jump right in and say what's on their minds. If they don't state their business pretty soon, I'll scream – or I'll tell them about the baby. Yes, I'll do that. I'll tell them and get it over with.*

Finally, Sven Anderson set down his cup and saucer and cleared his throat.

"Mrs. McNamara," Sven impaled Alice with his piercing blue eyes.

Alice gulped and fiddled with the button at her throat. "Yes?"

"We, Mina and I, have heard things on the island."

"Oh?"

"Yah. About our son and your daughter, Maggie here."

Alice looked like she wished the floor would open up and swallow her. Maggie held her breath, hoping her mother would not faint. Alice's face flushed and her hand went to her throat. "Yes? Er . . . wh - what have you heard, Mr. Anderson?"

"We heard that Maggie, "he motioned to Maggie. "That Maggie is going to have our grandchild."

Henry's mother, Mina, sat rigid as a post, twisting her hands together, her eyes filled with tears.

Maggie reached over and held her mother's hand. She looked directly into Sven Anderson's eyes. "What you have heard is true, Mr. Anderson."

Alice groped in her apron pocket for her handkerchief. Tears came too easy to her these days.

Sven tore his gaze away from Maggie's. "There, there, Mrs. McNamara," said Sven, patting Alice's arm. "Yah, now Mrs. McNamara, it will be all right."

He looked at Maggie, "How do you young people say? Okay?"

Maggie nodded.

"It is Okay, Mrs. McNamara." He patted Alice's arm. Mina dabbed at her tears with her handkerchief.

"We understand things happen. Yah, especially during war time," said Sven. Mina sat beside him, nodding her head.

"It is nature's way. We come to say we are glad you are having Henry's child. Henry's job in this war is maybe more dangerous than most, but all war is dangerous. Mina and I worry every day about Henry in France, flying those aeroplanes. Yah, he might as well fly in paper kites." Sven looked out the window at the harbor. Maggie's eyes followed his gaze, wondering if Sven expected to see Henry fly over the cottage in his homemade plane. Instead, they saw water brisk with white caps like the white peaks of meringue pie topping. White clouds scudded by in a sky turning from grey to blue.

Sven looked back toward Maggie. "It is all right, Maggie. Okay."

Maggie's tears started at that point. She nodded. *He means about the baby. It's all right about the baby. But what about Henry? It's not all right about Henry. The Army Air Corps should send him home. He's done his part. His chances are not good as an aviator.*

"We are happy we will have a grandchild. Sven raised his hands and looked toward the heavens. "*Hal-le –lu–iah!*"

He smiled at Maggie. "We know how much Henry loves you, Maggie. Mina and I want to tell you that the people who care about you are there for you – for all of you." His glance included Alice. "Never mind gossips on this island. What do they know about love, eh?" Sven smiled at Maggie. "You are strong and healthy. Henry is strong and healthy. Your baby will be perfect. Yah, our grandson will be perfect, you bet." Sven took a long drink of coffee.

Maggie's white face turned pink. She brightened and said, "Oh, so you think it will be a boy, do you?" she laughed as she teased Henry's father.

"Yah. He will be a fine boy." Sven smiled and looked around at the three women staring at him. His smile disappeared. A little frown took its place. Sven looked from one to the other, knowing he had not said the right thing. He combed his hand through his hair and shook his head.

"But, don'tcha know, a girl will be just as welcome. Yah, we will be happy with a girl or a boy." The three women relaxed. Sven smiled again. "We are glad, Maggie, that you are having our son's child."

Alice leaned back on the sofa and fanned herself with a napkin. "Oh, my, Mr. and Mrs. Anderson. You have no idea what a relief your words are to me."

"Yah, well, if we can help, just let us know."

Mina stood up to get the package by her coat.

"This is for the baby," she said in her quiet way, handing it to Maggie.

"For the baby?"

Mina nodded.

"Oh, thank you." Maggie untied the string on the brown paper-wrapped gift with hands that no longer shook, and found several hand made, hand embroidered baby garments.

"Oh, Mrs. Anderson," Maggie's tears flowed as she stood up to hug Henry's mother. "My baby's first clothes. They are beautiful. You made them, yourself?"

Mina nodded, a pleased smile playing around her lips.

"Look, Mama," said Maggie. "Aren't they beautiful? I love them." She held them close to her breast with one hand and squeezed Mina's hand with the other. "When our *son* is born, you must come over and dress him in these clothes. Will you do that, please?"

Mina nodded. "Yah, Maggie. That I'll do." She smiled and dried her eyes.

"And you, too, Mr. Anderson. You must come over and see our baby all dressed up in his beautiful clothes. Both of you come anytime to see your grandson." Maggie laughed. "Or granddaughter."

The Andersons sipped coffee, and Alice and Maggie sipped tea silently for a few minutes. Mina nudged her husband. He looked at her. "Yah, Mina, yah. In a minute, all right?" Sven finished his coffee and set his cup down on the table.

"Good kaffe, Mrs. McNamara. Thank you very much."

Mina nudged him again.

"Mina can't wait for me to tell you. She is so impatient, sometimes." Sven smiled fondly at his wife.

Sven cleared his throat. "You know I am a finish carpenter. The best on this island and maybe the mainland, if I say so myself." Sven looked around the room with a critical eye. "I have decided to build a bed for the baby. Yah, a crib. I have some fine bird's eye maple to make a sturdy crib. A wood lathe to turn the spindles. It will be a very good baby's bed. Okay"

Maggie grinned through her tears. "Okay, Mr. Anderson. That would be very, very okay. Thank you."

Alice went to the kitchen for the coffee pot. "More coffee?" She held the coffee pot in front of her.

"No, thanks a lot, Misses." Sven held up both hands. "Yah, well, we go now."

Alice set the pot back on the cook stove. The Andersons stood up and put on their coats. Maggie stepped forward to take Sven's and Mina's hands in hers. "Thank you, for coming, Mr. and Mrs. Anderson. Your visit means a lot to me and my mother."

"Yah, Maggie, you are welcome." Sven patted her cheek. "Everything will be Okay, I bet."

"Come over to the house any time, Maggie," said Mina. "I will help you sew more baby clothes."

"I'd love that," said Maggie, holding up the tiny garments for them all to see.

~~~

2000

I took the locked chest of letters and the little key to bed to read last night. When I was settled, I unlocked the tiny padlock and took out the first letter.
~~~

June 2, 1918

Dear, darling Maggie,

We are facing German squadrons of 14 aircraft called Flying Circuses, because of their remarkable tactical flying ability. We simply don't have the right equipment to fight them. The Fokker D VII is a better plane than anything the French or British possess. Even with fresh aviators from America, the Germans dominate the air. We engage them with everything we have. Even the men below in the trenches fire at the German planes, or the German soldiers fire at us if a dog fight takes us over enemy lines. We battle to the death like knights in the days of King Arthur's Round Table.

Yesterday, I barely escaped a squadron of German planes. They shot holes in my Camel's wings and nicked the oil pan. I managed to get away into a cloud and limp back to base, streaming oil behind me. I cut the engine in hopes that it would not be ruined and glided to our landing field.

It was a rum feeling, coming down at 125 mph with no power. I crashed the undercarriage of the plane. The ground crew ran over to help me out in case the machine caught fire. Fortunately, it did not burn, and they will be able to repair the plane, but Lord knows how long that'll take. One good thing though, there will be no empty chair at my place for dinner tonight.

How I miss you. Do you remember the tune, "A Long Way to Tipperary?" Play it and think of me, and I'll think of the sweetest girl I know.

Love,
Henry

June 25, 1918

My darling,

A group of French, British and American officers came to our base last night. They dined with us. We have the best food you could ever imagine – roast duck l'orange, wild rice, truffles, fresh green beans, and chocolate mousse. We are truly treated like heroes. Those poor Yanks in the trenches don't get anything like this. I've heard they have hardtack and have to dip it in the canned tomatoes they are issued in order to make it soft enough to chew and that's about all they have to eat, poor buggers.

After dinner, the officers spoke to us of our bravery and success, despite terrific odds. All the aviators received medals for number of enemy aircraft shot down, and for courage under fire. I was awarded the Distinguished Flying Cross. Newspaper reporters and photographers were here and wrote stories about us for papers in London, Paris, and New York

I miss you and long to hold you in my arms. In my dreams I smell the sweet clean scent of your skin and hair. Then I awaken to the stench of un-bathed flyers and soiled leather and canvas equipment.

I can't wait for the war to end and I will be home with you on Orcas Island.

Love, Henry

~~~

Soon Henry felt he had mastered the tremendous torque of his Sopwith Camel. It was a good aeroplane, quick to respond if the pilot kept his guard up and didn't let the engine flip him over. Some of the aeroplanes assigned to the Americans though, were planes that had crashed and had been re-built or were so worn the French and British had decided to replace them with newer planes. One of the American flyers, who happened to draw a Neuport 17 aeroplane, lost a wing as he flew into a tight turn.

The American aviators flew their varied planes in formation at 3,000 feet, on the watch for the enemy. Many of the German pilots used the Red Baron's tactic of coming out of the sun. Henry would rather have it the other way around.

He got his wish this day.

They surprised a group of Germans, a mélange of different airplanes: Fokker D VII's, a Hansa Brandenburg DI, and some Albatros D II's. Knowing the next few minutes were 'do or die', Henry, stiff and tense, touched Maggie's scarf tucked into his flying jacket for luck, and zoomed in out of the sun for the kill. He held the plane's stick between his knees while he fired the machine gun. The German pilot fought back, shooting at Henry's Camel, blinded by the sun. This time, Henry's machine gun case did not jam when he ran out of ammunition, and he quickly changed the
~~~

magazine to a full one while following the German who had headed toward a cloud. Once again, Henry placed the stick firmly between his knees and his machine gun chattered. Fuel evaporated from the German plane into the atmosphere. The plane lost power and glided to earth, traveling further than Henry had thought possible on the prevailing winds.

Henry followed and watched the Fokker D VII crash. He couldn't believe how terrible he felt. He was sure he had killed the pilot, a fellow aviator. His heart pounded. His hands sweat inside leather gloves. All at once he thought how glad he was to be alive. Henry dropped down out of the clouds and buzzed low over the wreck. The smell of gasoline filled the air, reaching its vaporous tentacles up toward Henry as his wheels barely skimmed over the German plane. The German pilot looked dead in the brief glimpse Henry had of him.

He climbed back up to help his comrades in the fight overhead, where he flew directly into a blast from another German machine gun. The Camel's body shuddered as it was riddled with bullets, its gas tank punctured. Henry's heart thudded as he limped back to base, trailing a thin stream of petrol. He watched the fuel gauge needle rapidly spin back down to zero, the oil gauge went down a little slower, but the temperature gauge registered in the red. He crash-landed on the field, destroying the fragile wooden skeleton of his aeroplane's undercarriage. Dust, oil, and gasoline fumes assailed his nostrils. Henry panicked as he tried to get out of the cockpit. The Camel's broken framework clung tenaciously to his legs. The ground crew pulled him from the wreckage as the flying machine ignited and exploded in flames.

"Thanks Mac," Henry told his crew chief. "You men are all right!."

Mac grinned, his teeth glaring white in his smoke blackened face. "We gotcha, Sir," he said. "Lucky. Yer a lucky 'un, fer sure."

Mac helped Henry to his feet and propped him up with one arm. "Can y'walk Sir?"

"I think so, Mac." Henry's voice quavered. "Just hold onto me for a minute. I'll be fine."

Henry tried his legs. They both worked. No broken bones. He stripped off the leather helmet and goggles and stood alone. "Thanks, Mac. I can make it from here, now." He wobbled to his tent to lie down.

Henry's commanding officer sat beside him that night in the mess hall. At least my chair isn't empty, thought Henry, rubbing one hand across the red-checkered tablecloth. Watching it tremble. He took a deep breath, put his hand in his pocket, and looked around the mess hall. The table was set formally for these aces, with silverware and wine goblets. Henry noticed a few empty chairs and thought how close his chair had come to being one of them. He seemed to have exceptional luck. In a war where the average pilot lasted twelve days, he had already passed that point. Subconsciously he touched his scarf – the scarf Maggie had knitted for him. He tucked the ends inside his tunic.

Henry put his napkin on his lap with shaky hands, as dinner was served. He picked at his roast squab and thought about how close he'd come to death. He thought about the flyer he had shot down, and as he forced himself to take a small bite of squab, guiltily remembered the men in the trenches. What were they eating that night? Hard tack maybe.

"We'll have another plane for you for tomorrow," the commander said. "A Spad 5A."

"Thank you, Sir," said Henry. He picked at his squab, not feeling very hungry.

"You may like the Spad even better than the Camel."

Henry bit into a grape. The sweet juice ran down his chin, and he dabbed at it with his napkin. He sipped a little wine. Henry did not feel like talking to the Major. He needed to think about the events of the day. Henry took a deep breath and sighed. "A Spad'll do fine, Sir."

Henry turned to look at some of the aviators where they gathered around one of his friends, Walter, who was singing and playing his banjo. Henry took a spoonful of chocolate mousse, re-filled his wine glass, and stood up. The singers' voices rose over the sound of people talking and the clank of dishes.

"*Mademoiselle from Armentieres,*
Parlez-vous
Oh, Mademoiselle from Armentieres,
Parlez-vous
Mademoiselle from Armentieres,
She hasn't been kissed for forty years!

Hinky-dinky, parlez-vous?"

The major stood, too, took Henry's arm and pulled him over into a dark corner beside the stove. He continued trying to talk above the raucous singing.

"That plane you shot down today crashed near our landing field and the ground crew ran out to see if the aviator had survived. No such luck, but they found this in his hand." The major held out a diamond necklace. "It was caught around a photograph he'd taken from his pocket."

". . . from Armentieres, Parlez-vous
She got the palm and the croix de guerre,
For washin' soldiers' underwear,
Hinky-dinky, parlez-vous?"

Henry held a hand over his ear on the side of the musicians, trying to block out their noise and hear the major better. He glanced at the jewelry and the picture of a pretty blonde girl. He shook his head and turned away to join the singers.

"Wait, Henry," said the officer holding out the necklace. "It was your kill. The necklace is yours."

Henry winced at the word 'kill'. It could have been him dead, trying to hold a picture of Maggie as his plane crashed.

". . . parlez-vous
She's the hardest working girl in town,
But she makes her living upside down!"

"Give it to the ground crew, I don't want it."

"Hinky-dinky-parlez-vous?" roared the singers, laughing.

"The men in the ground crew watched you nail him. They said to give this to you. Take it. Spoils of war and all that. I seem to remember you have a girl back home. A concert pianist? You could send it to her."

". . . She'll do it for wine; she'll do it for rum,
And sometimes for chocolate or chewing gum!"

Henry shook his head. "I wouldn't feel right."

"Hinky-dinky-Parlez-vous?" shrieked the musicians.

"You took his life. What difference does the necklace make?"

"I took his life, because if I hadn't, he'd have taken mine. That's war. But the necklace is a personal thing. . . Sir."

The singers stopped to catch their breath and pass around another bottle of Bordeaux.

"Oh, Henry, take the damned thing," the major's voice rang out in the now quiet room. People turned to stare. He stopped, his face red as he realized he had been shouting over the noise of the singers. In a low voice he said, "Take it. Send it to that girl. No one is going to give a hoot in bloody hell about this damned necklace."

Henry shook his head. "No, Sir!"

The officer sighed and slipped the jewelry back into his tunic pocket. "Stubborn, 'square headed', Swede." He smiled, and punched Henry's arm. "All right, but what am I going to do with it?"

"Give it to the War Relief Fund. Give it to the orphans in France and Belgium. Throw it away."

The officer snorted. "I'll think of something." He walked toward the door, stopped and turned back. "I have an idea. Why don't we make up a bundle of the aviator's things, his identification, the necklace, and the photograph with a note telling about his bravery in action and you can fly over their aerodrome and drop it. Brilliant, don't you think?"

"Absolutely. And what keeps them from shooting me out of the sky?"

"We'll tie a white banner to the tail of your plane – you know a flag of truce?" They've done that sort of thing with our downed flyers."

"I'll think about it. It seems to be the honorable thing to do." Henry extricated himself from the major to join Walter and his musicians.

The strains of "*There's a Rose That Grows in No Man's Land*" quavered through the smoky air. More men joined the singing. The poignant song soon had many aviators weeping. Henry decided to go to bed. He had needed the wild Mademoiselle tune to cheer him up, but this piece overwhelmed him with sadness. His throat tightened making it difficult to swallow, and he fought to control the tears that came into his eyes. As he walked slowly through the dark to his tent, he heard the men harmonizing

". . . Through the War's great curse,
Stands the Red Cross Nurse,
She's the Rose of No Man's Land."

~~~

2000

A Brahms Lullaby floated softly through the Indian summer moonlight. I slipped from my bed and tiptoed to the living room. Moonlight filled the room with a white glow and shimmered across the black mahogany of the open piano as the dulcet tones of the baby's song filled my heart to bursting, longing for the child I never had. I swallowed hard, but a big lump would not leave my throat. My fingers clutched the door frame, afraid of falling should I let go. Maggie, slender once more, played the piano, muting the tone with her left foot on the soft pedal while the toe of her right foot rocked a cradle holding a sleeping newborn child. Alice peeked into the room. She smiled, and turned back to her work, humming along with the music. *What a blessing the baby is. But I was so afraid for Maggie. Although some of the gossips on the island won't speak to us, I should have known our true friends are still our true friends. How could I ever have thought to give this baby up? What kind of a grandmother am I, anyway? Why does society impose such rigid rules that make us feel we must do terrible things like get rid of babies? Ah, little Hank is such a blessing. I think Maggie's right. A piece of paper and a few words spoken by a minister shouldn't make any difference.*
~~~

~~~

2000

One day, I invited Mike to go with me on a picnic. Sometimes when I painted or sketched alone, I lost track of time. It just slipped away from me. This time I took only my camera. I didn't want to become absorbed in a project, as he had to be back at the Gallery in a couple of hours. My little VW toiled up Mount Constitution through Moran State Park where I snapped views of the sea to paint later in my studio, the water shading from greens through blues to grays around other islands in Puget Sound.

We stopped by the lake. Mike carried the ice chest with sandwiches and pop and I carried a blanket to sit on as we wandered into the forest with its smell of Douglas fir, hemlock and cedar. I spread the blanket down on the ground. We ate looking out at the water and watched chipmunks and gray squirrels climb the fir trees and cut off the cones, dropping them like miniature bombs to the forest floor. Then they scampered back down the trees and packed the seeds into their cheeks to take away and store for winter. I longed to hold one of the tiny creatures, but they were shy of people and ran too fast. Mike reached over to hold my left hand and look at the POW bracelet. It slid down my arm. He traced the nearly worn-away engraving with his finger.

"Do you think thirty years might be long enough to wait, Sarah?"
~~~

"What?" I looked up into his blue eyes.

He held up my arm with the bracelet. It slid back up my arm. "It's been that long since you've heard from your husband, hasn't it? Don't you think that might be long enough to wait for him?"

"I . . . I don't know, Mike," I said, retrieving my hand. I brushed it over trilliums and yellow buttercups hiding among the fir needles on the forest floor. I stared at the wildflowers. "I don't know quite what to think." I picked a buttercup to hide my discomfort. Maybe I shouldn't have invited him to go with me. He might get the wrong idea. After all, what did I know about him? I glanced up at him as he gazed out at the lake. Not much, except he was quite handsome for a man his age – my age – early fifties, maybe a little bit older than me. Not gone to fat like so many older men -- and women. Lots of white hair. Neatly trimmed mustache. Clean and well dressed.

I buried my nose in the yellow flower. "As a child, did you ever hold a buttercup under someone's chin to see if the color reflects on their skin?"

Mike laughed. "No, I don't think I ever did that."

I moved the buttercup away, sneezed and reached for a paper napkin as I sneezed again, and wiped the flower's pollen from my nose. "As children, we said if it reflected, it meant we liked butter!" I held the buttercup close to Mike's chin. "Looks like you love butter." I laughed.

Mike took the buttercup from me and held it under my chin. "Seems to me you like butter, too, Sarah." He tipped my chin up. Our lips met in a gentle, lingering kiss. The first kiss for both of us in a long time – three years for him, three decades for me. I sighed, touched his lips with one finger and smoothed the neat mustache. Long-dormant primordial longings broke loose inside me. Feelings I had suppressed for years struggled to the surface of my consciousness.

"You liked it, didn't you?"

I shivered and nodded. "The moustache tickles, though."

"Want me to shave it off?"

I shook my head. "No, maybe I'll get used to it?" I looked up at him through my eyelashes. *Was this really me, being so coy?*

"Well, let's try it one more time."

This kiss was long and passionate. One of his hands brushed my breast. I gasped and moved away, unsure what to do. My feelings of longing hid, suppressed again.

His face fell. He looked out at the lake with sad eyes.

I reached up to touch his cheek. My bracelet slid up my arm. "Really, it was a nice kiss. I'm just not used to . . . being kissed, that's all. A little rusty, I guess."

Mike turned back to me and smiled. "We'll have to get rid of some of that rust."

I felt my face flush.

"Come on," he said, checking his watch. "Time to go." He stood and held a hand out to help me up. We packed up the remains of the picnic and folded the blanket for the trek back to East Sound where he had put a sign on his shop saying he'd be back by 2 p.m.

~~~

1918

Henry set the Spad down with a gentle touch on the landing field, and taxied to his place, fifth in the line of airplanes. He stood up in the cockpit, lifted his goggles to the top of his helmet, unfastened the helmet strap, and looked toward the canal. From the air, he had glimpsed a long entourage following the canal path, making its way toward the cemetery. Henry dropped the helmet and his leather flying jacket on the seat and climbed out as the ground crew ran to tie down the machine.

"This is it then, Mac?" He motioned toward the procession to one of the crew.

"Yes sir. They're burying the Red Baron today. If we hurry, we can go, too."

Henry nodded. "Let's do it, then. I'll help secure the plane."

"Thank you, sir." Crewmen scurried about, and with Henry's help, fastened the Spad to its place in line.

The slow somber beat of muffled drums could barely be heard.

Henry buttoned the high collar of his tunic as he and his crew hurried to the edge of the canal. The funeral procession appeared in the distance on the other side of the water. A British officer wearing a black arm band led the procession, followed by an honor guard of thirteen Australian soldiers of the
~~~

Number 3 Squadron, Australian Flying Corps, who marched in time with the drum beat, their rifles reversed. As the procession passed by, aviators and crewmen on Henry's side of the canal came to attention and saluted.

The drums continued their mournful dirge.

"Did they ever find out who actually shot down von Richthofen?" Henry looked at Mac.

"Well, sir," said Mac, "They's lotsa argument about it. Captain Brown, the Canadian squadron leader's sure he hit the red plane, but the Aussie ground troops say that the bullet that killed the Baron come from below. So, it musta been one a theirs -- one of the Aussie's bullets." "Ya know, sir, I keep thinking about all our gimpers the Red Baron done in. Eighty of 'em". The crewman pulled out a soiled handkerchief and blew his nose. "What about them, sir, if you know what I mean. Did the Krauts give 'em a honorable burial when they clicked it, like we're doin' for the Red Baron?" Mac stuffed the dirty handkerchief into his pocket. "No, Sir, I don't think so."

"They may not have had such an elaborate funeral as this, Mac, but I'm sure they gave our airmen a proper burial." Henry ran a hand that smelled of leather gloves over his face.

I certainly hope so.

Henry squirmed uncomfortably in his scratchy, wool tunic. He hooked one finger under the tight collar and tried to stretch it out a little as he watched a British tender carrying the Red Baron's coffin. The tender, its chain drive complaining, ground along in first gear behind the Australian honor guard. Wreaths sent in tribute by allied squadrons covered the wooden coffin. A platoon of British soldiers followed the truck, with a small British army vehicle bringing up the rear.

Henry and others standing across the canal moved in tandem with the funeral procession. By the time they reached the cemetery, a few French villagers had joined the group of mourners.

A British Army Chaplain wearing a surplice over his uniform led the Red Baron's casket bearers --- allied squadron leaders with the rank of Captain -- between two rows of Australian soldiers holding their rifles at "present arms". The procession moved on through the wrought-iron cemetery gates.

The Chaplain praised the courage and daring of Captain Manfred von Richthofen and prayed for his soul. Then the pallbearers lowered the coffin into the ground and covered it with earth. A large wreath, inscribed to Captain von Richthofen, "Our gallant and worthy foe", sent by British headquarters, was placed on the grave. Henry stood with other aviators, his crewmen, and the French villagers in respectful silence as the Australian honor guard fired a last salute.

Henry walked back to the aerodrome wondering if he would be given such an honor if he were shot down over German Territory. He was not an "ace of aces", as the Red Baron had been, but he was an "ace", with the required five kills to his credit. He thought of Maggie and Orcas Island as he made his way back and wondered what she was doing that very minute. Playing the piano? Flying kites on the beach? Reading his letters?

~~~

July 8, 1918

Dearest Maggie,

We buried the Red Baron, the German Ace, today. I can't remember when I've felt so low. This crazy war is a waste of good men, aeroplanes and materiel. The only thing I've accomplished is flying. But my love of flying can't take the place of my love for you. I'm lonesome for you and home. I think of our wonderful days on Deer Island, and the pain of not seeing you cuts right through me. You will let me know if anything came of our adventures out there, won't you? I need to know you are all right.

As soon as this war is over and I can get back to you, we'll be married. Say you will marry me, Maggie. I couldn't bear it if you denied me my fondest wish. I miss your touch, your scent, your wonderful tawny hair, all of you.

Love,
Henry

Maggie folded the letter and put it back in its envelope. She sat quietly contemplating the view of the harbor and their island. She sighed, tears welling in her
~~~

eyes. She realized she had not been fair to him. Henry deserved to know. She went to her room for stationery, a bottle of ink and a pen and sat down at the kitchen table.

August 12, 1918

My Darling,

You and I have a beautiful son. I have named him Henry after you, but we call him Hank. I didn't tell you because I didn't want to distract you from your duty. I asked your parents and mine not to tell you, either. How I have longed to share him with you. Our child looks like you with brown hair that bleaches almost blonde in the sun. He has your nose and blue eyes. He is my pride and joy.

Tears fell on the paper, smearing the ink. She dried her eyes, pressed an ink blotter on the page, and heaving a big sigh, dipped her pen into the inkwell again. The pen splotched ink drops on the next line when Maggie pressed too hard.

Mama was very upset at first, and some of the ladies on the Island will not speak to us, but our true friends are still our friends. Your mother and father have been wonderful and love little Hank as we do. I have simply ignored the wrath of those who think we were wicked to love each other. Every day I see your sailboat moored at your parent's dock and I think of you. I look out at our island and I think of you. I see you in our son, I count his tiny fingers and toes and smell his sweet baby scent, and I think of you. Please take care of yourself and come back to us.

Of course, I'll marry you.

Love forever, Maggie

~~~

2000

Thinking about all this made me want to cry. My head ached -- my heart ached. I had held on to the hope for so long that Johnny would return someday, it was hard to let it go . . .

Mike Hinton seemed like a very nice person. He was fun to be with. He was caring, compassionate and capable. Three very important "C's". I decided to go for a walk on the beach to clear my brain. It helped to be out with the seagulls and the sand dollars, the wind and the waves.

Mike arrived in his pick-up after the gallery closed the next day wearing well-worn Levi's and a blue and white striped hickory work shirt. He towed a flat bed automobile trailer. A couple of guys came with him to help load the Model T.

They opened the shed door and backed the trailer up to the shed, fastened the cable from an electric winch on the trailer to the front of the Model T's frame, lowered ramps in front of the Ford's wheels, and winched the car onto the trailer. Then they chained the car securely to the trailer and stowed the
~~~

ramps back up under the trailer. Mike's two friends got in the truck. Mike walked me around behind the trailer and the truck and gave me a lingering kiss, melting me into his arms. They took off. Red sky and orange tinged clouds dropped with the sun into the sea. I went back inside and wandered through Maggie's Cottage, thinking about Mike as I turned off lights and locked doors. The piano stood in moonlight flooding through the windows.

~~~

October 2, 1918

Maggie, my dearest,

I'm convinced the scarf you knitted brings me good luck, even though it is coming unraveled and has one or two holes. Long ago it lost your sweet scent that carried me back home to you and Orcas Island. Now, I am sorry to say, its odor is more eau de leather and aeroplane petrol than your perfume. Still I tuck the tattered remains inside my flying coat for luck. I have logged more than 20 days in combat against the Germans. Nearly twice what the average is for aviators in this war, and I credit it all to my good luck scarf.

I think the War is nearly over. The Germans are beaten, but they don't quite realize it yet. I miss you and think of you all the time.

Love, Henry
~~~

Maggie held Henry's letter close to her heart and thought of the hours she had struggled to knit that scarf. *It's no wonder it came unraveled. I didn't know what I was doing. The holes must be where I accidentally dropped stitches. Well, I know a little more about needlework now, than I did then. Maybe I should make a new scarf for Henry.* Maggie hummed to herself as she got out the hated knitting needles and a skein of blue yarn.

~~~

Henry piled into the muddy lorry with three other pilots. Walter tenderly cradled his banjo on his lap and plucked the strings to tune it. He struck a chord. Then another, and sang:

"How ya gonna keep 'em down on the farm?
After they've seen Par-ree?"

The others joined in with:

"How ya gonna keep 'em away from Broadway?"
Dum-dee-duh-dum, Paintin' the town?"

The men laughed as they forgot the words. They looked forward to a three-day-leave in Paris. The banjo player trilled another chord and struck up a new tune:

"Pack up your troubles in your old kit bag,
And Smile, Smile, Smile,"

They grinned inanely at each other.

"While you've a Lucifer to light your fag
Smile, boys, that's the style!"
~~~

Walter transitioned back to the first chord and shouted:

"What's the use of worrying? It never was in style – so-o-o-o"

Big trill on the banjo, then everybody roared

"Pack up your troubles in your old kit bag and . . ."

The men smiled at each other three times to finish the song while Walter played a C chord, a G chord, and another C chord, ending in an trilling arpeggio all the way up the neck of the banjo and finishing with a flourish. Someone produced a bottle of wine, uncorked it and passed it around the vehicle. They lit their fags -- their cigarettes, with lucifers -- matches.

Many songs later the lorry reached Paris in a shower of rain and stopped at the Grande Hotel Littre on the Left Bank of the Seine where they would be billeted for three days. Broad boulevards gave way to a narrow alley where the hotel stood, hidden from view.

The men climbed out of the vehicle as a group of American infantrymen walked around the corner.

"Bunch of doughboys over there," said Walter.

"What the deuce are doughboys?" asked one of the pilots.

"They're the ones trained in Texas that got covered with white adobe dust, so they call 'em dobies -- doughboys."

The other pilot laughed and said, "I'm glad I didn't go to Texas."

The pilots checked in and climbed the three flights of curved stairs to their rooms. Each room had a

French door in lieu of a window, the wooden frame thick with many coats of paint, opening onto a minuscule balcony and looking out over the roof of the hotel dining room. Gauze curtains blew in and out of the windows on a soft breeze. Henry unfastened the collar of his tunic and threw himself down on the iron-framed bed, luxuriating in the comfort of a real mattress. He breathed a deep sigh, reveling in the unaccustomed privacy of his hotel room and wondered what Maggie was doing at that very minute. He imagined her sitting at her piano, her taffy-colored hair piled high and her long, black skirt trailing to the floor as she played *Clair de Lune*, the tune filling Henry's inner ear as the image of Maggie filled his thoughts.

A rowdy rap on his door brought him out of his reverie. He stood up to open it, and the other men pushed and jostled each other inside.

"Come on, Henry," said Walter. "We're going to take a look at the city."

Henry smiled. "You fellows go along. I have something I need to do. I'll meet you later. Just tell me where."

"Ah, Henry's gonna get a present for his girl," teased one.

"Okay, Henry," said Walter. "We'll meet you for dinner at that seafood market restaurant on Montparnasse Boulevarde at eight. The frogs like to dine in the evening. No one serves dinner before 8 p.m."

"Tomorrow night we're getting tickets to the Follies Bergiere, so save some of your money, old pal," said Walter. "Don't spend it all on that girl." He slapped Henry on his back. They left with a great clatter of boots down the curved staircase.

The Eiffel Tower loomed over the city of Paris by the Seine River crowded with barge and boat traffic, muddy from rain. Henry looked for a jewelry store near the hotel. Buildings scrunched up close to each other on narrow streets and alleys between wide boulevards radiating from circles throughout the area. The houses hugged skimpy sidewalks where people walked their dogs and didn't clean up after them. Sewer pipes, added hundreds of years after the buildings had been constructed, snaked down the outsides of buildings, and leaked onto the sidewalks in places, spiking the air with the aroma of sewage mixed with the smell of dog-do. Wagons and carriages passed by, their horses adding to the pungent mix with droppings in the street. Now and then, Henry passed a wide doorway that opened to allow a carriage or an automobile into an inner courtyard. Thin strains of *Lilli Marlene*, a song written by a German soldier and popular with soldiers on both sides of No Man's Land, floated on the dank air through an open window. Henry could see a wind-up Morning Glory Victrola on a table inside a second story flat, its iridescent turquoise flower-shaped amplifier a bright spot of color glinting in the sun straining to emerge from the gray clouds.

Henry walked along, enjoying his leave and the view of the Left Bank. He passed an artist seated under an awning in front of a shop, his easel bright with color and his paintings displayed for sale. Henry stopped to look. Maybe this would be something he could send home to Maggie. But no, a painting was too bulky, too hard to package and ship, too impersonal. He decided she needed something more. Something that reminded him of her. A gift that would show his love for her. He wandered on, smelling the rain in the air and the city. He gawked around, not paying attention to where he walked, and accidentally stepped in a pile of dog manure, soggy with rain, releasing a pungent, sickening odor.

Oh, shit, he muttered. He splashed through several puddles, scraping his boots along the sidewalk to clean off the mess.

After walking what seemed miles, he found a jewelry store and went inside. A bell suspended over the door tinkled as Henry stepped into the dark shop smelling of dust, old furniture and fine clock oil. An old man dressed in black, his shoulders hunched over from years of repairing watches and jewelry, came out of the back room.

Henry was not proficient in French. He tried to explain in sign language what he wanted. The jeweler laughed. "Ah, Monsieur, I do have a little English. Come now, what is it you wish to know?"

Henry breathed a sigh of relief. "Merci. I want to buy a gift for my fiancé in America." Henry used his other French word and peered into a glass covered case full of rings, pins and necklaces. In the dim light, it was hard to tell one piece of jewelry from another.

"Oui Oui" The old man pulled a tiny key from his vest pocket, unlocked the case and lifted out the tray of jewelry, releasing a cloud of dust motes that made Henry sneeze. "What did you have in mind?"

"I thought of something like a brooch – a pin -- you know? Something delicate and beautiful and not too expensive, if you have it. "

"Ah, M'sieur, whatever suits you, and of course the Mademoiselle."

Henry pointed to a filigreed pin in an Art Deco design, set with a small pale translucent blue stone. "Her eyes are that exact color."

"Magnifique!" said the old man. "A nice aquamarine. Only 100 francs. Very affordable." He handed the brooch to Henry who turned it over, held it to the light and imagined Maggie wearing it. The pin was crafted in a lacy spider's web that started at each end with a quarter of an inch of gold wires laid close together. The wires fanned out into an intricate woven pattern to half an inch in diameter at the center where the aquamarine stone nestled in a gold setting.

"This design is Art Deco," said the jeweler. "You've heard, of course, of our famous French artist, Erte?"

Henry smiled and shook his head.

"No?" The man shrugged. "Erte is popular for his jewelry and his paintings of beautiful women in elaborately decorated costumes." He pointed to a print hanging on the wall of a woman wearing a fashionable costume dripping with peacock feathers.

Henry smiled and shook his head again. "Sorry, there is not much Art, as such, where I come from –

only the mountains and the sea and the deer and my beautiful Maggie."

Henry took a money clip from his tunic pocket and counted out the francs he had been saving it seemed, forever.

"Merci," said the old man.

"Now would you be so kind as to sell me a box and some packaging material so I can send this to my fiancé in the United States?" Henry held the pin up to the window light, fascinated with the way the sun glanced off each facet. "I need a piece of note paper and a pen and ink to enclose a note to her, if you have some to spare."

"Oui Oui, Monsieur. No charge for a box. Here. Let me help you." The old man wrapped the pin in tissue paper and put it in a small jewelry box. He packed the small box in layers of tissue in a larger box while Henry wrote his letter, folded the note, and put it inside. The old man sealed the package with gummed tape he moistened with a natural sponge that lay soaking in a little dish of water.

"Merci, merci," said Henry, smiling. He addressed the box to Maggie and left to find a post office. Late afternoon sunlight struggled through the rain clouds as Henry strolled back to the hotel. He stopped at the desk, asked to be called at 7 p.m., and climbed the curved staircase to his room on the third floor where he stretched out on the bed and promptly fell asleep.

The concierge tapped at Henry's door precisely at 7. Henry raised his head and looked around, disoriented for a moment. The simple luxury of this small hotel room baffled him, and then he remembered where he was. He sat up.

"Merci," he called. "Merci!" In three steps he was at the door and handed the man a franc note.

The concierge looked at the money and smiled. "No m'sieur." He shook his head. "Americaine aviator." He shook his head again. "Americaines help save Paris from falling to the enemy. He walked away smiling and shook his head as he held his arms out like wings, and made aeroplane noises, zooming back and forth across the hall.

Henry laughed and splashed cold water on his face from a bowl and pitcher of water on a stand. He dried his face, combed his hair, and picked up his room key fastened to a large metal bell-shaped object, to leave at the desk in the lobby.

Once again, Henry walked along the streets of Paris. The sun turned the sky blood-red to the west. To the east – to the battle front – the earth had already turned the same hue in places. The boulevard teemed with the early evening traffic of carriages, carts and wagons. Now and then an electric car moved eerily silent among the cacophony of steam-powered automobiles and combustion engine vehicles. A few chain-driven trucks groaned and clattered along, providing bass notes to the street symphony. Henry kept walking and wondered if he might be going in the wrong direction. He had not thought the restaurant was so far from the hotel. An outdoor bistro overflowed onto the sidewalk ahead, and he very nearly turned back to try the other way, when he noticed clouds of steam coming from the other side of the sidewalk café. Henry pushed on and found the fresh fish market with steaming kettles boiling crab, lobster, clams, mussels and shrimp. He threaded his way between fish ladened tables to the entrance of the restaurant and pushed open the door where he stood for a minute, trying to find his friends.

"Henry! Over here." Walter stood up and waved his arms. Henry smiled and worked his way between beautifully dressed customers, many of the women holding long ebony cigarette holders, and the men smoking cigars. Silver and china clattered as people shouted to be heard and waiters in tuxedos scurried around the dim, smoky room.

"We've ordered for everybody," said Walter. "Hope that's okey-doke with you, Henry. The specialty of the house," He waved toward waiters bringing silver trays filled with crushed ice and adorned with assortments of fresh crab, lobster, shrimp, steamed clams and mussels to their table. Wine, French bread and escargot had already been served and nearly demolished. The waiters set the trays on pedestals in the center of the table with pots of melted butter, and the Americans dug in with both hands.

"Wonderful," murmured Henry.

~~~

1918

"Maggie," called Alice as she walked into the cottage with the mail. "There's a package for you." Alice turned the small box over and showed her the postmark. "It's from Paris. From Henry."

"Henry? Oh, Mama, give it to me, please." Maggie sat on the sofa nursing her baby. She reached out with her eager free hand for the box and turned it over, reading Henry's handwriting, longing for him. Wondering what he was doing at that moment while she waited for the baby to finish nursing. She put the box on the sofa beside her and held Hank up to burp, wiped milk from his chin and laid him on her lap while she buttoned her blouse up properly. Then she opened the package. A note and a pin.

"How beautiful." Maggie held the brooch up to the sunlight.

"Aquamarine suits you, Maggie."

"Oh, Mama," Maggie blushed. "I guess Henry remembers me, after all." She opened the note. Alice set the pin down and lifted the baby from Maggie's lap. She walked around the room, crooning to her grandson while Maggie read her letter.
~~~

November 1, 1918

My Darling Maggie,

I'm on furlough and have been wandering the streets of Paris's left bank all day in sporadic rain, searching for a jewelry store. Finally, I came across this little shop – a hole in the wall – where I found a gift that reminds me of you. The stone is the same color as your eyes, the same as the blue sky on a sunny day, and its gold filigree reminds me of your hair. It's the right color and twists around in tendrils the way your hair does.

I miss you and love you more than the sun and the moon and the stars. More, even, than flying. Your letters to me are worn and ragged from reading them over and over. I look forward every day for mail call, hoping for another one.

At night I dream of sailing with you on Deer Harbor. I long to be with you at our special spot on Deer Island. My heart aches from loneliness without you. The thought of you keeps me going in this accursed war. I'll come home as soon as I can when it's over, and we shall be married.

Love forever, Henry

Henry tore things in the tent apart. Clothes, bedding, leather jackets and goggles flew about the small space. He ran his hands through his hair in exasperation. "Where the hell is it?"

"What's the matter, Henry?" Walter leaned his head inside the tent flap. "There's a flock of Heinies heading our way, and if we hurry, we can catch them." Walter waited a minute. He ducked his head out again as he heard no reply, just more things flying around inside the tent.

"I can't find it, Wally," Henry poked his head out the tent door.

"What is it, Buddy? If you tell me, maybe I can help. Okay?"

"My lucky scarf. The one Maggie knitted for me. It's gone. Disappeared. Vanished." Henry gnashed his teeth in frustration.

Walter took his head out of the door and watched as his fellow pilots ran to the landing field pulling on leather coats and fastening helmets.

"Come on, Henry," Walter called. "Maybe you left it in your kite."

"I wouldn't do that," said Henry. He searched his pockets frantic with worry and retrieved a small piece of yarn from his flying coat.

"Well, let's at least see if it's on the plane." Walter grabbed Henry's arm and towed him toward the field. Henry jogged head down, searching the ground for a trace of his scarf.

"Mac," he called to his head ground crewman. "Have you seen my scarf?"

Mac shook his head. "No, Sir, not a sign uv 'er."

Henry groaned. "All I have is one little strand of it." He held it up for Mac to see. "Do you think there's enough good luck in that little bit to get me back safe?" He made a face and grinned at the crewman.

"Undoubtedly, Sir." Mac grinned back. "You'll be right as rain with that bit, Sir."

"All right, Mac. Anyone who can keep these planes flying must know something about luck, right?" Henry climbed into his Spad and looked in vain around the cockpit for the scarf.

"Switch on, Sir?" Mac called.

"Oh, right!" Henry turned the switch on, still searching for his scarf.

Mac turned the prop to start the plane. The propeller backwash caught the tiny bit of wool and blew it out of Henry's hand.

The squadron taxied onto the field, Henry fifth in line.

~~~

2000

Last night, I read another letter from the small chest in the hall closet. The envelope was not addressed to Maggie, but to Henry's parents. It looked as though it had been wadded up into a ball and then smoothed out again.

10 November, 1918
Mr. and Mrs. Sven Anderson
Orcas Island, Washington State, U.S.A.
~~~

Dear Mr. and Mrs. Anderson,

I regret to inform you of the death of your son, Henry Anderson who was shot down over the Argonne Forest today. Henry was an outstanding aviator much liked and admired by his colleagues. We are returning his personal effects his Identification Card, Aviator's Certification and Rank, and some French francs.

Please accept my condolences.

Sincerely,

Major C.J. Roberts

United States

Expeditionary Forces

P.S.

The necklace was found in a German plane Henry shot down last week. I did not know what to do with it, so I am sending it to you with his other things. Perhaps his fiancé, the concert pianist he spoke of so often, might wish to have it.

C.J.R.

~~~

Sven and Mina Anderson, Henry's parents, sat on the sofa, their faces white and drained as they showed Maggie and her parents the letter they had received from Henry's commanding officer. Svens fumbled with a telegram, pulling it awkwardly from his shirt pocket
~~~

and offered it, also. Maggie crushed the letter up into a ball. *No! Not Henry,* her voice screamed inside her mind. The letter dropped to the floor. She held her baby close, trying not to be hysterical. Her father read the official War Department letter and silently handed it back to Sven. Somehow Maggie had known Henry would not be back. She had kept this dreadful premonition inside her, but deep in her heart, Maggie had been sure he would not come home.

"We want you to know, Maggie, how much we love you and the baby," said Sven in his sing-song Scandinavian manner. "Without you and little Hank, there would be nothing left of our son."

Maggie nodded. She leaned over to kiss the top of the baby's head. "I . . .," She took a deep breath and tried again, choking on the words. "Mr. and Mrs. Anderson . . . I . . . loved Henry very much, and I'm proud to . . . to have his son. The love Henry and I had, was not something sinful. I feel so lucky to have had that little time together with him, and now, we have his son." Maggie buried her face in the baby's neck, absorbing his sweet baby-scent, and hiding her tears

Sven leaned over and patted Maggie's head. "Yah, well we know, Maggie. We know. You betcha."

"It's a hard thing you have to tell us, Sven." Maggie's father said, putting one hand on Sven's shoulder.

Alice nodded mutely, her hands tight against her lips, her eyes brimming with tears. She put her arms around Mina, Henry's mother, and rocked her back and forth the way she rocked the baby. The way she had rocked Maggie as a child. The two women wept quietly together. Maggie stood there, clutching her baby, her face ashen.

"Henry's commanding officer sent this for you, Maggie." Sven said. He pulled the diamond necklace from his coat pocket and handed it to her.

"Oh," said Maggie sitting down. "What do I want with a necklace? What good is that? I just wanted Henry to come back home safe to me – to us." The jewelry fell to her lap through unfeeling fingers as the dam of tears burst. "Henry, Henry," she sobbed. "Just a day longer and he would have come home safe."

She handed the baby to her mother. The necklace dropped to the floor as Maggie stormed around the cottage, tearing at her hair. She ran out the door and down the road to the beach where she and Henry had flown kites and airplanes, where they had hunted sand dollars and star fish. Maggie ran on the sand in the cold wind from the sea, her voice keening with the seagulls' cries.

Alice gave Henry's mother the baby to hold, and stood up to go after Maggie, but Alexander said, "No, Alice, let her be. She needs time alone with her grief."

"But, Alexander, she doesn't even have a coat!" Alice tried to pull away from him, but he held her close.

"Let her go, Alice. It's better this way."

Alice fell back to the sofa and cried. The diamond necklace glittered from under the tea table, and she leaned over to pick it up. Its many facets shone ice-blue in the pale winter sunlight.

"Come, Mina. We go home, now." Mr. Anderson took the baby from his wife's arms. He looked deep into his grandson's eyes and kissed him on one cheek. Then he gave the baby to Alice, picked up his hat, and helped his wife to stand. Holding her hand, he walked with her slowly from the room, across the blue-gray painted porch and helped her down the steps. Alexander and Alice watched them metamorphose into old people, supporting each other as they made their slow journey back down the road to their empty house and the dock with Henry's sailboat still moored there.

~~~

2000

My Volkswagen Bug and I spent nearly every day during the summer, traveling all over Orcas Island. I packed a lunch, sometimes crackers and cheese and an apple with a chocolate bar for dessert, other times a tuna sandwich, a pickle and some Oreo Cookies. Whatever happened to be in the fridge. A bottle of water. A can of pop. Water-color materials. Canon Camera. My baseball cap. I parked the car beside a scenic spot to photograph, sketch or paint.

The other day I walked far out along a beach carrying my cap, my paint box, a small bottle of water, and a block of watercolor paper. I set them down in
~~~

the lee of a driftwood log, reveling in the smells of the sea and the warmth of the sun and sand. Gulls cried and wheeled overhead. The wind blew my hair around making it stick up all over like a scarecrow. I jammed my baseball cap over the tangled mess. Seashells and sand crabs lay underfoot. I slipped off my shoes and socks and ran along the hard-packed sand just before the water line. My toes scraped over sand crab holes, making dry, whistling noises. I splashed in the surf, forgot about painting and walked far out into the waves, getting my Bermuda shorts wet and freezing my feet and legs. Maybe it would be nice to just keep on going, now I was numb with cold. Just keep walking out into the Pacific Ocean and swim all the way to the China Sea and Johnny.

Come on now, Sarah. Don't be an idiot. . .

Instead, I ran back to the log and leaned up against it, feeling its smooth, bleached, weathered surface, knotholes and splits in the wood filled with white sand. I shut my eyes, remembering our wedding – Johnny's and mine -- on the California beach back in 1968. What had happened to everyone? I knew where Vermillion . . . ah, that is, Mystic and Lyle were. Those two were on the fortune-telling circuit, but I really didn't count them as my *friends*. Where were the others now? Frankie and Sue? Tex and Bonnie? Maybe the guys were dead long ago in Vietnam. I slid down to sit on the warm sand, sand sticking to my wet shorts, and leaned back against the log as visions of old friends danced before my eyes.

A re-run of the wedding party on the California beach played inside my head. The stoners, the beer guzzlers, and the dancers on the shore falling down in the foaming surf. The make-shift wedding cake. Our private driftwood haven a mile down the beach. This log reminded me of one wall of our bridal suite on the California beach where we held each other close and whispered eternal love. I rubbed one hand over its smooth weather-beaten surface. Tears welled in my eyes making it hard to see. I brushed them away with a sandy hand. Why hadn't he written more? At first, I wrote to him every day. Sometimes twice a day. After months of no word from him, I wrote every other day, then once a week. Once a month. The first telegram stated he was missing in action. The letter, nearly a year later stated John Hanaeki was presumed dead. My bracelet slid down my arm, clicked against my wristwatch and stuck there. Johnny. I sighed, pulled the chain link loose and sat in the sun with the ghosts of my memories.

~~~

After a day of sketching and painting, I stopped in at the gallery to see Mike.

"Sarah, I'm so glad you came by. You have another check for some paintings that sold this morning." He opened the cash register and pulled out a check for $150 made out to Sarah Hanaeki.

"But this is for the total amount," I said. "You have to take your commission off, first."
~~~

"It's okay, Sarah. The lady had already made out the check and discovered it was her last one. I'll catch up with you next time."

"You sure?"

Mike nodded.

"Thanks, Mike." I put the check in my purse. "I've been all over this island painting and sketching. I should have something to show you in a few days."

"Good. And I have something to show you. Do you have time to stop by my house after I close the gallery?"

I nodded. *What did I have to be home for? Home was not a place where a husband or a child waited to be fed or talked to or loved.*

"Okay. I'll just empty the cash register, except for enough cash to start tomorrow, and we'll be off." Mike counted the money and checks and put them in a bank deposit bag with a deposit slip. He took the keys from his pocket. "Ready?"

"Yes. I'll follow you."

"I have to go through the drive-through window at the bank on the way, but that won't take long."

"Ah, Mike?"

"What?"

"Well, aren't you going to close the money drawer on your cash register?"

"No. I don't leave much change for the next day. I figure if someone breaks in to steal the money, they can have it, but the cash register is complicated and kind of expensive. Just don't break the cash register. These blamed computers are too expensive to repair."

"That makes sense. I guess."

"All right. Let's go."

I followed Mike to the bank and then to his house. We parked both cars on the driveway. He opened the garage with his garage door opener.

We went inside.

The sun hung close to the horizon, turning the sky orange.

"Ta, dah!" Mike turned on the garage light.

There stood the Model T, shiny as a new penny, her brass polished, and the dark green-nearly black of her paint reflecting depths of color.

"It's beautiful, Mike. I walked around the car touching the fenders and brass headlights. "You've done a wonderful job." I looked over at him and grinned. "Does it run?"

"Well, we're working on that. But it won't be long now. The guys have taken the engine all apart and steam cleaned everything. We just need to reassemble it and put in new oil and gasoline."

Mike walked around to the back seat that had no cushion. "I took this seat out – remember the one with the mouse's nest in it? It's at the car upholsterer's right now, being repaired. I told them no vinyl. Has to be leather like the original."

"Well, it's going to be perfect, I know."

"Yep. Sarah, look here at the tires. It took some doing, but I found new ones – 30X3 inch tires for the front and 30X30.5 inch for the back."

"Oh, my, they are beautiful, but what about the expense? I mean, rebuilding the engine and new leather upholstery and tires and everything? It must be costing a bundle." I thought of my dwindling retirement money and the things I still wanted to do to Maggie's Cottage. "Here," I said fishing the check he just gave me out of my purse. "I'll sign this over to you. That should help a little."

"No, Sarah. I won't take it. Let's just wait and see what it comes to." He laughed. "Maybe you'll decide to sell the car to me."

I looked with longing at the beautiful antique. "I don't know about that, Mike. It's absolutely gorgeous." I stood back a few feet to admire the car. "It would be fun to join a Model T club and go on tours in it, wouldn't it?"

"I think so. Did you have a chance to check the attic for vintage clothing, yet."

"Yes. There are some things. They look rather small, though. Were people smaller seventy-five years ago than they are now?"

"I guess it's possible, what with all our good nutrition and vitamins and such."

"Well, come over on your day off and we'll see if they fit. There's a man's black suit – so old it looks almost rusty. Also, a woman's dress trimmed with lace and taffeta ribbons. The waist is so tiny, I'm sure I could never fit into it. Women then must have tortured themselves wearing corsets. I don't know how they stood it. And the hem of the dress is hobbled – it's not very large around – so whoever wore it must have had to walk in teeny-tiny steps." I sighed. "I'm certainly relieved women have been liberated from all that." I laughed. "I'm not exactly an advocate of burning bras, mind you, but I'm glad clothing is more sensible, now."

Mike laughed. "I agree. I'll be over on Monday. Maybe the clothing can be altered to fit. D'y think?"

"Maybe. Do you know a good alterations person? I don't think my sewing skills are up to much more than making curtains for Maggie's Cottage."

"I'll ask around." Mike rocked back and forth on his heels.

"How about staying for dinner? I'm a pretty good cook, if I can barbecue something. Let me check the freezer. I think I've got a couple of steaks, and we can make a salad. Okay?"

"That would be nice, Mike. You're sure it's not too much trouble?"

"Nope. You're never too much trouble, Sarah."

I felt my face turn red and heard my bracelet click. Mike grabbed my hand. "Come on inside," he said. He pressed the garage-door opener button to close it. Mike opened the freezer compartment of his refrigerator and found two steaks sealed in plastic Ziplock bags, turned the hot water on at the kitchen sink, and pulled out a large pan.

What in the world? I thought.

Then he put the steaks still sealed in plastic in the pan, filled the pan with warm water and let it sit. "There. While they thaw out, I'll check the barbecue on the patio and see what we have for a salad."

Mike made it all look so easy. A bottle of wine. Some French bread, also retrieved from the freezer, wrapped in foil and set on the back of the barbecue to heat. In an hour, we were seated on the patio with a candle on the table and a little scrap of sunset along the horizon in the west.

~~~

One day, while I drove my Volkswagen Bug around the island looking for interesting things to paint, I discovered a World War I airplane museum. An elderly man wearing a Veteran's cap from World War II on his balding head, and a row of war medals pinned to his shirt pocket, rose with difficulty from his chair next to a card table, as I walked inside the old hangar. His steps were slow and tentative. He leaned on a cane as he moved in obvious pain.

"Good morning," he said. He smiled and winced as he drew closer. "Arthritis is bad this morning. Takes me a while to get moving." He laughed and stopped in front of me and rested both hands on the cane. "I'm a docent here at this air museum." He pointed to a name tag pinned to his shirt. "Name's Bob. Bob Bailey." He nodded toward the card table where a Mason jar holding a one dollar bill sat next to a stack of colorful World War I airplane brochures. "If you'd like to make a contribution, it'd help with the electricity and heat for these planes – can't let 'em get too cold in winter, y'know. Damp air's not good for 'em."

I had left my purse locked in the Bug but found a couple of dollar bills in my jeans pocket. I stuffed them into the jar, wondering how on earth he could acquire
~~~

enough contributions in this out-of-the-way museum to make a dent in an electric bill these days. The smells of dust and old fabric, petrol and oil hung over the interior of the hangar where airplanes sat like ghost ships from the past in the dim light filtering through dirty windows.

"Thank you kindly," said Bob. "Be sure you pick up one of our brochures on your way out." Bob shuffled over to the light switch by the door, turned it on and illuminated the old hangar with a flood of fluorescent lighting bringing the airplanes and all the dark recesses and corners of the building to life. I wished I'd had a little more money to put in the Mason jar.

Fragile airplanes constructed of wood and fabric, painted bright red, blue and yellow stood tied down like delicate butterflies impaled on pins in a collection. Others were painted in the red, white, and blue colors of the United States Army Air Corps. I looked closely at one not painted a bright color, but still the neutral tan tone of the dope-painted fabric. Someone had scribed an "M" intertwined with an "H" in fine black calligraphy on each side of the plane. I was certain it was the same one as the airplane in a picture I'd found in the old *Fredrick and Nelson* dress box from Maggie's linen closet. Henry and Maggie's aeroplane.

"These planes over here are from World War I." Bob waved his cane at a group of three airplanes. That'n there's a Spad. And the next one is called a Sopwith Camel. The last one's a Neuport." I nodded, fascinated and wandered through the display, in awe that aviators had actually gone to war in such fragile machines. Maggie's fiancé had flown in planes like these. The thought brought a lump to my throat. Henry and the other World War I pilots hadn't had a chance without a parachute in their frail craft.

"Now you take this here plane," the docent took my arm, leaned on me for support and propelled me with shuffling steps to the old fabric and wood airplane with "M and H" painted on its sides. "This plane was built by Henry Anderson, the father of a friend of mine, Hank McNamara, way back in the early part of the twentieth century. Before World War I. In fact, Hank's mother helped sew the fabric for it."

"Really?"

"A-yeah. Sewed it on her mother's Singer Sewing Machine. A treadle, y'know – no electric sewing machines then. Had to pump a foot treadle to keep the thing going. Must 'a been hard to sew fabric on a machine like that.

"Henry, Hank's dad, flew with *The Hat in the Ring Squadron* during World War I in France. A-yeah, he flew in a Sopwith Camel and a Spad, like them two over yonder. He was shot down just before the Armistice." Bob let go of my arm and leaned on the sign in front of the plane.

"Hank McNamara and I played football together at the high school here. Hank worked with his grandfather, old Sven Anderson, a finish carpenter who lived down the road from Maggie's Cottage. They both liked to build things. Hank's father, Henry, did, too. He built this airplane and also a sweet little sailboat he used to take Maggie sailing in." Bob coughed and swallowed. "After the Japanese attacked Pearl Harbor, Henry's boy, Hank, signed up for the Army Air Corps. Guess he wanted to be a pilot like his dad, although he never knew him."

Bob stood and looked at the airplanes, fragile as moths in the bright overhead lights.

"I went into the Tank Corps myself." He sighed. "That was during WWII, the big one." The old man patted the side of the aeroplane, sending up a little cloud of dust.

"Hank was killed in a battle over the South Pacific during the invasion of Iwo Jima." Tears welled in his eyes. "Lot of boys from this island never came home. Such a waste."

The old man took out a handkerchief and blew his nose. "I was lucky. I served with General Patton in North Africa, and then in Europe." Bob gazed out the hangar door looking into the past. "That goddamned Patton! Oh, excuse me, Miss, but Patton didn't let anything stand in his way. He just barreled through, trying to get to Berlin before the Russians. We even outran our own supply trucks." He laughed. Can't move armored cars and tanks without fuel, nor soldiers without rations."

"Oh, I'll admit, he wasn't the most considerate General. I suppose you've heard how he yelled at that shell-shocked boy and slapped him? The kid couldn't help it. His nerve was gone." The old man sniffed. "There was a big stink over that, I'll tell you. Patton had to apologize to the kid. It really riled him to have to do it." Bob wiped his nose with his handkerchief, folded it carefully and put it in his pocket. "But I have to admit General Patton got the job done."

"I don't know much about World War II," I said. "I do know about the war in Vietnam. My husband was reported killed over there."

Bob looked up at me. "Oh? I'm sorry to hear that."

"Thank you, Bob. It's strange that neither his body nor his dog tags were ever found."

"Well, that's the way war is. Things happen that can't be explained."

"You know, I have the strangest feeling that he's still alive – somewhere. That sounds sort of ridiculous, doesn't it?"

"No, can't say as it does. You never know what'll happen in a war." Bob found a bench to sit on. "But that war – that Vietnam thing – was the biggest goddamned mistake our country ever made, if you ask me." Bob frowned and stamped his cane on the cement hangar floor. "If we was gonna be in it, we should 'a fought it like Patton would 'a done it. Give it everything we had and get the damn thing over with. Instead, we just pussy-footed around "helping" the South Vietnamese." Bob's voice rose an octave and he moved his body around in a mincing manner on the bench. "Got a lot of our good boys killed and messed up a bunch more. We probably prolonged that war with our "help". It had to come to an end sooner or later. And it came later. Too late for some."

"I think you're right," I said trying to swallow a huge lump in my throat.

I wandered around the museum brushing tears from my eyes while Bob sat on the bench, resting.

These planes would make a good subject for paintings. I could use Puget Sound for the foreground and put the forest in the background. But they're much too intricate for a quick sketch. I walked back to where Bob sat.

"Do you mind if I photograph the airplanes? I paint watercolors for a gallery in town, and I think they would be a great subject to paint."

"Go right ahead. Shoot!" Bob laughed.

I spent fifteen minutes photographing the airplanes. Then I walked back to Bob.

"Thank you for showing me around. I just recently moved to Orcas Island and bought Maggie's Cottage at Deer Harbor. You must know the house if you were a friend of Hank McNamara."

Bob's face lit up. He grinned. "That I do. I've been there many a day after school. Me and Hank ate cookies Hank's mother baked. She had an old wood cook stove that baked the best pies and cookies."

"I know. The stove is still there, and although I had a small electric stove installed for when I want to cook in a hurry, I like to bake in the wood cook stove, best."

Bob leaned over to me in a conspiratorial manner as though he didn't want anyone else to hear, and said softly, "Y'know, they never married – Hank's mom and dad. Hank's dad, Henry, volunteered and was shipped out to France before they had a chance to get married." He sniffed and wiped his nose again.

"Caused a scandal, it did, her having that baby and not being married," he said. "Lots of folks wouldn't speak to Maggie, even after Hank went to war twenty-four years later."

"That's really too bad." *Poor Maggie.* My heart ached for her.

Bob leaned on his cane with both hands and struggled to stand. I took his arm to help.

"Maggie McNamara was quite a piano player. Made a good living with her music."

I didn't tell him Maggie's ghost played for me once a month when the moon was full.

As we walked through the door, Bob reached over and turned off the lights leaving the hanger in the eerie light from the windows. *So, he is frugal with electricity.* We stood in the sunshine and looked at Puget Sound. He shook his head. "Must a' been lonely for her after Hank got killed. Her folks and his both gone by then, too."

"Yes, I imagine it was lonely. Sometimes I'm lonely at Maggie's Cottage, but then I go out to explore the island like I did today and have a chance to meet nice people like you. The tour was really interesting. Thank you." I shook his hand and headed for my car. Then I turned around and walked back to where Bob stood leaning on his cane.

"You know, I found a photograph of that plane in there, the one with "M and H" painted on it, in a box of old pictures in Maggie's Cottage.. I'd be pleased if you would come and see me some day and I'll show you the pictures. I'll bet you'd know a lot of the people in them." I tore off a sheet of paper from my sketch pad, scribbled my name and telephone number on it and handed it to him. "My name's Sarah Hanaeki. Call first to make sure I'm home."

Bob nodded. "That'd be great."

"I can make cookies, too." I grinned. "In fact, I found a recipe for butter cookies in Maggie's kitchen drawer. They are really good. Maybe you'd like some of those?"

Bob looked off into the past once more. He nodded. "I remember Maggie's butter cookies. They'd just melt in your mouth."

Bug and I ventured past East Sound to the lovely resort of Rosario where I sketched the white, Victorian Mansion trimmed with intricate "gingerbread" that turned the building into a frosted wedding cake set among the fir trees. I looked forward to painting the negative space around the ornate trim back in my studio, letting white paper sparkle through to show the lacey patterns. I wandered through the grounds and inside the old mansion where a musician played a grand piano in the dining room as people dressed in their best ate luncheon. Could Maggie have played the piano here at the resort to supplement her income? I wanted to know more about her.

As I further explored the building, music from an Aeolian pipe organ filled the air from a concert in progress in the music room. I slipped inside the door and found a seat, immersing myself in the music. Later, I wandered back outside and looked over the Marina crammed with yachts and power boats. A seaplane tied at the pier seemed to beckon to me as it bounced in the breeze, tethered to the dock, eager to take off. I gathered my sketching material and walked down to the water to sit in the sun and try to capture the ambience of the place.

Weeks later, when I had completed three watercolors to my satisfaction, one of Rosario with lots of white gingerbread, one painting of the whales, and one from the mountain peak, I took them to the gallery.

"Sarah!" Mike said. "How nice to see you again." He held my hand. My bracelet slid on my arm. "You've brought some paintings." He nodded toward the large plastic bag I carried. "Have you been eating any butter lately?" he teased.

I felt my face turn red and laughed. "Not much. How about you?"

"I'd rather wait until you're with me," he said.

I retrieved my hand and slipped the watercolors from the bag. My POW bracelet slid down my arm and made a small sound as the links hit each other.

"Click."

Johnny.

"These are beautiful! Just what we need." Mike picked up a card with my name lettered in calligraphy, Sarah Hanaeki, and added the name "Rosario, $600". He set the painting on an easel in the gallery window and placed the card beside it, then added titles and prices to cards with my name on them to the other two paintings and arranged them on easels near the check-out desk.

"Do you do all the calligraphy?"

"It's one of my hobbies." Mike grinned. "Winters are slow on the island, so I have a lot of time to practice. Comes in handy." He gestured to other work in the gallery.

You're very good. Calligraphy is too precise for me. I'd rather splash watercolor around."

"That's what I like about your painting, Sarah. It's so loose and free. It's *wet-looking*, yet it has good basic structure underneath to hold it all together."

"Thank you."

I wandered around the shop, interested in what else he had on display. Some oil paintings, fragile hand-blown glass in myriad colors, sculpture, hand thrown pottery, and one room of Indian crafts: baskets, hand-woven rugs, arrowheads, and beadwork. My watercolors fit right in with the rest of the things.

A man and a woman came into the gallery. I hung around the sculptures near the back of the main room while Mike helped his customers.

"We love the picture of Rosario in the window," said the woman. "That's where we had our wedding." She smiled and added, "We're back this week to celebrate our Fiftieth Wedding Anniversary. At Rosario."

I didn't know they held weddings at the resort. Interesting. I looked closer at the couple. They looked to be in their seventies. White hair, frail bones. Both wearing Nike walking shoes and matching sweat outfits. Once in a while their hands touched. Eyes caressed each other. A huge sigh escaped me. Is this the way Johnny and I would have been, had he come back home? I blinked away a tear and looked up to see Johnny's image change into the sight of Mike looking at me, concern in his eyes.

I wondered if these people might have known Maggie. But they would be about 30 years younger than Maggie. Besides, they looked more like visitors than native Islanders.

"We'd like to buy it," said the man.

Mike smiled and nodded. "Maybe you'd like to meet the artist?" He motioned me to come forward as he went to the window to retrieve the watercolor and carried it to the desk. "This is Sarah Hanaeki," he said. "She's our latest watercolorist here on Orcas Island, and her work is outstanding."

I blushed. "Thank you, Mike." I held out my hand to the man and his wife.

"Paul Wilson," he said, "And this is my wife, Catherine."

"If you would like to have Sarah dedicate the painting to you, I'm sure she'd be glad to do that," said Mike.

"Oh, yes," I gulped. "I've already signed the painting, but I'd be glad to dedicate it to the two of you. Do you think on the back? Or maybe on the mat? The mat would be a good place, I think."

They agreed. Paul paid for the watercolor while I wrote:

To Paul and Catherine Wilson
On their 50th Wedding Anniversary.
Best wishes,
Sarah Hanaeki

~~~

1918

"It's a beautiful necklace, Maggie," said Alice, turning the strand of diamonds toward the sun. Reflected light radiated from the many facets of the stones causing an icy brilliant pattern to dance on Maggie's bedroom wall.

Maggie deigned to look at the necklace. "It is gorgeous, isn't it, Mama?" She took it from her mother, held it up to her neck and looked in the mirror. "But I have no use for such a thing." She let the necklace fall with a careless clatter to the top of the dresser.

"Perhaps it would look nice with the black silk dress you plan to wear for the concert in Seattle next week," suggested Alice, toying with the string of diamonds, moving it around on the dresser top with one finger.

"I have my aquamarine pin that Henry sent from Paris. I'll wear that." Maggie smoothed her dress over her waist, satisfied that her figure had returned to its normal size.
~~~

"But, Maggie . . ."

Maggie sniffed. "No, Mama, I don't want it. It belonged to a German flyer – someone who tried to kill Henry."

Alice brushed a tendril of hair back in annoyance. "The major said in the letter that it was found in an aeroplane that Henry had shot down, is all."

"The aeroplane had to have a pilot in it. Think about him for a moment, Mama. Maybe that German aviator bought it for his fiancé, like I'm – like I *was* -- Henry's fiancé." Maggie pulled her long-tangled hair up into a bun on top of her head and turned this way and that in front of the mirror to see how this hair style looked. "I wonder who she was. What does she look like? Does she feel devastated now that her aviator is dead, the way I do, with Henry gone?" Maggie stuck a few wire hairpins into the bun and stared at her reflection with hollow eyes.

"If it hadn't been for this accursed war, we might have been friends." Maggie extracted the hairpins and let her hair fall back down. She turned around to look at her mother. Her eyes glittered with tears as she picked up the necklace and watched the play of light on the diamonds.

"But now, Mama, I hate all Germans. She scrunched the necklace into a wad. And I hate the aviator who had this necklace with him. I even hate the girl he bought it for." She wadded the necklace up tighter. "I detest and abhor the Germans for what they have done to our young men and the lives of practically everyone in the whole world." She looked down at the diamonds sparkling in her hand, opened the top drawer of the dresser, threw the necklace in where it clattered against the mahogany, and slammed the drawer shut. Maggie put her arms on top of the tall dresser and buried her face in them. Her shoulders shook with sobs. "Only one more day, and Henry would have been safe, Mama. I just keep thinking about that. Only one more day."

"I know, Maggie. I know." In tears, Alice folded Maggie into her arms and held her close.

~~~

2000

I had barely dropped off to sleep after a long day at the beach painting, when the music of Chopin, played with the expertise of a professional, filled the cottage. I awoke to my room bright with the white light of the full moon, my heart pounding. I caught my breath and realized my little ghost had returned. I tiptoed to the living room. Maggie sat enveloped in moon beams, playing with intense feeling. Her black silk evening gown fitted at the waist, low-cut to show cleavage, flowed in a draped skirt fashioned with a short train. She had twisted her taffy hair into a bun piled high on her head and held in place with wire hairpins. A few tendrils had escaped and coiled down to frame her face. At her waist, she wore an Aquamarine Art Nouveau pin, her only decoration.
~~~

I gasped at the sight of her fresh beauty and lost myself in her music. The aquamarine stone sparkled . .

. . . as clear and pure as the notes she played on the Baldwin Concert Grand.

Maggie finished the Concerto and dropped her hands to her lap. The audience applauded. She stood up, lifted the train of her dress in her left hand and walked to the apron of the stage where she stood alone. She smiled as she gazed around the baroque Seattle theatre, the ornate balcony, the private boxes draped in red velvet, and dropped into a deep curtsy. The audience stood and applauded. The stage manager brought her a bouquet of red roses. Maggie held the blossoms in her left arm and blew kisses with her right hand.

"Encore! Encore!"

Maggie smiled again. "With your permission, I'd like to play something for our men still in France. I pray they will all come home soon. Please join me if you feel like singing." She went back to the piano, sat down, arranged her long skirt, and placed the bouquet on the bench beside her. Then she played tunes popular during "the war to end all wars", among them: *Over There, When Johnny Comes Marching Home, Again, Lillie Marlene,* and *It's a Long Way to Tipperary.* Remembering the way Henry sang this song brought tears to her eyes, "*It's a long way to Orcas Island – to the sweetest girl I know.*"

The audience sang along with Maggie, and then applauded louder, many weeping. Maggie stood and dropped into another deep curtsy, her eyes glittering like diamonds, her smile wavering through tears, as she thought of Henry flying his Spad; of Henry shot down over the Argonne Forest.

Of Henry dead.

~~~

1968

The two Viet Cong guerilla fighters traveled fast – too fast for John in his weakened condition. Steam rose from the jungle as the sun climbed higher in the sky. Now and then a bird called. The soldiers begrudged the frequent stops to rest and argued between themselves. Each time, one of them pointed his AK-47 rifle at John's head and made noises like a rifle firing. He laughed and jerked the rifle up into the air, causing John to flinch. The soldiers' argument became heated. The air, heavy with condensation, turned into a light shower. John strained to release the thin rope tying his wrists behind his back. His heart pounded, but he stood tall and glared at his shorter captors while rain and sweat trickled into his eyes.

After many miles of travel, the trail became steep and wound into the mountains where they reached a platoon of North Vietnam soldiers holed up in a cave. John dropped to the ground, exhausted. His head throbbed and his side ached. The soldier who had pretended to shoot John in the head slid a dull knife under the rope binding his hands together and cut
~~~

through them, sawing back and forth through the tough hemp. John's numb hands had no feeling left in them. He lay there, panting with a painful stitch in his chest where his rib had been broken in the helicopter crash. The knife finished its work with a jerk, causing pins and needles to course through his hands and arms.

One of the North Vietnam soldiers walked over and stood a moment. He kicked John in the side, rolling him over onto his back. John screamed. The V.C. guerilla leaped to his feet and thrust his rifle into John's chest, growling at him. The soldier who had kicked him stared into John's face and said something John could not understand. The man kicked him again and stalked away. John shut his eyes tight, trying not to make a sound. *Fuck, man! Hurts like hell!* John took shallow breaths, trying to control the pain. *I've seen that guy somewhere before -- but where? Gotta think, man. Shit! They all look alike—South Vietnamese and North Vietnamese. Even Viet Cong. All look the same. Fuck!*

John forced his eyes open. The soldier who had kicked him sat in a corner like a cobra. Watching. Waiting. John's eyes met his in a flash of recognition. He was the spy – the man he and Greg had dropped off on the beach of the little lagoon. The man narrowed his eyes at John, warning him not to let on they knew each other. John closed his eyes again. He breathed in short gasps and doubled up, melting into the agony of his throbbing side.

"Don't look at me and speak softly." The spy's voice was so low it was nearly imperceptible. He stood beside John the next morning as they relieved themselves in the bushes. "I'll try to get you out. That family you stayed with back in the Cambodian village? They'll take you in. Remember the way?"

"I think so," said John staring at the two piss streams. "But how did you know about the village? What the fuck are you doing here? Who are you? I thought you were like, a spy or something."

"Quiet! Don't look at me!" the man whispered as he glanced out the corner of his eyes.

Satisfied they were unobserved, he said, "My name's Kim." The man spoke without moving his lips. "And I'm a spy for the South Vietnamese. We'll have to go along with these troops until we get a chance. If they find out you're a door gunner, they'll kill you. Only pilots are worth capturing."

John gulped. "How can I get back to Da Nang?"

"Look at the stars for directions at night, the sun during the day. The North Polar Star will show just above the horizon. Keep going southeast. You can do it." He tied the drawstring on his North Vietnam uniform pants and turned away. "Too bad about the aviator. He was a good man."

~~~

2000

On a Monday morning filled with fog in September, Mike called. "It's my turn to take you on a picnic, Sarah. Can you meet me at the boat dock in East Sound?" I heard the mournful plaint of a foghorn
~~~

in the distance and the faint dismal clang of a bell buoy. "By the time you get here, the sun will have burned through. I'd come and pick you up, but I want to have things ready when the tide changes in forty-five minutes." I could almost hear him smiling. "And that's all I'm going to tell you about our picnic!"

"Whoa! Sounds mysterious, but what about the gallery?" My POW bracelet slid down my arm. *Click.*

"This late in the season, I close the shop on Mondays. The few tourists here for the week-end usually go home on the Sunday ferry."

"All right," I said. "What can I bring?"

"Just yourself and your camera in case you see something to paint later. Oh, you might want a swimsuit and towel."

A swimsuit? How long had it been since I'd worn a swimsuit? I laughed and said, "It's been ages since I even tried to get into a swimsuit, Mike. Are you sure you want to swim?"

"Absolutely. See you in half an hour. Gotta run." Mike hung up.

I dug through boxes in my closet and finally found a swimsuit. Maybe it was too small now. I held it up in front of the mirror and shuddered. Oh, well, maybe I could just say I don't feel like swimming.

Camera, sunscreen, swimsuit and towel packed in a tote bag. Sunglasses. I drove the fifteen miles from Deer Harbor up to the pier at East Sound, parked, and looked around for Mike, but couldn't find him. I got my tote bag, locked the car and went to sit on a bench in the sun burning through fog. Someone on a sailboat moored far down the dock among a sea of masts, waved. I waved back. He waved again and motioned me to come as he stepped from the sailboat to the dock and walked toward me. The man wore white shorts, a navy blue T-shirt, white canvas sneakers, and a navy blue, gold-braid trimmed yachting cap with a visor.

I ran toward him calling. "Oh, my, Mike! I didn't recognize you in that hat."

Mike ran the remaining distance toward me and took my hand. "Come on, Sarah, the tide's right. Let's go."

We hurried down the dock to the sailboat that appeared to be about 30 feet long. It looked large enough to be self-contained, with a cabin and decks in front and back, and walk-ways around the sides. Mike tossed my tote bag aboard, jumped aboard, and turned around to help me in. A stiff breeze flapped the loose sails and blew away the remaining wisps of fog. I shivered.

"Are you cold?" He looked at me with concern.

"No, just a little bit scared, I guess. I've never been sailing before, although I have been surfing, but they're different things." I held on tight to the edge of the sailboat and looked around. The mast soared high into the sky where the wind whistled eerie music around it, and gulls drifted on thermals. "Do you have life jackets?"

"Yes, ma'am. Just lift up that cushion. They're stowed under the seats."

I peeked under a cushion to see them. "Are you sure you know how to run this thing?"

"Sure, as can be," Mike laughed. "And in a pinch, I have an auxiliary engine."

I watched Mike start the motor and ease us away from the dock, maneuvering carefully away from other boats moored there. As the tide caught us, he cut the engine and reached for the sheets.

"Sarah, please stand here and hold the wheel steady while I set the sails."

"Me?" I gulped.

"Yes, you," he laughed. "You are perfectly capable of holding the wheel straight. You can drive a car, can't you?"

"Well, yes, but . . ."

Mike nodded to me and left the wheel turning free in the water. I leaped from my seat to grab it and hold it steady as he set the sails, first the main sail, then the jib. He was quick about it and hurried back to relieve me, standing behind me, putting his hands over mine. I breathed a sigh of relief along with the scent of his after shave. My knees turned to water. I resisted the desire to lean back into his arms.

We were off.

We sailed down the channel that nearly divided Orcas Island in two parts. Blue sky. White caps. Bright sunshine. Fluffy clouds and sea birds overhead. I ducked from under Mike's arms and took photographs as we moved along running from one side of the boat to the other. After awhile, we passed Rosario, and still later, the town of Olga. We made our way around the end of the island going east and entered Obstruction Pass where a sandy beach greeted us.

"We can stop here, if you like," said Mike un-cleating the sheets to let a little wind out of the sails and slow the sailboat down. "Or go on up the coast to Pt. Lawrence. "

"Oh, let's keep going. This is so nice. Just the wind and the sails snapping in the breeze and the creak of the sailboat as it moves in the waves. It's wonderful. So quiet."

"Aye, aye, Cap'n," Mike grinned. He pulled the sheets taut again. The sails snapped and filled with wind.

We sailed north by northwest up the side of Orcas Island and stopped at a sandy cove. Mike furled the sails and powered in on the engine just to be on the safe side, checking the depth of the water with sonar as we went. He dropped anchor and shut down the motor. Quiet surrounded us except for waves lapping the sides of the sailboat, and the wind piping a primitive tune around the metal mast. We were alone in the cove.

"We can have a swim before lunch, if you'd like," he said.

"That'd be nice." I lied. I worried about how I would look in my swimsuit. I hadn't had time to try it on before leaving the house. After all, I was no longer eighteen. Or twenty-eight, for that matter. . . Even forty-eight. . . Oh well . . .

"You can change in the cabin," said Mike, indicating the short staircase.

"Right," I nodded and headed with apprehension down the steps carrying my tote bag, wondering if I could just accidentally drop my swimsuit overboard. But no, Mike would jump into the water and bring it back, and then I'd have to struggle into a cold, clammy swimsuit. I shivered at the thought and wished I had "forgotten" to bring it.

I looked around the neat, compact cabin. A tiny sink and a two-burner gas stove, a small table and benches built into one side. A mini bathroom complete with shower. Behind folding doors, a king-sized bed. Cupboards wherever there was room for them.

By the time I came back up on deck, Mike already stood there in his swimsuit looking handsome and fit. Well, a little bit of a tummy, but not bad for a man his age. I had a bit of a tummy, too. Either he had worn his swimsuit under his shorts, or he was quick to change. Mike grinned at me, stepped up on the stern of the sailboat and dove into the water. The splash hit me like sleet in a January storm. Cold! So . . . cold! I wondered if I'd be able to get into such icy water. Puget Sound was far north of the warm Santa Barbara surfing areas I had known with Johnny.

The only way was to jump right in, so I did. The frigid water took my breath away. We swam around the sailboat and over to the beach where we lay side by side on white sand in the hot sun.

Mike leaned over me, propped his head on one hand, his elbow digging into the sand, and traced a sandy finger around my chin. "You are very beautiful, Sarah, you know?"

I felt my face flush. To my dismay a giggle escaped me. "No, actually, I don't know. Maybe once, but you are speaking to someone old enough to be a grandma, for Pete's sake!"

"Well, you are. You're a beautiful woman." He leaned closer to kiss me. I gasped. His kisses took my breath away, even more than the cold water had.

Click, click, my bracelet scolded . . .

Mike's kisses traveled to one ear, then my neck. The strap on one side of my swimsuit slipped down. He kissed me on my bare shoulder. I wriggled away near tears. "I'm sorry, Mike. I just don't know if I'm ready for this, you know?"

Mike sat up, sighed and nodded his face downcast. "I know. I felt that way when Corrine died, too. It took me awhile to get over her death, but Sarah it has been more than thirty years for you!"

"Mm—hmm." I brushed the tears away and got sand on my face. "If only I knew for sure there was no hope. If I knew Johnny really was dead, then I think I could close that part of my life and get on with a new one." I smoothed a spot in the warm sand swishing one hand back and forth like a windshield wiper.

"The hardest part is not knowing for sure." I pushed back my wet hair and got more sand in it. "Was he killed in a helicopter crash? Or was he taken prisoner? Was he tortured and held in a bamboo cage too small to stand up in and too short to lie down in, as I've heard some of our men were? Did he die of malnutrition – did the enemy starve him to death?"

I looked out to where the waters of the Puget Sound seemed to nearly touch fluffy white clouds on the horizon. "Sometimes I imagine John is right here beside me, and if only I could reach out in just the right way, I would be able to touch him." I stretched my left arm away from my body. The bracelet links caught, pinching my wrist.

I tried to straighten the links out. "That sounds pretty weird, doesn't it? Almost as bad as a ghost that plays the piano in the moonlight."

Mike reached over, took my hand, and straightened out the bracelet. He kissed the inside of my wrist sending electric tremors throughout my body.

I stood up and ran into the water, glad of its frigid temperature. Mike followed. We swam back to the yacht and climbed aboard. I scampered downstairs to change while Mike changed on deck. I wondered if it would be all right to take a quick shower but decided against it. After all, this was Mike's boat. He hadn't said anything about using the shower. Maybe he didn't carry enough water for a shower, quick or not.

When I came back up, I felt a little bit foolish. After all I was a grown woman. Why not enjoy life while I could? But something held me back. "I'm sorry, Mike. Maybe you'd better take me home."

"I'll do no such thing," he said. "In my opinion, you just need a little more time. Maybe we can find out what happened to Johnny. I'll get on the internet when business is slow and see if I can find out anything. We'll be friends first, and then see, okay?"

"Okay." The tears came unbidden.

Mike opened a bottle of Riesling and poured two glasses. He handed one to me and said, "Here's to future boating picnics together."

I sighed, trying to hide the fact that I was crying. Then I hiccupped. "Thank you."

Mike reached over and brushed away the tears, rubbed his nose against mine and made a face at me. I laughed. He kissed me on the tip of my nose and I reached up to hug him, spilling a little wine on my lap.

We sipped the wine while Mike laid out lunch. Sesame crackers and Brie cheese with thin-sliced salami and apples. All at once I found I was hungry. We sat in the stern of the sailboat and enjoyed our lunch. My hair, full of salt water, dried in a sticky mess, but I didn't care. I put my baseball cap over it.

"Now for the dessert," said Mike, a mysterious smile on his face. "My favorite-- after fresh-baked apple pie, that is."

"Ta-da!" He held up a package of Oreo cookies.

"Oh, Mike, You are a goofy guy," I laughed. "Oreo cookies are one of my favorites, too." I picked up one. "How do you eat them? It's an art, you know."

"I don't know. You tell me," he said.

"First you twist the cookie a little to take it apart. Then you eat the part that has no filling on it. Then you eat the filling, and finally you eat the other cookie part. Or . . . or throw it away. Simple." I demonstrated by tossing the denuded cookie to the gulls.

I helped Mike set out the bright red, white, and blue spinnaker sail, and we sailed back down the Coast of Orcas Island, going downwind, sipping wine and eating dismantled Oreo cookies.

~~~

1968

Although John made tight fists and tried to keep his hands apart when the soldiers tied his wrists together behind his back with heavy cord, he could not get loose. The Viet Cong traveled toward Hanoi, taking him with them. Rain made the trek miserable but did make it possible to stretch the cord a little. He was at least able to keep the circulation moving in his arms.

I wonder where they're taking me. We're going north. If we get to Hanoi, and they find out I'm not a pilot, I'm done for. They kill fuckin' door gunners! Rain ran down John's face. He sniffed, and wished his hands were free so he could wipe his face. He leaned over to try to wipe it with his shoulder. The spy eased his way back down the column and walked with John.

"You see the bend in the trail up there?"

John nodded. Rain ran down into his eyes. He shook his head to get rid of the heavy downpour.

"There's a fork off to the left. Take it, hide, and wait for us to get out of sight. Then head back south. Got it?"

John nodded. "Yeah. But what about my hands? I won't get far if I can't use them." John wiggled his fingers, trying to keep the blood moving. He ducked his head as a cloud burst drove rain like bullets.

"I'll cut you free. Steady as she goes." Kim walked behind John, shielding him from the men behind, and put the point of his knife under the cord binding John's
~~~

hands. He cut through with one quick slice. "Don't make a sound. Watch out for land mines."

They trudged in silence for a few minutes. A fresh deluge of rain splattered on the broad foliage making a noise like machine gun chatter.

"Now!" the spy hissed.

John veered off to the left. The heavy wet foliage hid him immediately. He stopped a few feet from the "Y" in the trail, hunkered down, held his breath, and waited. The last of the Viet Cong troops passed him, slogging along unseeing in the deluge. When all was quiet, except for the splat of rain drops on broad leaves, John slipped back onto the main trail and back tracked, headed for the village five days away, rubbing his arms to get rid of the pins and needles, and wiping his face as he ran.

~~~

The village people welcomed John back. A smile flitted across Chi's face as she found cotton shorts and smocks for him like the other men wore. She carried them to her house and motioned to John to follow her. John put on this disguise while Chi hid his uniform with the First Cavalry Horse Patch on the sleeve, folding it flat at the bottom of a giant rice basket, and filling the basket to the top with rice. She set a straw cone-shaped hat on John's head and smiled up at him, her eyes shining bright. John bowed and said "*Thank you,*" in Cambodian. Smiling, Chi returned the bow.
~~~

Chi's brother, Sovann, took John to the rice paddies, gave him a limber switch, and showed him how to ride the paddy rake. John's extra height and weight helped hold the rake down under the water as he and the water buffalo worked the paddy back and forth. The first day, John gagged at the smell of human excrement used for fertilizer. Sovann laughed at him.

"*You get used to it,*" he said in Cambodian, pounding John on the back.

After a few days, John became accustomed to the stench, and developed a deep appreciation for the patient water buffalo. His Polynesian heritage helped him blend in with the others, although he was much taller. Each day, when he finished his work on the rice paddies, he unhitched the rake from the buffalo, and drove the animal into the freshwater stream where they both had a bath. Then he turned the animal out to graze and went home to Chi and her brother.

After work John used the Montagnard axe and his engineering skills to build a system of flumes from hollow bamboo to carry water to all the little houses. He tinkered with decorative waterfalls and dippers that filled from the bamboo pipes, and then tipped to continue the flow of water. He put a floor in Sovann and Chi's house and built some furniture. A table. A few chairs.

~~~

2000

On a warm Monday morning, I watched through my new kitchen garden window as Mike's car drove into the back yard. I went out on the back porch to meet him, my dish towel still in my hand.

"Hi, Sarah," he said. "I've got the check for your latest sales at the gallery."

"Thank you, Mike." I smiled and motioned for him to come in. A soft breeze wafted off the harbor and ruffled my hair.

"It's really nice out here," he said. He sat down and patted the step. I sat next to him and enjoyed the view of the boat basin with the yacht masts sparkling against the dark green-nearly black-of a Douglas fir forest. Mike handed me the check.

"$700! Wonderful! I can use this." I put it in my jeans pocket. "There's still a lot to do around this place.

"Have you found anything else interesting like that Model T?"

"Well . . . there's a boat underneath the house."

Mike grabbed my hand and headed for the front of the house. I gasped as electricity flowed between us and had to run to keep up with his long strides down the hill around to the water side of Maggie's Cottage. Lattice work covered the spaces between huge timbers that supported the southeast corner of the living room where the land sloped sharply toward the harbor. We stooped to get under the house through a broken place
~~~

in the lattice, where a large area was high enough to stand in. I could barely make out the name "*Maggie*" in the faded and peeling blue paint on the boat's stern.

"Now this is something we can work on here." Mike let go of my hand. I held my hand to my face, feeling his warmth still on my palm. Smelling his scent. Mike walked back under the pilings to look at the boat.

"It's about 14 feet long, Sarah, with a main sail and a jib." He came back out and held my hand again. I caught my breath. "Duck your head," he warned as he drew me in under the latticework. Mike rubbed his free hand over the old gunwale. "The keel seems sound. No dry rot. It just needs to be sanded and painted."

I walked around the boat, tentatively touching it. "How can you get away from the gallery to work on it?"

"During the summer I usually hire a college student to help. When Elizabeth gets home from the University, she'll want her summer job back. I can have her watch the gallery mornings while I work on the sailboat. When it's finished, we might take it out in Deer Harbor to that little island. What do you think? Want to do that?"

"It sounds wonderful, Mike, but I don't know much about sailing, and I'm not that great a swimmer, either." I shivered and held his hand tighter.

Mike brushed a lock of hair from my face and said, "Don't worry. I'll bring life jackets. Then if it tips over, we won't drown."

I laughed. "You mean we can just freeze to death!"

We walked back to the shed, still holding hands. I felt I didn't want to let go. I'd been alone too long. I found I liked the idea that Mike cared about me.

"I'll put the boat up on sawhorses so I can work on it. There's room right there under the front of the house.

~~~

1968

"John," Sovann used his English name. Then he rattled off in Cambodian, *"If the Viet Cong come again, you must hide. We send the young boys to the edges of the paddies and to the forests and cliffs to watch. They warn us if Cong soldiers are near. Then you must go to the caves in the mountain." Sovann* pointed toward a densely forested hill.

John looked at Sovann and Chi. "I don't understand," he said. "Er-r . . . No comprende. . ah ." John shrugged his shoulders helplessly, knowing they would not understand his smattering of high school Spanish, or for that matter, the Polynesian language his family in Hawaii had spoken. He stood looking askance at them, arms dangling helplessly at his sides.

Chi ran to get a boy. They hurried back together, the boy grinning wide. "*This boy, Sa'ang, watch for Cong,*" she said, "watch for Kymer Rouge." Chi mimed what the boy would do. She leaned forward, peered into the distance, and shaded her eyes with one hand. "*This boy go fast to you.*" She clapped her hands at the boy. *"Run, Run!!"* Sa'ang ran around the compound, laughing.
~~~

"*No laugh! Serious!*" scolded Chi.

Chi picked up a large stick and held it against her shoulder like a rifle. She marched around in a circle frowning. Then she pretended to find John and poked him with her make-believe weapon. "*Surrender!*" she commanded.

John nodded. He finally understood what they tried to tell him.

Chi let out her breath. She pushed her hair away from her face and grabbed John's arm. "*Attendez! If this boy, Sa'ang, say 'Cong', John run, hide.*" She pointed to the mountains. "*Cave. Sovann show. Go!*"

John nodded and followed Sovann who had already headed for a path that led to the mountains through a heavy tropical forest. John hurried before he lost sight of Sovann who pointed out other trails that twisted and turned and that John would not have seen by himself, they were so faint in the dense foliage. Eventually, they came out on the mountain of many caves.

John nodded and grinned. "*Biet!* I understand," he told Sovann. He held out his hand in a 'high five'. Sovann grinned and slapped it in return.

One night when only the stars lit the earth, Chi lay wide awake listening to her brother's sleeping sounds. Sovann snored gently. Satisfied that he was in deep slumber, she slipped naked from her wooden bed and holding her thin blanket in front of her, trailed it across the room on tiptoe to where John lay sleeping. He turned over and was surprised to find Chi had slid under his blanket beside him. She placed one finger on his lips and snuggled close. Tiny moans escaped Chi's lips as her fingers explored John's body. John sighed and thought of Sarah. Half asleep, his hands roamed over the slender form close to him. But this was not Sarah. Guilt filled his sleep-hazed consciousness. Sovann slept on at the other end of the room, his snore still purring as gentle as a kitten.

A cock crowed at first daybreak. Sovann got up and staggered half-asleep across the room to go outside and relieve himself. He stopped short by John's sleeping board and rubbed his eyes. He peered through the dim dawn light. Yes, his sister was there with the American soldier. Sovann shrugged. *What will be, will be.* He scratched his groin and proceeded outside.

That day, Chi moved her blanket to John's bed. John tried to tell her he had a wife in America. She didn't understand or didn't want to understand. His indiscretion gnawed at him. Each night Chi placed a finger over his lips to hush him as he tried to explain he already had a wife he loved in America. Chi snuggled closer. John sighed. *Shit, man! Might as well live while I'm alive. We could all be dead tomorrow with those fucking Khmer Rouge soldiers roaming all over the place let alone the Viet Cong who come around once in a while.*

~~~

2000

Mike called. "The Model T is running, Sarah. She purrs like a kitten. Like a Singer Sewing Machine. How about a date?"

"Oh, Mike," I laughed. "You are so funny. Of course, I'd like to go for a ride in the Model T. Where shall we go?"

"Well, I thought if you wouldn't mind driving to my house, we'd go out to dinner at the Pizza Parlor. It's such a nice evening. The sunset will be spectacular. I'd rather not go too far with her the first time out. That's why I wondered if you'll meet me here."

"Okay. I'll be there in half an hour."

We drove the Model T through town and had fun waving to people passing by. Mike tooted the bulbous horn. The antique car rattled and shook its way down Main Street to the Pizza Parlor. We parked where we could keep an eye on it, ordered our pizza and carried our food to tables outside where we could watch the setting sun cast its warm glow over the automobile.

A gibbous moon hung low in the sky, enhanced by starlight twinkling in the clear atmosphere as we left the Pizza Parlor. Mike lit the kerosene side running lights and tail lights, so oncoming cars would be able to see us poking along the road like a large green turtle. The gas headlights worked, but really didn't give much light. Without the moon's help, we might have ended up in a ditch. We were lucky there was not much traffic, but
~~~

what little there was slowed down when they passed us. People grinned and stared at us in our ancient chariot, like we had somehow landed in the 21st Century from a hundred years ago.

~~~

1968

Viet Cong soldiers continuously traveled down the Ho Chi Minh trail along the Cambodian border. John decided he had to find his way back to the base at Da Nang. Chi wrapped several rice balls in cabbage leaves for his trip, her face an unfeeling mask, but she brushed away tears from her eyes.

John had mastered the Cambodian language a bit better by this time. Now his angst over being untrue to Sarah was compounded by the fact that not only was he already married, but that the U.S. Army frowned on taking home war brides.

In Cambodian, John said, *"Don't cry, Chi. I'll send for you. I'll take you with me when I go back to America."* John had no idea how he could do this thing but decided at least to try.

What would Sarah think if I brought Chi home? Guilt over what he had done to Sarah enveloped him the way the jungle enfolded its broad leaves and tendrils of vines about him. *Sarah'd kill me if she knew, but fuck, man, I'm here, and Chi's here. Sarah's stateside. I've got to live while I*
~~~

can. No telling when I'll be at the receiving end of a sniper's bullet, or step on a land mine. I could be dead any day now.

Chi wiped her tears with her hands and wiped her hands on her smock, smoothing the fabric over her stomach. No one, not even John, had noticed the slight bulge. She decided to say nothing. He would not be back.

John and Chi made love one last time. The sun set filling the air with a golden glow. John kissed Chi good-bye and went outside where he bowed to the other villagers, thanking them for their help. Then he slipped away after dark, jogging along the paddy dikes by starlight, keeping the faint twinkle of the North Star hanging low on the horizon at his back. He reached the dense forest just before dawn and holed up in a nest of foliage for the day. Late in the afternoon, voices awakened him. He looked out of his hide-out to find Viet Cong soldiers camped a few yards away. John sucked in his breath. He closed his eyes, hoped he was invisible, and waited.

John noted where the guards were stationed, and when the camp had settled down for the night, slipped silently from his leafy sanctuary, and sneaked in a round-about fashion away from the Viet Cong encampment. In the dark, he stepped on a dry branch. The sharp snap alerted one of the guards who fired by reflex toward the sound, nicking John's arm.

John scrambled away to climb a tree, leaving a trail of blood. The camp came alive as soldiers searched the area but could not find him in the dark. Up in the tree, John twisted his shirt sleeve tightly around the wound, holding one corner of the fabric in his teeth, and leaned against the tree trunk, waiting, wondering what to do. His arm was on fire. He could be tracked by his bloody trail. He scrunched his eyes shut tight.

Fuck!

After a very long time, the camp settled down again. Johnny slipped out of the tree and away from the forest. He traveled back along the paddy dikes as fast as he could, worried about leaving a path; not wanting to lead the soldiers to the village, but not knowing where else to go for help. He veered into the murky paddy water to hide his trail. The new bright green shoots of rice looked silver in the starlight. They blurred and ran together in front of him. Sweat ran down his face and the middle of his back. He swallowed hard and tried to keep from falling down. Rain clouds formed overhead and emptied themselves over the land. *Better stop and rest a minute.* Johnny hunkered down in a clump of bamboo and elephant grass at the edge of the rice paddies and fainted.

Johnny lay unconscious, hidden by the bamboo. The sound of footsteps and the rattle of equipment awoke him as the Viet Cong soldiers traveled along the paddy dike nearby. John put his face down into the mud and froze, staying there long minutes after he could no longer hear them. The rain clouds followed the soldiers as they headed north. Starlings flew overhead. In the distance, a farmer switched his water buffalo as he worked the paddy. A crow cawed.

Johnny pulled himself up. Muck sucked at his feet but had not touched his wound. He stood up hunched over, his whole-body aching, and took a few steps toward the village. The soldiers were nowhere in sight, so he stood straighter and forced himself to walk faster. The fresh stream he and the water buffalo had bathed flowed at the edge of the dikes where it was diverted when needed to flood the paddies. Johnny stripped naked and washed off the mud, rinsing his uniform in the water. The bullet wound bled. When he felt clean again, he carried his soggy underwear and uniform toward the village, dripping a trail of blood and water. A small boy spotted him and ran to alert the villagers.

Chi hurried to meet him, ts-tsk-ing over his wounded arm. Tears ran down her face as she helped him to her house.

"Sovann!" she called. *"Sovann! Come. Help Johnny."*

Johnny's arm was swollen and red but had bled profusely. The bullet had barely clipped him. She and her brother washed the wound in cold tea, letting it bleed more to clean it out, and bandaged his arm. Johnny became dizzy and lay down on the wooden bed.

A few days later when he had recovered enough to move around, Johnny and Chi sat together outside her house and watched a sliver of new moon reflecting on the rice paddies far below the village. John put his good arm around Chi. She nestled close to him. The stench of the paddies lessened in the cool air. Night birds called. Far in the distance thick forests covered the mountains. Chi moved Johnny's hand down toward her stomach and pressed it on the slight bulge.

"What?" Johnny spoke in the little Cambodian language he had learned. He sat up straight. *"Baby?"*

Chi nodded.

"Ah, Chi." This time Johnny spoke in English. He shook his head. This miracle Sarah had always hoped for had happened here in a foreign land where children of American soldiers were ostracized. Johnny sighed. Could he leave now? Leave his child to be discriminated against by people who wouldn't want it around? Could he take Chi and the baby home with him? Sarah certainly would have something to say about him bringing home another wife, let alone a pregnant one. Johnny shook his head to clear it. He rubbed his good hand across his face.

"You don't want baby?" Chi looked up at him, her smooth forehead creased with worry. *"Not have . . . baby?"* Her eyes filled and she looked down. Tears dropped on her hands and on Johnny's good arm. She sighed, choking as she stood to leave. *"I see medicine woman."*

Johnny held on to her. "No, Chi. No. Don't do something stupid. Of course, I want the baby. A baby is a miracle."

"Mi-ra-cle?" What is mi-ra-cle?" Chi twisted her hands together, tears running down her cheeks.

"A miracle is a thing of wonder," Johnny said. "Don't worry, I want the baby. Everything will be all right."

He held Chi in a tender embrace, wondering what to do.

~~~

2000

Up in my attic workshop, I checked the POW Website on my computer to see if there had been any news lately about the First Cavalry's soldiers missing in action during the Vietnam War. No news of the 2400 American POW/MIA's unaccounted for since 1973. Nothing. I still hadn't given up hope. I went downstairs to the bathroom and washed my face. Brushed and flossed. Put on my nightgown and climbed into bed, the white goose down comforter snug around me. A thin crescent moon hung over the harbor. I read one of Henry's letters to Maggie. When my eyes grew heavy with sleep, I put the letter away and turned out the lamp. My bracelet clicked. I felt the clasp, checking to make sure it was secure and ran one finger over John's name, rank and serial number, engraved in the stainless-steel bracelet plate, nearly worn off now.

~~~

1919

Alexander dragged himself up the porch steps and into the house. Stars reflected tiny points on the water of Deer Harbor like diamonds scattered from a broken necklace. He collapsed in one of the big chairs by the fireplace.

"Bad day?" asked Alice.

Alexander nodded. "Five more taken with flu. The hospital is overrun with sick people. I don't know how we can take care of so many."

"Boppa," called his grandson stretching his arms toward his grandfather. "Want Boppa."

"Hush, Hank," said Maggie. "Boppa's tired. Wait a bit until he rests."

The little boy snuggled under his mother's chin and put his thumb in his mouth. Maggie rocked him back and forth as she walked into her bedroom. Soon he fell asleep. She put him in his crib, covered him and stood over him, watching him breathe, cheeks rosy, blonde curls damp with perspiration, his turned-up nose like his father's – like Henry's.

Hank awoke, feverish and cross. Maggie held him, giving him sips of water. His feeble cry could scarcely be heard. Exhausted after several hours, Maggie handed the baby to her mother to hold.

"There, there, little Hank. Nana's here," said Alice.

Hank threw up all over his grandmother. Diarrhea ravaged his body. His temperature soared.

Maggie struggled to clean up the mess and make him comfortable. He cried and fussed. Sips of water came right back up.

Alice stripped off her soiled clothes, had a quick bath, and pulled on a robe. She went to the telephone on the kitchen wall, lifted the receiver and turned the crank on the side of the wooden box three times, the hospital's ring.

"Hello," she shouted into the telephone. "Hello? This is Dr. McNamara's wife. Please let me speak to the doctor."

"He's busy? Well, have him call home immediately. Our grandson is terribly ill. I don't know what to do."

"Yes, we've tried that. Cool sponge baths, sips of water. He just throws up everything and he's burning up." Tears ran down Alice's face. "I'm afraid he has the flu like everybody else who is sick on Orcas Island. He's so little. Just a baby. We can't let anything happen to our precious little one. Yes, thank you. Please have him call." Alice sat down on a kitchen chair and sobbed.

~~~

1969

Fine gravel rattled against the woven split-bamboo window covering in the little house. John awoke and froze, all senses alert to a Viet Cong raid. The bamboo cover rattled again. Chi sat up clutching her thin blanket to her breast. She looked at Johnny in the dim starlight glowing through pinpoint cracks in the window covering, her eyes large and frightened. Then she held one finger to her lips, wrapped the blanket around her and slipped off the wooden sleeping platform. Her hands shook as she completely covered
~~~

John with the second blanket and slid the bamboo window screen open an inch. Chi peered out into the night, her heart pounding in her throat.

Kim, the spy, looked back at her. *"Johnny,"* he whispered.

Chi nodded. She slid the bamboo covering shut; let out her breath, surprised to find she had been holding it, and shivered in the warm night air. She tiptoed back to tell John. He pulled on shorts, slipped out the door and walked around to the side of the house. Kim motioned him to follow. They made their way a short distance from the village and hunkered down in the deep foliage of the forest.

"Viet Cong come by here often?"

Johnny nodded. "Part of the Ho Chi Minh trail's right over that hill."

"I need your help. I want to leave my spare radio with you. If you see any Viet Cong, notify my contact. I'll give you the code. He'll let the base at Da Nang know. How many. What direction they go. The whole drill."

Johnny stared at him in silence, thinking of Chi and the unborn baby. Beads of sweat formed on his brow. He chewed on his lower lip.

His indecision made Kim nervous. "Hey, Man! You help me it'll go good for you when this mess is over. Right now, they might think you're missing in action. *Or* they might think you're a deserter. *They think you're dead, but you don't know that and I need your help.*

"I know about you and that girl. If you work as a spy for the government, you'll get an honorable discharge when you get back stateside." Kim punched Johnny on his arm. "As they say in Chicago, the land of mobs, 'this is an offer you can't refuse', buddy. Whaddya say?"

Johnny looked down at the ground and thought a minute, palms sweaty. A frog hidden in the underbrush croaked and jumped away.

Johnny nodded. "Okay. I'll do it. But I can't have the radio in the village. If the Viet Cong or Khmer Rouge found it, they'd kill everybody, for sure. Just the fact that these people have taken me in endangers all their lives. The Cong wouldn't like it a bit if they found me *and* a radio." John heaved a sigh, wiped one hand on his pant leg and rubbed his face.

"The little boys warn us when the Cong show up, and I go hide in one of the caves up there." Johnny gestured toward the mountain. "I'll stash the radio in one of them. It'll be handy, and no one here needs to know about it. There're lots of caves. I can move the radio around each time, so the Cong can't zero in on it."

Kim clapped him on the back. "Good. I'll let your battalion commander know where you are and what you're doing. It'll go on record that you're helping me. Let's go hide the radio. Then I have to get the hell outta here."

"One question," Johnny detained Kim with a hand on his arm. "How did you learn to speak so much like . . . like an *American?*"

Kim laughed. "L A Public Schools. UCLA. My family immigrated to California when I was a kid."

Late one afternoon, seven-year old Sa'ang ran to Johnny. "Cong," he gasped. "Viet Cong!"

"Where?"

Sa'ang pointed to the north.

"How many?"

Sa'ang looked puzzled.

Johnny held up his fingers. "How many?" He ticked them off, one, two, three . . . "Oh," Sa'ang grinned and held up both hands, fingers spread out, four times.

Johnny nodded. "Thanks," he said, ruffling up Sa'ang's hair.

Johnny grabbed his Montagnard axe, tucking it under his belt as he ran, and slipped onto a seldom used forest trail. The thick foliage enveloped him completely. He jogged deep into the jungle, zigzagging through the now-familiar trails toward the cave with the hidden radio. He ran the antenna out the cave entrance, trailed it as high as he could reach, and contacted his battalion command.

The radio crackled with static. "This is Yogi Bear," Johnny identified himself. "Calling Boo Boo Bear. Do you read me?"

"Roger, Yogi. We read you loud and clear."

"Forty Cong troops headed south from the border." John looked at the sun. "It's about 3 p.m. solar time. They should be past the village by now. "

"Roger. Boo Boo Bear over and out."

"Yogi Bear, over and out." said Johnny.

Johnny reeled in the antenna, closed the radio and moved it to a cave a mile further from the village. He hid the radio and went still further to another cave to rest and wait until he judged it was safe to go back.

Chi's child was born. A boy.

~~~

2000

I tied Henry's letters back in bundles with the ribbons Maggie had used – blue, faded to silver, but still showing flashes of blue where the ribbon had been tied. The lock of baby's hair tied with more faded ribbon. I put the letters back. Something moved in the bottom of the chest. I opened the lid, but it was empty. I had emptied it myself. I shook the chest and heard a definite movement. The bottom of the wooden box seemed thicker than it needed to be. I turned it upside down and looked it over carefully. A small catch, hidden inside a mortised joint underneath the box, glinted in the lamp light. I looked around for something to release the catch. A nail. A needle. Something thin and sharp.

A finishing nail on the kitchen windowsill, left over from having the windows changed was just the right size. I pressed the catch with the point. A secret compartment in the bottom of the chest popped open. Inside, wrapped in tissue paper, was a necklace. I held my breath and lifted it to the lamplight. Each gem
~~~

sparkled like the stars shining over Deer Harbor reflecting on the water. They caught the reflected splashes of color from the Tiffany lamp and sent their bright colors dancing around the room. Diamonds. I was certain they were diamonds. One of the photographs of Maggie advertising a concert showed her wearing a diamond necklace. This gift from Maggie would certainly help me with the expense of restoring the cottage. But was it mine to use? Did I have to declare it and give it to the Music Scholarship at the University? I didn't think so. Virginia had definitely said the cottage and all its contents belonged to the buyer – me. Only the money I paid for the sale of the property would go to the University.

Tears welled up in my eyes. I had become extremely fond of the cottage and wanted it to be perfect. My retirement money was disappearing like a drunken sailor's pay. I decided to sell the necklace and invest the money in Mutual Funds . . . and maybe some Microsoft stock. Now I could relax, enjoy the wonderful view, paint tons of flower fairies for the tourists, and live my life out here watching the sun set on the water, while I waited for the full moon and Maggie's ghost to wander into my living room. I checked the secret compartment in the little chest once more and found a safety deposit key and a piece of paper stuck inside. The crisp parchment felt fragile and crackled as I unfolded a birth certificate for Henry Alexander McNamara, dated June 12, 1918. Mother: Maggie McNamara. Father: Henry Anderson.

~~~

The next night I read a letter from Henry's commanding officer dated November 10, 1918, the day before the Armistice. Wrinkles showed it had been scrunched up, and then smoothed out.

Dear Miss McNamara,

I regret to inform you that your fiancé, Henry Anderson, was shot down in an air battle over the Argonne Forest. Henry was an excellent pilot, an honorable man and a fine person. Please accept my condolences on your loss.

I am aware that Henry's parents should receive this information, and they will get a letter, too, but my fellow officers and I felt you deserved some notification, as you are all Henry could talk about.

Very truly yours,
Major C.J. Roberts
United States
Expeditionary Forces

The full moon filled the room with white light. Once again, I awoke to hear Maggie play. I wanted to go to her and hold her in my arms, but I knew she would disappear if I did that. Together, we wept.
~~~

~~~

1969

"John," called Sa'ang. The boy's face creased with worry as he trudged up the hill to the village. He looked much older than his 12 years, more like a wizened old man than a child.

"Hey, little buddy," called John. "What's happening?"

Sa'ang's body shook as he held in his sobs.

Johnny knelt down and took hold of Sa'ang's shoulders. "You know you can tell me if something's bad."

"Kim," said Sa'ang, choking over a lump in his throat.

"Okay, what about Kim?" Johnny had not seen the spy for many weeks.

"P-Pol Pot," stammered Sa'ang. The tears fell down his face. John enfolded the child in his arms. *"K-kill Kim."*

"Sorry, Sa'ang," he said.

Sa'ang sobbed. *"Tie Kim's hands together behind his back. Hang him from tree. Rope through arms."* He buried his face in Johnny's shoulder. His body shook with long, shuddering sobs.

"After long time, Kim's bones poke through." Sa'ang put his hands behind his back to demonstrate how Kim's shoulders had been dislocated. *"Kim not talk. Kim die."*
~~~

Johnny shivered. He rocked Sa'ang back and forth, tears running down both their faces.

"Kim not tell about you, Johnny." Sa'ang wiped his nose. *"Know about your radio, but Kim not tell."* Sa'ang wiped his eyes. *"How know about radio?"*

"They have ways to locate a radio beam. That's why I move the radio every time I use it."

Johnny held his breath. He knew if Kim had told the Viet Cong about him the Khmer Rouge would have massacred every person in Chi's village.

~~~

2000

The box of old photographs tore on one corner as I carried it to the coffee table. I made a mental note to tape it up when I had finished looking at the pictures. Sepia-tone prints mixed in with black and white photos. Early colored prints faded to yellow fell out with later shots still bright and clear. One pile of sepia, one pile of black and white, one pile of colored.

Some of the photos had names and dates on the backs. Alexander and Alice McNamara, in a wedding portrait. Alice wore white satin and stood beside her seated husband who was dressed in black, her hand on his shoulder. Maggie, a little girl of about eight dressed in the clothes she wore the first night she played for me. Other pictures showed her growing up. Soon she appeared in black and white photos with Henry. *A handsome couple.* Henry's sailboat with "MAGGIE"
~~~

painted across the stern. Henry's aeroplane, with Henry at the controls and Alice in the passenger seat.

Baby pictures of Hank. Hank as a little boy with blonde curls, short pants, and sturdy little boots. Hank growing older.

Hank in the uniform of the United States Army Air Corps in World War II.

Letters from Hank to Maggie were stuck in the bottom of the box. I pulled one out.

January 5, 1945

Dear Mom,

We're at Pearl waiting for the next strike. Where am I going? Sorry, can't tell you. But I can tell you something that isn't a secret. I met a wonderful girl here in Hawaii. We plan to be married as soon as I get back. Here's a photo of the two of us. I know you will love Nanilei *as I do. We'll be coming home to Orcas Island as soon as the war is over. It shouldn't be long now.*

Love,
Hank

I studied the picture of Hank, handsome in his United States Army Air Corps uniform. A pretty Hawaiian girl wearing a short print dress and high wedge-heeled ankle-strapped sandals with platform soles, stood close to him. Straight black hair fell shimmering to her waist the way mine had in the 1960's. I turned the photograph over. Nanilei Hanaeki and me, Hank McNamara, written in Hank's bold handwriting. *Nanalei Hanaeki? Johnny's name. My name, too. How could she be Hanaeki?* I sat and stared at the photo. Could she be one of Johnny's extended Hawaiian family? Did I see a resemblance between the girl in the photo and Johnny?

I ran to the bedroom for Johnny's photograph where it sat on the dresser and held the two photos close together. *Yes, the same eyes and smile. John had told me his mother was Hawaiian and that she'd had him out of wedlock, a scandalous thing in the 1940's. And his father had been a pilot in World War II. Hank McNamara in the picture wore the uniform of the United States Army Air Corps. Could it possibly be?*

No. Of course not.

I held the two pictures close together, again. *Oh, my God! Yes, it might be possible.* How I wished Johnny could see this photograph and tell me if these people were his parents.

I hurried to the small bedroom closet where I had stored Johnny's things, pulled out the box of photographs from college, and laid them on the bed. A few photos from Hawaii. One group photo showed Johnny with many of his extended Hawaiian family. There were so many people in the photo it was hard to tell. I found Johnny, but I couldn't tell who any of the others were. Maybe the woman standing next to him was his mother. She looked like the girl in the other photo of Hank and Nanalei.

~~~

1945

Maggie put Hank's letter down. She picked up the photograph of him with Nanalei and smiled to herself. She knew Hank would choose a pretty girl, and this one looked like she was more than pretty. She looked very intelligent. This was the girl who would be Maggie's daughter-in-law. She sighed, remembering the other war when Henry didn't come back. She turned the photo over to read Hank's inscription on the back. Maggie closed her eyes and prayed that Hank would come home. If he didn't, there would be no one left for her. Maggie put the photo with others she had saved in a dress box from the fine Seattle store, *Frederick and Nelson.*

~~~

2000

The things in Maggie's linen closet took hours to wade through. One envelope held four funeral cards each titled "*In Memoriam*". The first was for Maggie's father, Alexander, dead of influenza during the epidemic of 1919. The second one was in memory of Alice, dead in1921. The last two were for Henry's parents who passed away in 1925, a week apart. Poor Maggie, I thought. How did she manage after that? She had little Hank to rear and no one to help her.

A box from The Bon Marche Department store held several concert programs with photographs of Maggie seated at a grand piano, dressed in a black silk gown, an Art Deco brooch pinned at her waist. She must have earned her living playing piano concerts. Perhaps she played dinner music for the Rosario resort. But maybe her father had been able to leave a little nest egg for her – maybe a few securities that he'd planned to use for his retirement.

I drove my VW Bug to the bank in East Sound with the safety deposit key I had found in the small locked chest and asked to talk with the bank manager.

"Last Spring I purchased Maggie McNamara's little house at Deer Harbor known as Maggie's Cottage," I said. "In her will the money from the sale of the property went for music scholarships in Seattle. The realtor who sold the place to me emphasized that everything else in the house and property would belong to the buyer -- me." I chewed on a fingernail and looked at her.

"The house contained all Miss McNamara's personal belongings, including photographs and letters. While going through some of the things, I found a safety deposit box key. Does it belong to this bank?" I handed the key to the manager. "Or is there another bank on the Island?" I shrugged my shoulders. "Maybe it's a Seattle bank."

"It's really hard to say," the manager said. "Safety deposit keys are all made by two or three companies, and they all look pretty much the same. What did you say the woman's name was?"

"Maggie McNamara."

"Let's look it up." She checked on the computer for Maggie's name. "There's an Alexander McNamara," she said.

I nodded. "He would have been Maggie's father."

The bank manager took Maggie's key and went to the vault with the bank's key.

"The key is the right one," she said, when she returned, "but according to the law, I can't let you open the box unless I have proof you are the rightful heir."

"I'm not the heir, but I think my husband might have been," I said. "He was . . . k-killed . . . in Vietnam." Actually, saying the words out loud like that made it hard to breathe.

"You'll have to see an attorney. Privacy laws are so strict we can't even open the box without a court order." She typed something into her computer. "It appears the rental of the box has been an automatic withdrawal the first of every year from a bank account in Maggie McNamara's name," she said. "If the rent hadn't been paid since her death, the court would have taken over the box.

"Well, that was lucky, wasn't it?' I said. "All right, I'll see if I can find an attorney. I've only lived here on the island a few months, but the woman who sold me the house can help me with this."

The bank officer gave back the key. We shook hands and I left.

~~~

On a soft February day, Mike called from the gallery. The crocuses were popping up around the edges of the English flower garden outside my kitchen window and greeting the pale winter sun with their bright yellow, white and purple blossoms. I pulled myself away from the window and its promise of Spring time to answer the telephone.

"I think you need to come into the gallery right now, Sarah," he said.

"Why?" I felt confused. *What was the rush? It was February, the off-tourist season. Did someone want to commission a special painting?*

"There's someone here I think you'd like to meet."

"Oh?"

"Yes. He noticed your painting in the gallery window -- the one of the small island out in Deer Harbor -- and asked about you."

"Really?" I said in disbelief.

"Really. It seems you both have the same last name." I heard a faint chuckle in Mike's voice.

"What? The same last name?" I nearly jumped out of my skin. Then I calmed down and said, "It can't possibly be Johnny, can it?"

"No, I think Johnny was much taller than this man. Didn't you tell me he was half Polynesian? They are not tiny people. No, I believe this man is shorter, and besides, he is much younger than Johnny would be now, if he had lived."
~~~

"Johnny had dozens of Hawaiian relatives. It must be a cousin or nephew," I said, chewing on a fingernail. "What's his first name?"

"He hasn't told me that," said Mike, "but this 'cousin' is wearing a ring like yours. If I remember, it matches exactly."

My heart leaped into my throat. *Johnny! Could it be Johnny? I had just finally accepted the fact he had been killed in Vietnam, besides, hadn't Mike just said he was shorter and younger than Johnny would be now.* "I'll be there in fifteen minutes," I managed to croak.

I grabbed my purse and car keys and ran out to my Volkswagen Bug. Opened the door and threw myself into the driver's seat. Turned on the key, pushed in the clutch, and pumped the accelerator. In my hurry, I flooded the engine. I sat with my trembling hands on the steering wheel and dropped my head on them while I let the gasoline dissipate. Then I tried again. Bug coughed and the engine started. I eased down to the road and drove too fast, slipping past stop signs without coming to a complete stop, hoping I wouldn't get a ticket.

Finally, I could see the gallery with my painting of Deer Island on an easel sitting in the front window. I parked in front. Jumped out. Slammed the car door. Ran inside. A young man stood with his back to me, talking to Mike. He was dressed all in black – black shoes, black slacks, and black long-sleeved buttoned shirt, neatly tucked in. Shiny black hair worn a little long, but in a clean, trim cut, not shaggy. From the back I thought he looked like Johnny . . . I *wanted* him to be Johnny . . . but then I realized he really was not as tall as Johnny. Much shorter, in fact. He talked with his hands and used the same mannerisms as Johnny. He turned around. Not Johnny, but very close. Much younger than Johnny would be now. About thirty, I guessed.

"Hi," I said, out of breath. I smiled and stretched out my hand. "I'm Sarah Hanaeki."

"I'm pleased to meet you. My name is John Hanaeki," he said.

"You're . . . *Joh-.John* Hanaeki?" My heart leaped into my throat.

"Yes, I am. I also have a Cambodian name, spelled C-h-a-n-n, and pronounced Jahn. Your friend, Mike, here tells me your husband, Johnny Hanaeki, was killed in Vietnam during the Second Indo-Chinese War. The Vietnam War."

"Yes. That's right." I gazed at him in wonder. My eyes skipped to Mike, questioning him. He smiled a little smile and shrugged.

"My father was an American soldier in that war, and my mother named me for him. Do you suppose they might have been the same person? If this is true, I'm sorry to be an embarrassment. My mother and I didn't know he had a wife in America." He rubbed a hand through his hair and laughed. "Language was sort of a problem then."

"It's possible they were the same person." My hands shook. I took a deep breath. This John Hanaeki looked so much like Johnny; it was like seeing a ghost, but a small ghost. My life had filled with ghosts. "Mike told me you're wearing a ring like mine." My left hand trembled as I held it out to show him my hand-carved silver wedding band.

He held out his right hand. There was Johnny's ring on this man's finger.

I felt dizzy and reached out to Mike for support. He put his arm around me. "It's all right, Sarah. Maybe now you'll find out what happened to Johnny." He guided me to a display cube. I sat down on a corner, sharing the cube with a small, Pacific Northwest Indian totem pole.

"This was my father's ring," John said. He held out his hand and admired the ring. "My mother gave it to me when I came to America to go to college." An explosive silence thrummed in the gallery. I sat, stunned.

"Ah . . . why don't . . . I . . . ah . . . close the shop for the day so we can go to your house, Sarah?" offered Mike. "It's late and it's the off season. It won't hurt to close early. You can show John the pictures of Hank and Nanalei Hanaeki." He turned to the young man. "We think they were your father's parents. If that's true, they'd be your grandparents."

Mike paused a moment. "Sarah?"

"What . . ." I sat in a daze, my mind a muddle. "Oh, yes. That's a good idea." I took my car keys from my purse. "John? Does that sound okay with you?" John Hanaeki nodded and took my elbow to walk to the door. I couldn't stop looking at him, he looked so much like . . . Johnny, *his father. Johnny had a child! But* <u>*we*</u> *didn't have any children. Although we had been married a whole year before he went overseas, we had no children. The fault must have been with me. I couldn't have any children!* My heart ached for the children we didn't have. I reached out to this child of Johnny's, a child no longer, but a grown man.

"Yes, Mrs. Hanaeki. That sounds fine."

"Oh, dear, Mrs. Hanaeki' sounds so *formal.* Please just call me Sarah."

"All right, Sarah." John smiled and looked at my little Volkswagen. "Your car looks pretty small for all of us. We could all go in my van if you like?"

I chewed on a hang nail and looked up at Mike. He nodded.

"Okay. My car will be all right here for a while."

Mike took the gallery keys from his pocket and locked the door.

At Maggie's Cottage, we went in through the kitchen door. The baby grand piano stood in the corner of the living room windows right in our line of vision as we walked in. Mike went ahead to kindle a small fire in the fireplace.

"Sarah! You have a piano." John reached the instrument in several long strides. He sat down and lifted the lid covering the worn and yellowed ivories. Then he played. He played beautifully. *Maybe he and his father both have Maggie's genes.*

"Do you play?" John looked up at me. Mike stood and put the screen in front of the burning logs. He brushed off his hands.

"I play a little, John, but not like that. That was wonderful."

"Thank you." John played an arpeggio up and down the keyboard. "This is how I earn my living. I'm a musician. We just finished a gig in Victoria, and decided to take a little vacation touring the San Juan Islands on the way home to L.A. We have one more booking in Seattle before we head south. Wasn't it lucky we decided to get off the ferry at Orcas Island?"

"I'd say it was fantastically lucky," I breathed. I looked out the corner windows as the winter sun dipped toward the west filling the sky with shades of red and apricot.

With trembling hands, I put the tea kettle on the stove and got out the cookie jar. While the water boiled, I said, "Please tell me about Johnny – your father. What happened to him? I've waited so long. I didn't give up hope that he would come home until just recently." My bracelet clicked as I worked.

John stood up, walked to the kitchen doorway, and leaned against the frame. "My father was door gunner in a helicopter that crashed near the Cambodian border. Some of the people in my mother's village pulled him from the wreckage, but the other crew members were already dead. The helicopter exploded and burned. Johnny was injured in the crash with a big cut over his left eye and a broken rib. My mother sewed up the cut with silk thread and she and my Uncle Sovann bound his rib cage with strips of cloth so the broken rib would heal. Mother told me the cut over his eye left an ugly scar. She thought maybe she hadn't done such a good job of sewing! " John laughed gently. "But Johnny lost consciousness when she stuck the needle through his skin, and she thought she had better hurry. Several weeks later, he tried to get back through the Viet Cong soldiers to his base but was wounded again."

The tea kettle whistled. I poured a little boiling water in a ceramic teapot and swished it around, warming the pot. Poured out the water and added loose tea leaves. Then I poured hot water over the tea leaves and let the pot steep. "Go on, John," I said, nodding.

"My mother told me my father was a good man. He helped the people in the village by bringing a water system to all the houses with bamboo piping. Until then, the women had to carry water from the creek. He also learned to ride the rakes in the rice paddies behind the oxen. It took awhile to get used to that." John shifted his feet and shoved his hands into his pockets.

"Mother told me he also helped an American spy, who was of Vietnamese descent, but born in America. Kim needed someone to send messages on a CB radio, so my father did that. He hid the radio in a different place every time he used it. If the Viet Cong had caught him, they would have tortured him and killed him. He was very brave to do this thing."

John walked into the kitchen and looked out the garden window at the crocuses. "Maybe my father thought he could not get back through Vietnam to his base and come home to you. He tried once and was wounded again." John leaned against the kitchen counter. He looked at me, as if he was undecided about how to tell the whole story. Then he continued.

"After my mother and uncle helped him recover from the wounds he got in the helicopter crash, he and my mother fell in love. Although they didn't marry, they had a . . . I guess relationship about sums it up. Maybe he had tried to tell her he was already married in America, but he spoke only a little Cambodian, and she spoke a few words of English. When he found out my mother was going to have his baby – me -- he didn't want to leave us. Many Asian people resented the American soldiers and their Asian/American children, you know. My father did not want his child to be discriminated against."

My mind whirled as I imagined how it would feel to be pregnant and know my neighbors might abuse me and my child because of his father's heritage.

Not good.

Tears trickled down my cheeks. I grabbed a tissue from the box of Kleenex on the kitchen counter and wiped my face.

Johnny loved me! How could he have gotten a Cambodian girl pregnant? I threw the damp tissue into the garbage under the sink and slammed the cupboard door. Mike caught my eye and shook his head, ever so slightly. I frowned at him.

Why didn't Johnny just stay away from her and come home to me? When had he stopped loving me? I did not stop loving him. How could he have done this to me? Why?

But then he would never have had a child.

I took a deep breath and stood up straight. *After all, it was not this young man's fault. He didn't ask to be born.*

I set the teapot and cups and saucers on a tray with a plate of Maggie's butter cookies.

"Let me help, please," offered John.

My hands shook so much, I was glad to have him carry the heavy tray into the living room. Mike and I sat on the couch by the coffee table. John sat on the piano bench on the other side of the table. I poured tea, rattling the cups on their saucers with my shaking hands, and passed them around. The tea was too hot to drink. We sat and held our cups while it cooled. John took a bite of cookie. Except for the crackling of the fire, silence filled the room.

I took a deep breath. "You know, I have waited all these years not knowing what happened to Johnny," I held up my left arm. My POW/MIA bracelet clanked. "You see this bracelet?"

John peered across the table at it. "Yes. It has my father's name on it. That must be his rank and serial number, too, right? Just like . . ."

I rudely interrupted him. "Right! Do you know how long I have worn this bracelet?" *as if it were this young man's fault!*

John shook his head in silence, his eyes wide, awed at my anger.

"Well, it's been about thirty years! Thirty years of not knowing what happened." Tears splashed into my cup of tea. I dabbed my face with my napkin. "Oh! How hard it was not to know."

"Sarah, I'm sorry he couldn't get word to you that he was still alive in Cambodia. Things were bad there as well as in Vietnam, what with Pol Pot and his Khmer

Rouge soldiers. Had my mother known Johnny had a wife in America, she would not have fallen in love with him. Well, maybe she would have, but she probably would not have had me. And from my point of view, I think that would have been too bad." John laughed.

Mike reached over to hold my hand. He squeezed it gently and patted my arm. He looked into my eyes as if to say, *it's not John's fault, Sarah.* Mike shook his head imperceptibly.

I cried softly for a bit using up tons of Kleenex, besides my paper napkin.

"Of course, it was not your fault, John. You were not even born when Johnny was reported missing in action. Then I got another letter from the Army stating he was presumed dead, as the helicopter had crashed with no survivors. They couldn't have known your people in the village had rescued him."

"I'm sorry," said John. "I wish I could have changed that for you, but you see I didn't know he had a wife in America."

I sat up straight, straightened my clothes, and pulled myself together. Taking a big breath, I said, "Please tell us about you and your father, John."

"Are you sure you are all right, Sarah? I know this has been a big shock to you."

I smiled through my tears. "I'm okay. I just have to get used to the idea that my husband was un-unfaithful to me, and that he has been dead for a long time."

"You're sure?"

I nodded, wiping away the tears.

"Well, I was born in 1969. There was fighting in Cambodia as well as in Vietnam. You probably knew that. You know, Pol Pot, the Leader of the Khmer Rouge? The Communists? They wanted to take over the country. They were always stirring up trouble and fighting with Prince Sihanouk's troops. They helped the Viet Cong in Vietnam. After I was born, my parents and my Uncle Sovann decided to flee with me to Thailand."

The tea had cooled a bit. John gave it a tentative sip.

"I wasjust a baby a few months old, so I don't remember that trip, but my mother and uncle told me how they traveled at night and hid from the Khmer Rouge during the day." John drank some tea. "The Khmer soldiers were all pretty young and ruthless – some of them just kids. They did what Pol Pot told them to do." John grimaced. "They had no qualms about killing anyone – young – old -- babies. It didn't matter to them."

John ate a cookie and sipped more tea. "My father wanted to get to Bangkok where there were facilities to help American GI's get back home to America. He planned to try to take us all with him." John looked over at me, a worried frown on his face. "I don't know if he could have done that, since now I know he was already married to you. Will the United States allow a man to have two wives?"

"No," I shook my head with a sad little smile. "I'm afraid not, John. I don't know what Johnny would have done about that." I sat in a daze, thinking about the possibilities. "M-Maybe we would have gotten a divorce." At this thought I wanted to rip my POW bracelet from my arm and throw it as far as I could. I burst into tears again.

John shook his head and set his teacup down. "I'm sorry, Sarah. If they had known about you, I'm sure my mother and uncle would have tried to contact you through those people in Bangkok." He reached over and patted my hand.

"One afternoon, when my family awoke in a hiding place, my mother and father and uncle heard me cooing and gurgling. My father found I was looking eye to eye at a cobra ready to strike. My father picked up his Montagnard jungle axe and threw it at the snake, killing it. The axe whizzed right over me and nailed that snake to the ground."

"It's a wonder he didn't hit you with the axe." I shuddered.

"He was very good with that axe. It came in handy on that trip many times." John sipped his hot tea. "As my father came out of hiding first, as usual, that evening, he met a patrol of Khmer Rouge soldiers. My uncle had no weapons so my father told him to take my mother and me and get away while he fought these tough guys. He had only the axe. He used it well, but it was no match for their rifles."

"Mother and Uncle Sovann hid under the bank of a river, burrowing into the tree roots hanging over the edge, and hoped I would not cry. Mother said she was prepared to cover my mouth if I let out one whimper.

Of course, she would not have smothered me to death, just kept me from yelling.

"After they heard rifle shots, Mother and Uncle Sovann could hear the soldiers thrashing around in the underbrush jabbing at piles of dirt and leaves with their bayonets, trying to find us. They would have killed us all. But we stayed quiet and hidden. Hours later, when the soldiers had gone away, my uncle went out leaving mother and me safely hidden and found my father and two of the soldiers dead."

"At first, my mother cried and carried on so, my uncle was afraid for her sanity. When she had exhausted herself with crying, she took this ring from my father's finger to save for me." John held out his hand and looked at the ring. "They used the axe to dig a grave and bury my father. It was really hard to do without a real digging tool." John drained his teacup. "So instead of burying the soldiers, Uncle Sovann threw their bodies into the river to get rid of them. He didn't want to leave a trail other Khmer soldiers might see and follow." John sat deep in thought for a few minutes. Then he looked up at me and said, "Mother still has the axe. She hung it on the wall of our house in Bangkok for a decoration."

I sat and cried quietly for a few minutes. Then I wiped tears from my face. "Thank you for telling me this. I needed to know what happened to Johnny. I needed to close that part of my life." I poured more tea with shaking hands and we all sipped our tea in silence for a few minutes. I thought of all the years I had wasted thinking of Johnny and waiting for him to come home.

"Mother and Uncle Sovann both worked hard to make a home for us in Bangkok. When I was old enough for school, they managed to scrape up enough money to send me to the Catholic School. The nuns taught the children to read and write English. People in America say I have very nice handwriting, thanks to Sister Celeste. I was so lucky to go to that school. Sister Marybeth taught music. They had an old upright piano that she kept in tune herself, and when she discovered my talent for music, taught me everything she knew about playing the piano. The nuns encouraged my mother and uncle to try to send me to college in America in order to learn more about music. I know it was difficult for them to pay the tuition, but after I enrolled at USC, I organized a small group of other student musicians, and we earned extra money playing for different affairs, like school dances."

I went to the kitchen and put the tea kettle back on the stove. Mike went over and stirred up the fire, putting a couple of pieces of wood on it. John stood and stretched his arms and legs. We all sat back down as John continued.

"One time, when I was sixteen, my uncle and I went on a hike, back-tracking the route he and my mother had taken to Thailand. We tried to find my father's grave, but things had changed. And Uncle Sovann had hidden the grave so well, no one or no animals could dig it up."

"I'm sorry you couldn't find it. I might have made a trip over there to see it, but I don't know what good it would have done Johnny or me." I brushed away a tear. "You know, it's like Johnny just vanished from the face of the earth."

I felt drained. I went back to the kitchen and poured more hot water into the ceramic teapot. Could I possibly let go of Johnny now? In a way, Johnny had been as much a ghost as Maggie's ghost playing the piano. I felt my bracelet. It did not click on my arm. I walked back with fresh tea and set the pot on the coffee table.

"He really is dead, then." Tears flooded my eyes again. "For years I've hoped he lived and would come back to me, but he really is dead." The tears spilled over and ran down my face. I dabbed at them with a paper napkin. "I wanted so much to have him come home." I sighed. "I guess I thought if I wished hard enough he would come back, but that's not the way things happen, is it?"

I stood up and reached over to the kitchen counter to grab another tissue and blow my nose. "Thank you for telling me about Johnny -- about your father," I said, tears streaming down my face. I mopped my face and threw the tissues in the garbage under the sink. This time, I did not slam the cupboard door.

"I'm really sorry, Sarah. I'm sure he would have got word to you if it had been possible. He was killed when I was a baby, so all I know is what my family has told me."

I tried to open the clasp on my POW/MIA bracelet, but it was stuck.

"Do you want to take it off, Sarah?" Mike stood up.

"Yes, Mike. Now that I know Johnny's really been dead all these years, I want to take the bracelet off."

"Let me help."

Mike took out his pocketknife, opened the smallest thin, pointed blade, and forced the lock open. I unfastened it and slipped the bracelet off. It felt strange not to wear it. I frowned, rubbed my arm and looked up to find them both anxiously watching me. I smiled at them showing their concern for me with their anxious looks. John, so like his father, showed his caring in his eyes. Mike, so patient. So loyal.

I walked over to the piano and held John's hands. "Thank you, John." He stood up and held both of my hands in his. Something clicked under his shirt – some kind of a necklace. "What's this, John," I laughed and lifted the chain visible around his neck.

"Oh, this was my dad's, too. Mother saved it for me, as well as the ring." He pulled it up from his shirt and showed it to me. "See? The chain has his dog tag on it."

"Ohmygod! It is Johnny's dog tag! Look, Mike. Of course, they couldn't find them in the crash. Johnny was wearing his dog tags when the village people pulled him from the wreckage."

Uncle Sovann buried one of the tags with my father's body and saved this one on the chain for my mother to give me."

John lifted the chain over his head and handed it to me. "This and his ring are all I have of him unless you can count my musical ability. Mother said he played beautiful music on bamboo flutes he made."

I sat down on the coffee table and held the dog tag.

"See? It has his name rank and serial number on it just like your POW.MIA bracelet."

I gulped back more tears, nodded and gave the chain back to him. He looked from the dog tag to me.

"Sarah? Um . . . would you like to keep this? After all, he was your husband."

"Thank you, John. That is so thoughtful. But no, I've lived with Johnny's name, rank and serial number for over thirty years on my bracelet. You keep it. He was your father." I stood up and helped him put it back over his head.

"I want to show you the photo of Nanalei Hanaeki, John. I think she might be your relative – maybe even your grandmother." I went to the hall closet and brought out the box of old photos. Shuffled through them. Found the one I wanted.

"Here," I said. "Here she is, with Hank McNamara who I think was your grandfather."

"Really?" John looked at me in disbelief. "You're sure that's who they are?"

"Pretty sure, John. Maybe I should try to contact the Hanaekis in Hawaii to find out."

"If you do that, Sarah, please let me know." He reached in his shirt pocket and pulled out a business card. The card was printed with a black baby grand piano:

John Hanaeki.
Jazz Blues Classics
Music for all occasions
San Diego, California

~~~

That night the full moon filled my house, but Maggie's ghost did not appear. In the past, whenever the moon was full, Maggie's ghost had returned. Each time, she changed imperceptibly. By the end of my first year at Maggie's Cottage, the ghost of Maggie playing the piano in my living room had become frail, thin, and bent over. Getting up from the piano bench became difficult for her. Even so, her music soared through the cottage. But now, she did not return. Perhaps she felt safe now that her last living descendant had been in her house and played her piano.

~~~

2000
"Yes, what can I do for you?"

"I came in a few weeks ago to see about this safety deposit key. Do you remember?"

"Oh, yes, Sarah Hana. . . something Hawaiian, isn't it?"

"Yes. Hanaeki. This is my husband's son, John Hanaeki, by . . . by his second wife."

John looked sideways at me with a funny little grin on his face.

"How do you do?" The manager rose and held out her hand.

John reached out and shook the manager's hand. "Ma'am," he said.

"We were able to get a court order to open the safety deposit box. John had his father's dog tag from the war in Vietnam."

I handed the court order and key to her. "I brought my marriage license, too, to prove that I'm John Hanaeki's wife and the letter from the army stating John was presumed dead." I put both documents beside the court order.

"All right," she said. "Please sit down." She read the court order while we waited. "It looks as though you, Sarah are to receive this inheritance, what-ever-it-is, as your husband John would have been the legal heir. The State of Washington's community property law entitles you to his estate. His son John is also a legal heir and would then inherit from his father or from you, if his father is deceased."

She pushed her glasses up on her nose and looked at me. "Since his father is deceased, it will be up to you to decide what would be a fair and equitable share for

John, or if you think he should wait until your demise, to inherit."

I looked at John, then at the manager. "I would like to share it by giving John half," I said. "I know his father would have wanted it that way."

John's eyes widened. "Sarah, you don't have to do that! You hardly even know me."

"I knew your father, John. That's enough for me." I grimaced. "Besides, there might not be anything in the safety deposit box at all."

The manager stood up and we followed her to the vault. She used the bank key and I used Maggie's key to unlock the box. Then she left us alone. I looked at John and held my breath. Opened the box. Inside were several packets of oil stocks purchased in 1910, now maybe not worth the paper they were printed on, or maybe worth a million dollars. There was also a stack of $1000 bills, and ten twenty-dollar gold pieces.

John's eyes grew round. He looked at me in surprise. "Can this be true, Sarah? Half of all this is mine?"

I smiled. "Yes. Of course, gold coins are not allowed anymore. We might want to save them for keepsakes, or cash them in at the bank. We can check on the price of gold per ounce, now. We'll divide them and the rest."

"I can't believe it.. . . " John sat down with a dazed look on his face. "Now I can go back to visit Cambodia and help the village there. After Saigon fell, Pol Pot took over Cambodia and decided to turn the country into a huge Communist collective farm.

Everyone from the cities had to go out and work in the fields – *the killing fields* --. Doctors, lawyers, priests -- everyone.

"Pol Pot is dead, now, and Prince Sihanouk is back. My wife, Mayuko, and I try to go every two or three years and take enough money to do some good. A big sack of rice is only $5, and will sustain a family for many months, but this year my family's village has asked for a bridge. This money will help get the materials they need to build it."

He wiped his eyes with his hands and grinned. "Don't mind me. I'm just happy I can help them." Our little boys will be old enough to go with us this time and find out how lucky they are to live in America."

"But what about your mother, John? What happened to her?"

"She and Uncle Sovann are still in Thailand. They save their money to help the village. When Mayuko and I go, we plan it for a time when my mother and uncle can be there. I hope to bring them to America someday, but immigration laws are difficult." John picked up the stack of thousand dollar bills and ruffled through them, making a little breeze.

"At first I stayed on a Student Visa even though my father was an American soldier. We had no birth certificate or any other papers to prove that's who I was. Then, when I finished college, Mayuko and I decided to get married. Of course, since she was born here of Japanese parents, she's an American citizen and

I could stay as her husband. As soon as possible, I became a naturalized citizen."

John and Mike both came to dinner that night. I turned on the Tiffany lamp, sprinkling the room with confetti color. John played Maggie's piano for us, and I felt as proud of him as if he were my own son, and not just Johnny's boy. The next morning, he left for Seattle to play his last gig on the tour, and from there to Los Angeles, promising to bring Mayuko and his two sons to see me at Maggie's Cottage during the summer. If I couldn't have any children or grandchildren of my own, I could sort of adopt Johnny's child and his two little boys and be a stepmother and step grandmother. I could hardly wait to show the boys how to fly kites on the beach.

~~~

Mike worked all his spare time in the high space underneath the living room of Maggie's Cottage on Henry's old wooden sailboat. By the end of April, he had the boat cleaned, sanded, caulked and painted – cobalt blue up to the water line, and white. We had ordered new sails and sheets from a local marina that arrived in the mail. He came to the kitchen door one day holding a can of cobalt blue paint and a fine, lettering paintbrush.

"I think I'll re-name this boat *Sarah"*, he said.

"No, Mike. The boat's name is *Maggie.* Let's not change it, now. It's bad luck to change a boat's name."
~~~

"You think so? You believe in luck and ghosts and . . . what else, Sarah? Fortune tellers?" Mike's eyes twinkled as he teased me.

I laughed as I thought of Vermillion – that is Mystic. "Ghosts, yes. The rest, I don't know."

"All right, then. *Maggie*, she shall be."

Mike removed a section of lattice work so he and some of his friends could slide the boat out from under the house and carry it across the road and across the beach to Deer Harbor where they waded into the water with it, careful not to scratch the new paint. They helped him step the mast and rig the sails while the small boat, *Maggie,* tugged at her mooring line.

When this had all been accomplished, they untied the boat, climbed aboard and took off into Deer Harbor for a trial run. I ran along the edge of the beach waving life jackets at them, but they didn't pay any attention to me. They were having too much fun. They sailed far out into the harbor, tacking back and forth the way Mike had shown me on his larger sailboat. All I could see were the small triangles of white sail. Then the sails disappeared. The boat had tipped over. Splashes and shouts of laughter came from the area around the upturned keel as they turned the boat back over.

When they got back, they pulled up the dagger board, furled the sails, anchored the boat out in the water, and waded to shore.

"That was a great trial run," said Mike dripping water all over the beach and me. "Next time, Sarah, you and I will take it to that little island out there."

I gulped. Did I really want to go bobbing out in the choppy bay in a little chip of a boat? I managed a smile. "I'll make a picnic lunch for next Monday."

The picnic basket was ready when Mike arrived Monday morning. Fried chicken, apples, cheese, bottled water, and home baked cookies. I wore shorts, a t-shirt and a sweatshirt. Mike wore a swimsuit with a short- sleeved shirt unbuttoned down the front. We both had on flip-flops.

"Are we planning on swimming?" I shivered when I noticed his swimsuit. I knew how cold the water was, even in May.

"No, I just thought this would be easier getting into the boat. We'll have to rent a place to dock it so we don't always get wet when we want to use it. Maybe the boat basin across the bay there has a slip small enough for Maggie."

I looked out at the water between the boat and the edge of the beach. Mike had already tossed two life jackets in. He grabbed a stadium blanket from his car and the picnic basket and we walked to the beach. Mike put the things down on the sand and said, "Put your arms around my neck, Sarah."

"What?"

He scooped me up in his arms. "I said, put your arms around my neck, Sarah." He nuzzled my neck and nibbled my ear. I shrieked and kicked as he waded out into the water. His after-shave smelled good. His mustache tickled my cheek. I felt tempted to rest my head on his shoulder, but at about that time, he deposited me inside the boat.

"Just sit tight, now. I'll go get the lunch."

While I waited, I put on a life jacket. After watching Mike and his friends sail, I didn't want to take any chances.

Mike untied the line from the pile of driftwood and waded back out with the picnic basket and the blanket. He pulled up the anchor, turned the prow of the boat away from land, gave it a little push, and climbed aboard. Dropped the dagger board. Raised and uncleated the mainsail and the jib and untied the rudder. We were off.

"Now on this little boat, when I say "coming about", you need to duck your head under the boom and move to the opposite side. We have to tack in the wind. Okay?"

I nodded.

"Coming about", called Mike.

I moved over to the other side, the boom holding the main sail barely missing my head. Away we skimmed over the water, crosswind. After three or four tacks, we neared the island. Mike let the wind out of the sails and we drifted into a little sandy cove. He pulled up the dagger board so it wouldn't scrape bottom and break and beached the prow of the boat in the sand. I cringed as I heard the sand grinding the new paint. Then Mike jumped out and tied the prow line to a driftwood log. He came back and I handed him the picnic lunch and the blanket. I took off my life jacket, too warm in the hot sun reflecting on the sand and water and stepped onto the seat to climb over the gunwale. Mike was right there to help me out. He threw me over one shoulder and packed me over to dry sand. I didn't even get one big toe wet.

Mike stood there holding me like a sack of potatoes.

"Put me down!" I giggled, pounding his back with my fists.

"Not until you pay the toll fee," he laughed.

"What toll fee?"

"One kiss for every time I carry you across the water. You owe me two."

"You nut," I laughed. "Okay. Two kisses." I slid down through his arms. My t-shirt slid up as my breasts moved down over his bare chest until our faces were level. Lips met in a spine-tingling kiss.

"One more," he murmured.

Another kiss.

"And one for good measure," I laughed as I kissed him a third time, loving the way he smelled. Loving being with him.

The wind freshened, blowing sand on us. We took our picnic into the center of the log pile where the wind could not reach us and shook out the stadium blanket. I took a small tablecloth from the top of the basket, spread it over the blanket, and set out the lunch. Sea gulls cried above us, diving for clams, soaring high to drop them on the rocks and break their shells. Then they dove down to snatch the succulent clam before another gull could snatch it. The sun warmed us. I put the remains of our lunch back in the basket and set it in the shade of a huge log.

Mike stretched out on the blanket and pulled me toward him. The gulls called and the wind sighed, seeping in around the drift logs, seeming to make Maggie's music. Could this little nest have been Maggie's and Henry's? I felt safe in the little den of driftwood, so like the driftwood sanctuaries I had known on the Oregon Coast. No bracelet to scold me with its little clicks. No feelings of guilt about Johnny. I lay down next to Mike and snuggled close. The wind's music crept around the logs. We were alone in a world of our own, nothing but sand, water, wind and sun in our private driftwood world. Just the two of us.

~~~

After the night John played for us and moonlight streamed again through the windows, Maggie's ghost did not appear. She hasn't returned. Her music is silent. My cottage is empty without her. Maybe Maggie's ghost has finally found what she was looking for. Perhaps she has been able to let go because the last living member of her family, John Hanaeki has come home; just as I have been able to let go of Johnny now that I know for certain he's not coming back. I miss her.
~~~

Maggie's Cottage, a real place on Orcas Island in the State of Washington is now a vacation rental home. The piano sits in front of corner picture windows in the living room. The cottage has been remodeled with a huge country kitchen and a deck tacked onto the back of the house. The original kitchen is now the dining room. The living room, downstairs bath and two bedrooms are basically as I have pictured them. A second bath and two bedrooms with dormer windows looking out over Deer Harbor now occupy the attic. The basement containing concrete laundry tubs, has a dirt floor, except for one section under the front of the house with its own outside entrance that is a sort of dorm room. The oriel windows Sarah installed in this story do not exist, except in my imagination.

The characters in the book are fictitious. I have used Maggie's given name, but McNamara is a fictionalized name. I have no idea what the real Maggie looked like, so I have made her up. She really was a concert pianist, and the piano was hers. I recently learned that she was married to a doctor, but I did not know this when I invented a doctor to be Maggie's father.

My husband and I spent a weekend at Maggie's Cottage with a group of friends a few years ago. I was enthralled with the old baby grand piano that was still in perfect tune, its finish dull, its ivory keys yellowed and split, but its tone still beautiful, and enjoyed playing it while looking out the corner picture windows at Deer Harbor and Deer Island.

Made in USA - North Chelmsford, MA
1299034_9798722399250
01.19.2022 0908